THE SELFISH BETRAYALS

From inevitable to impossible

A Novel by

Abhishek Kapoor

For my two little ones

"We did not get the opportunity to hold each others' hands but don't worry, earth is the place where your dad still is and will do all he can for you. I know wherever you both are you are doing it for me too!"

THE SELFISH BETRAYALS

A Novel by

Abhishek Kapoor

Copyright ©Abhishek Kapoor, 2019

SWA Registered

All rights reserved.

PAPERBACK PRINTED IN INDIA BY

Bhakti Prakashan

Shri Ram Krishna Pragya Bhawan, 8/87, Arya Nagar,

Kanpur-208002

ISBN

ISBN 978-93-5361-182-8

Although he has worked on several film scripts in the past, as a fiction author, **The Selfish Betrayals** is the first novel written by **Abhishek Kapoor** and is dedicated to his **two little ones** who were unfortunately lost a bit too soon. A meticulous student since the very beginning, he completed his schooling from Seth Anand Ram Jaipuria School, Kanpur and engineering from PESIT, Bangalore. He started his career with an IT giant and then switched to another before venturing into entrepreneurship. Apart from the regular work, he also has keen interest in film making and sports, especially cricket and table tennis. Some of his short films have done quite well at various film festivals and have also been aired on national TV.

Get in touch with him with your queries, suggestions, ideas, reviews and feedback at **writetokapoor@hotmail.com**

"Centuries come, centuries go; people come, people go; time comes, time goes; movies come, movies go; but what remains forever is a book well written. I am excited to present my first book to you, just like an international cricket batsman is, to score his first run. Remember, all the runs that he scores in the span of his career, are the outcome of the effort he had put in prior to his selection.

There are two things that have given me the confidence to write books. First, the habit of writing the lengthiest essays in every English Language examination and second the art of storytelling, which I learnt from working on several scripts and screenplays and also direction of films.

Kanpur, my home city, is perhaps one of the most underestimated cities in the world. This book is a little reflection of the city and its people.

Happy reading"

- Abhishek Kapoor

Contents

I	Betrayal is intangible truth	7
II	Redemption lies in remembrance	29
III	Aim big, small aims are a crime	55
IV	Do good and good will return	92
V	Is the road to success same as the road to failure?	114
VI	Can someone blaze inside with outer ease?	161
VII	Fight for right	207
VIII	Being affluent is a curse or a blessing?	233
IX	Time moves so slow yet so fast	261

Chapter I

Betrayal

is

intangible truth

The eerie darkness of that bizarre yet serene night in the otherwise noisy industrial town of Kanpur, located within the territories of the imperial state of the magnificent Taj Mahal, would never escape any ordinary man's memory as an incessant black curtain draped over the eternal sky. Though the courageous and faint moonlight seemed to overcome its struggle to get to every unsheltered corner of the town, somewhat lessening the inky gloom, it was not bright enough to dull the luminous stars that appeared as speckled twisted, amorphous shapes glittering confidently in the heavens above.

The holy Ganges acted as a perfect symbol of how far some irrational humans had come. What was once lethally polluted and even referred to as dead by some lamenting experts continued its heroic venture to team up with life - fish and plants. The many delicate shades of the submerged pebbles shining due to the radiance of the moon were more priceless than any incalculable jewel in the jewel box of any undisputed queen in a fairy tale. Just to watch the sleeping young ducklings at the corner of the river was a balm to a sane mind and a reminder to all that we must protect what we have and cherish it.

This night was so still and peaceful yet the gorgeous women with treasured long and straight hair would not like it much as the outright calm would not let their silky hair fly to enhance their sultry enchantment. It was that kind of a night when even a feather would fall without drifting one way or the other. Even the brown leaves were utterly motionless as if they belonged to a canvas of any absorbed illustrator. The inelegant and awkward silence had taken over the otherwise vociferous town with a clumsy feel of melancholy as if the calm had given complete authority to the demons singing premonition melodies in the hells above.

As midnight came trailing the entirety was buried by the city folk as they had gone into a long trance, filled with dreams and nightmare. Only an isolated mature white owl, sitting in its grand mansion on the top of a hollow banana tree in the corner of the lush side of the prominent Green Park, seemed to be amused by its own creepy hoot, as if justifying the spurious stories of nocturnal owls taking away kids who don't sleep.

Who can think of global issues when their own child has been stolen from them? The battle against illicit drugs had been false for so long, the laws against them were just a screen for keeping the money in the hands of wretched criminals. A couple of seasoned police officers, one a dynamic inspector and the other a middle aged constable, in the corner of an abandoned street just let free into the dark two vicious criminals who had serious charges of drug smuggling on them. There were deceitful smiles all around that section of the public road. Evidently, the criminals must have offered a good amount of cash to the officers and in return the scandalous duo was not hesitant whatsoever to liberate the devils, permitting them to blend into the society as sugar dissolves in milk. Maybe, they knew deep within that they will be handsomely paid once again to catch the same culprits. Money, after all, is only loyal to money.

When a person or a group, entrusted with a position of authority turns dishonest and bribery takes over like alcohol takes over the control of the brain of an irregular drunkard, it becomes fair to blindly assume that a criminal activity has taken place. Who was the criminal in this case, will remain an unanswered one crore question forever with four options – the corrupt officers, the criminals, the sleeping citizens or all of the above.

Meanwhile, outside a luxurious multi storied apartment in one of the most classy and elite locality of the municipality, there was a lone costly car, an age old antique, rather a collector's dream, parked in an uncharacteristic cramped up visitor's parking. The parking was just outside the towering boundary walls of the campus, in between the two gates, one for entry and the other strictly, for exit. The impenetrable walls surrounding the entire apartment were made of solid brick and coated with the darkest shade of blue. They perfectly served as the border between the rich and the not so rich.

Judging by its appearance, the parked car seemed to belong to the later part of the 1960s or maybe the early 70s but it looked right of a Hollywood suspense cum horror movie. It was a two door grey colored serious sports vehicle with an elongated version of the bonnet. The giant grill, which apart from exemplary style, served as the outlet for the heat waves ejecting from the hefty engine, was right in between four circular headlights, two on either side, fitted into their sophisticated rectangular box. It was indeed a high valued collector's item due to its age and quality.

A couple of security guards in their modish blue uniforms had already posed for their social media selfies with this aesthetically graceful Challenger. Not only were they expecting a lot of likes and comments from their obliged friends, they even had a serious discussion about the car. Their detailed arguments ranged from technical ones to historical ones. Maybe the technology of those days required big and powerful engines, or maybe it was just the class which the younger lot need to learn as quickly as they possibly can. One of the animated guards was of the opinion that the car would powerfully roar when the mighty engine revs up while his witless co-worker thought that it would whir like an electric fan. Anyway, the car seemed invaluable to its owner and perfectly suited the posh apartment, outside which it was parked.

The apartment was indeed colossal, probably the tallest and the most high priced property in the simple unembellished town. The immense white structure had a glorious naval blue colored bell made into the wall near the top floor, the twenty fourth. Though it was merely the builder's logo, it was so high that some ordinary people thought that it signified affluence. They thought that if a common man reached that emblem, he would be regarded as the Sultan of success.

Success, no doubt is not an accident. It is indeed a result of hard work, perseverance, learning from failures, loyalty and perfection, but can never be classified logically. A rich business tycoon may have achieved financial success but not necessarily romantic success, or a vice versa scenario for a low paid gentleman. But, in the not so far-sighted working minds of the common citizens of Kanpur, success just meant financial success.

Just one floor above the branded unattainable bell was the most exclusive and lavish penthouse, perhaps the costliest one of the city, so boastfully displaying and glorifying the achievements of its owner. That house was one of those ones which rich people buy when they get paranoid about having too much money. But, money is a manifestation of power while power is a manifestation of fear, so one cannot be free of fear while he has money.

To the hungry, money may mean food, to the sick, it may mean medicine. To any full time employee it may be the paper and metal he traded his life for, and for the employer, it may just be a not so significant financial gain but it is always a cold thing of no value whatsoever in the motionless hands of the dead.

Anyway, thoroughly unmoved by the events and affairs of the outside world, on an extravagant Pink Ivory chair which resembled the eternal throne of any royalty, inside the chilled air conditioned bedroom of an ambitious and glorious pool side suite of this grand paradise, just by the side of the cushy and lush bed, there relaxed an appealing, charismatic man, dressed in macho infernal black tuxedos along with matching buffalo leather fancy shoes with pointed toes and perfectly stitched thick soles.

In his early thirties, this jazzy guy had an exclusive flawless aura about him despite his slightly muscular body. His eyes were black but not soulless or lifeless, instead they were like two pristine stones of Onyx. His posture was strong, erect and graceful, as if he had the backbone made of steel. The man had a tremendous jaw line, similar to the ones that action heroes of Bollywood flicks work hard to get. He was eminently handsome and a regular to the gym nonetheless. His bone structure was symmetrical, cheek bones high and prominent. Despite his pastel brown skin his nose was exactly at the appropriate place to match his dark black curly hair, set in place with the silky and shining hair gel.

The watch he wore on the wrist of his left hand, was none the less expensive. The gold in it glinted casually in the bright light fitted inside the dome shaped structures on the perfectly whitewashed designer false ceiling. The rational choice of opting for this genuinely stylish and sophisticated watch in the modern age of smart watches and gadgets, hinted at the exemplary class and taste of the young man. To the birds and cats this watch may be no more interesting than a rock, probably less important than a worm, but to well-informed cultured humans it was a real substantial antiquity.

The reassuring soft instrumental music in the background from those exaggerated speakers, fitted into the ravishing wooden roof of the dining room adjacent to the bedroom, would comfort anyone's ears, just like how a deep sleep after two days of ceaseless endeavor refreshes the entire body of a menial workhorse. The aroma of the branded designer candle sticks in the hand carved soapstone beige incense and candle holder subdued the scent of the perfume of the personable good looking man with a clean cut perky face. A slight look towards the floral net work of the holder was enough to make an estimation of its utopian cost.

The man had a half full glass of whiskey in his robust hands and was sipping the intoxication in the most virile manner while the soothing bottle and two other glasses were kept on the sleek glass table next to him, one filled with the booze till the brim, whereas the other contained nothing but emptiness.

The sleek table, by the way, looked like a rich porcelain plate, standing strong on three pencil thin stilts. The ends of the stilts curved up and curled exactly like gnome shoes. On the top, apart from the high quality glasses, there was a surprisingly humble desk calendar. It was thick as every day of the year had its own personal page. Maybe the affluent require specific sheets to mark their important days as finding and circling particular days on a common month sheet is too cumbersome. Anyway, the date as displayed silently by that lonely calendar was the fifth day of August, 2018.

The almost soundless golden knob turned and the washroom door, opposite to the neatly dressed man and carved out of wood, opened. Walking through it entered into the room a graceful and well cherished lady, on the wrong side of forty. She was splendidly dressed in a fancy and high priced pink night gown. Though she was slightly pudgy, she carried herself so admirably that even most of the appealing teens would engage into spiteful conversations after seeing her through the corner of their wary eyes.

Her eyes were the type of brown that was like a sweet chocolate, the chocolate that melts at the slightest bit of heat from love, happiness, or anger. But that chocolate can also grow hard from the cold harsh reality that is apparent in this unpredictable world. The foundation that she had applied all over her average looking, round and brown face helped her to hide all the scars and blackheads below it. She clearly had finished the time consuming makeup with some mascara and black eyeliner.

Walking enticingly towards the desirable man's personal space, she had just the right look of heat in her chocolate colored eyes. She had let open her long and curly amber hair which added a lot to her charm. Her hands and legs were smooth and pampered, just like the rest of her body. She had tiny palms with long and bony fingers, like that of a skilful pianist who played the perfect melody for every occasion. Her sharp nails were coated with dark shade of pink, matching with her night dress.

Though her silver colored glittering shoes had pencil shaped heels and uncovered pointed toes that revealed the beautiful dark brown nail paint perfectly, it must be a talking point at the kitty parties. The soft leather must have been tremendously comfortable and high backs were reassuringly expensive. The three inch heel had the perfect balance of femininity and practicality.

"Thanks Monty, for being with me at times when my mood is lousy", she said in her alluring voice as a naughty smile blossomed on her thick lips, exposing her cream colored teeth. Although she was a North Indian, she spoke perfect English. Her accent was so pleasing to the ears of the listeners, especially due to her speech patterns and rhythm. Her voice was the perfect combination of loudness, pitch and the quality of sound.

There was no doubt whatsoever that Monty was the one whose mere presence had pulled the affection seeking lady into that room. The brown eyes met the black stones, not once, not twice but six times in those warm sixty seconds. Staring at her partner was the only thing that kept her brain alive, giving her observations which might assign her characters and dialogue.

"When I see you, it is as if speed and time come so close to each other, as if the progress of time collapses into one tiny speck of dust and explodes at the speed of light. It's as if my Universe begins and ends with you. I could run forever, search forever, but in the end, every path my soul takes, leads right back to your heart. I love you my man, Monty C Dhingra!"

Monty kept glaring at her with his ever so revealing black eyes as he raised his left brow in the process. Perhaps staring was the only medium of communication he wanted to use for the extra special moment. He looked fixedly with wide open eyes at the lady as if her head was transparent and he was fascinated by an object three inches behind her skull. The air that left the slight gap between his red lips was warm enough to comfort the lady. The red color of his pristine lips was exactly the one that the bodies of fire engines have painted on them.

With an acceleration in her heart rate, that had nothing to do with fear but everything to do with what her body and mind wanted, she continued, "My husband Rajendra is like the unhealthy drug you need to take even when you don't want to and it spoils your day, while you, my macho man, are the healthy one, who puts my mind into a frenzy of sparks."

As she unhurriedly sat on the cushy bed in front of Monty, the fine charmer slowly picked up the glass full of whiskey from the table using his right hand and cautiously offered it to her. She was delighted by the caring nature of her romantic partner and took it leisurely from his hands with a gentle touch of compassion on his tough fingers.

"This medicine you present to me heals me, and though I am addicted, I feel safe, because you are here," she said taking in the first sip of the alcohol, decorating the ordinary glass with the maroon color of her branded lipstick, the shade resembling the hue of seeds of a freshly cut pomegranate.

"They say that there is no excuse to be bored, but unfortunately, I have one. My husband," she continued," he is a nerd, a typical boring business man. I don't enjoy his company at all. And in fact, I can never share my mental and private feelings with him, like I can with you my dear."

Comparable to a true and authentic gentleman, Monty stood up from his royal throne straight on his muscular legs, and looking directly into the gullible eyes of his romantic companion, he bent down on his left knee. His right hand took out a fake plastic rose from the inner pocket of his tuxedo and with a flawless body language and eye contact, presented it to his sweetheart, saying, "Naina, I know how much you crave for Strawberry ice cream. I also know how every couple goes out to the ice cream parlor together. Obviously, we cannot do that, we cannot go out together in public, but trust me we can have so much more fun here. Trust me Naina you will not be able to forget me till this rose is alive."

There was no hint in his accent of his Punjabi heritage, not even in his voice. He could be reading a user manual and be as good as any digital personal assistant. Everything he said flowed as smooth as a meadow river and that deep quality of voice just added to his decent charm. At this special moment, words rolled out of his tongue as a timbre of warmth, each one wrapped in a deep heavy voice.

Naina frowned slightly, not because she lacked trust but because she was taken aback by the absurd gift and such unanticipated cheeky words, but running out of options in her mind, she accepted the preposterous rose from her drunken admirer. Though it was a counterfeit copy of the original, it was sprayed with a delightful perfume that gave it the feel of the real one. As she looked down towards the spurious leafy green stem of the deceptive blossom, she right away noticed a tiny circular logo on which the three letters – MCD, were imprinted. She did not seem to understand what that corporate identity type of thing actually meant, so promptly pointing towards the emblem, she asked, "To be precise, what does MCD stand for dear Monty?" But there was no answer.

Naina took to a couple of seconds to carefully scrutinize the fictitious crimson souvenir with a green leaf, made of high quality rubber, attached to its end. That much time was enough for Monty to stand up back on his feet. He stood still for a few slow deep breaths, inhaling from the nose and exhaling from his mouth as if he was a bit nervous, but did not want to show that he was nervous. He finished sipping the last drop of his celestial bitter drink, and raised his empty fragile glass high up with his left hand, his eyes closed, resembling those of a wise and experienced

Yogi in transcendental meditation. A couple of feet could be added to the anticipated six feet and had that inanimate glass been a despondent man suffering from Acrophobia, he would have lost consciousness then and there.

In a rather baffling turn, Monty, in the most perplexed shriek, shouted at the top of his authoritative voice, "Cheers! Cheers to our new relationship!" With this boisterous proclamation, he dropped the destitute defenseless glass, leaving it to take a rapid and abrupt free fall to the cemented floor below and break into numerous small and big pieces with just one loud crash, similar to the death cry of an innocent and unaware juvenile when struck by the fierce bullet of a deadly terrorist.

Just like emphatic noise of firing of a gun prompts the athletes to start their run at a big racing event, the loud sound of shatter of that unfortunate and powerless glass was perhaps a signal to convey the precise time. All of a sudden, the main metallic silvery door of the exclusive suite banged open with a sound as loud as the sudden burst of one of the loudest fire crackers on Diwali, and hastily entered two gentlemen, one in early fifties and the other a twenty something youth. The elderly man with a dark complexion and a round tummy, dressed in spotless white kurta pajama was apparently the lady's fuming husband while the expressionless youth who accompanied him was wearing a tucked in full sleeved, shabby and wrinkled grey shirt and faded blue old jeans.

From his resentful expressions and hostile walk towards the couple, it was clear the bald middle aged man, was enraged at his credible wife. The restless and fidgety manner in which he conducted himself gave the impression that he had been waiting impatiently since ages for this very moment. With the brown knuckles of his left hand clenching the fist too hard and gritted teeth from effort to not lose composure, the hunched form of the husband exuded an animosity that was burning like hot lava coming from a recent volcano eruption.

Somehow with his right hand, he reached the pocket of his white silky churidaar pajama and took out a bundle of hot currency notes and throwing them flat on the sleek table, next to the calendar, he said, "Your work is over and thanks for it. Mr. Monty C Dhingra and Mr. Chetan Prasad, you both may now leave my home."

Naina's brown eyes widened. She was as stunned as any levelheaded person would be if a black colored rat came out of his trouser's back pocket. She sat there motionless, unable to breathe, unable to speak, unable to cry and not even able to fight. All she knew was that she had been tricked by lewd and devilish Monty on the orders of her skeptical and dubious husband. Only the feeling of betrayal bounced around inside her round skull. Her chocolate eyes were about to melt due to the heat of frustration. However, she failed to realize that in her attempt to find love, she herself was also in a similar process of betraying her rather boring husband.

Chetan picked the money from the sleek table unhurriedly from his right hand, but neither did he utter a word nor did his prompt action make any kind of noise. His motionless eyes turned towards the heavy calendar on the table. He gazed at it very carefully and then slowly turned the page over by a gentle flick from the rugged index finger of his left hand, after realizing that midnight had already passed some minutes ago.

The calendar now indicated the correct date. It was indeed the sixth day of August, 2018, and the fond Sunday made sure of avoiding any attention as it slowly changed into Monday, the day which is not the most solicitous one for most of the common people.

Chetan remained expressionless and it appeared that he would continue to be poker faced even if the earth stopped its rotation. He was a tall fellow, lean as a greyhound, flat-flanked, in color neither dark nor fair but somewhere in between. All ten brazen nails of his thin and seemingly weak hands were probably a product of hard work, dirty, uncut and unshaped. His eyes were deep-set and looked out from a face that was burned to the color of a brick. His nose was straight and large, cheeks well hollowed and covered with thin lining of facial hair, more due to being a lazy lump than a style freak. The face would have been more articulate if only his personality was not that of a deadpan.

And then the impossible happened! Unexpectedly, Chetan Prasad reacted! He reacted only on seeing the gorgeous Naina and her pink lipstick, and that too with stare on her eye catching night attire, followed by a cunning and devious smile, like a sly fox.

They say that a desperate man on a mission will never waste time on miniscule things, so with blind trust on the outrageous husband, Chetan did not feel there was any need to count the hot cash. He just picked those valuable notes with his right hand and passed them to his smart boss with his left hand, swapping the hot cash like a proficient magician between his own willowy hands.

Monty accepted the fees paid by the dismayed client without any fuss and moved out of the sumptuously rich suite through the open main door with the money held tight in his left hand. He took giant steps towards the door without even bothering to look at the heart broken dismal lady with whom he had a sincere romantic relationship just a few seconds back, accompanied by wily Chetan, who slammed the door from out as hard as he possibly could, leaving the couple all alone inside, to inevitably clash in private till the harsh morning.

Just outside the main door, Chetan let go his seriousness like an amateur actor goes absolutely out of his character when the cameras are turned off. From the deadpan he was inside, he now turned completely articulate, though maintaining that cunning smile on his darkened lips, darkened maybe from months and years of smoking.

Like the slow motion views third umpires look for before making their final decision on an appeal for a close catch during a cricket match, Chetan in the most relaxed manner, took out a protracted cigarette from the pocket of his wrinkled shirt, and handed it over to Monty. From the back pocket of his compliant jeans, using his left hand, he withdrew a lighter and suddenly changed pace to light the cigarette for his boss.

Monty sucked in the first puff deep into his lungs, remembering all the warnings but caring for none. The rich odor of the injurious smoke permeated the verandah, wisps of silver grey smoke curled and danced their way through the thick, hazy air as if excited to escape the area above their heavy heads. The ash sprinkled across the shining tiles when he flicked the filter as if each floating piece were a moment of his life sheared away.

The chief still had the pile of his well deserved cash in his sturdy left hand. Without even looking at it, he gifted Chetan some notes and the latter accepted them graciously, keeping them in his jeans pocket as quick as a famous actress' wink without even bothering to count them. Perhaps in their elite minds, counting and calculating was so middle class, anyway it was unavailable to the poor and meaningless to the rich.

The four physically tired feet took short and steady steps across the glossy tiles of the corridor, dusty canvas sneakers next to the shined pointed-toe buffalo leather shoes towards the elevator. On reaching their destination, Chetan pressed the buttons of two different lifts but both arrived at the same time. Monty took the one on the left while Chetan took the right one, and they moved in as if they never knew each other.

Monty's elevator was a dark and creaky thing that moved like a lazy snail and smelled of sour milk. Someone had switched off the light inside it and Monty did not bother to switch it on either. It was not the one used by the building staff but was dirty after the whole day's toil. The walls of this elevator were made of glass so he could watch the security guards on the ground floor expand from ants to bears and then to humans as it reached the end of its excursion.

On reaching the ground floor, Monty came out of the elevator, with the special cigarette still fixed in the gap between his tremulous lips and walked towards the gate of the apartment through the arched portico, passing the salutes of the enthusiastic security guards. His footsteps echoed sharply around the deserted square, sounding overly loud in his own ears, like the booming heartbeat of a condemned prisoner.

He was walking through a place of incredible cleanliness, as uninhabited that night as the path of a ship in the middle of the Indian Ocean. Instead of seeing the guards, he saw nothing - no light, no shadows, just empty white. Every surface was dustless and the ceramic tiled floor reflected every detail of the passage. The atmosphere was placid, almost silent.

There were no doors, no windows in the walkway, only more walls stretching away like some infinite asylum. Walking became running in an attempt to get quickly to the way out, with his eyes following to where the white became darkness.

The last security guard at the imposing exit gate of the apartment, with a prodigious wavy moustache arranged in perfect curls, did not appear to show as much zeal as his painstaking companions. Instead of the frisky salute, he murmured near Monty's ears, "Till when Mr. Monty will you keep solving these miniscule messes? Wish you luck for some bigger offences."

Monty heard the croaky rough voice of the middle aged guard, who probably had a sore throat, but chose not to respond and continued his walk, like an online video game player who is unwilling to quit even after regular calls from his mother for dinner.

The Challenger in the cramped visitor's parking belonged to Monty and he unlocked it using the traditional gold plated key, as the automatic central lock system was so much the future in those days, free from anxiety or much responsibility. Neither there was a single facial expression of regret or guilt on his face, nor was there any confusion in his body language.

Though the period car smelled of stale beer, the interior was sublime and steering, pure gold. It was a large round metallic wheel fitted with two protruding gear shaped shafts, one used for the actual four gear system and reverse shift, while the other one was the emergency handbrake. Oh the forefathers of this gentleman must have been a class apart to choose to buy that beast!

He sat on the most beautiful, comfortable and straight backed drivers' seat of his irreplaceable and prized possession, coated with brown leather, and slowly took a couple of relaxing deep breaths. The alcohol and the smoke had really set in by this time. He felt like he was at the top of the world and his mind was getting slow and fuzzy.

Precisely a couple of seconds before the amazing and prepossessing rush to the other world was about to get activated, all the godly delight concluded abruptly as the left door of the warm and congenial car opened with an unpleasant and disturbing sound. It was Chetan. He sat into the car with a dull, heavy thud next to his chief but his characteristic tricky smile on his coffee colored lips seemed to have faded away and what was left was the original blank facial expression. This time even Monty's face did not convey any emotion and inscrutably, he turned the key and switched on the headlight. The right ones were perfectly bright but the inner left one failed to light up, but that was not a concern for the regulars.

"Focus on the front windshield Sir, and not the deceiving rearview mirror" said Chetan is his raspy voice, like that of an old man, though his face was pretty young. But there was absolutely no reaction from the chief. Maybe the bad is more potent and contagious as humans always give an impression that they generalize bad more than good.

The three headlights shone out bravely into the black night, only to be swallowed by the pressing dark in some parts of the not so well maintained bumpy road they chose to follow to drive into the uncommunicative and restrained dark night with the lit up cigarette still in the middle of Monty's pristine and immaculate lips.

Chapter II

Redemption lies in remembrance

As the vociferous car engine sung to the dark and deserted main roads of the sleeping town, Monty relished the roaring winds that surprisingly seemed to dry up the shining gel on his nicely trimmed curly black hair and simultaneously whistled in his round and unconcerned ears. The subtle tilt of the philanderer's proud head was much adorable as he turned the big round steering towards the left, then towards the right but mostly keeping it straight.

However, there was an atmosphere of absolute gloom inside the slowly moving car on a boring long drive back to the headquarters. An unpleasant and disagreeable feeling of dejection and despondency had crept into the elegantly and cautiously designed automobile just like the damp into bare timber during the rainy season. The thick and dense white smoke from the cigarette hung in the air inside the enclosed car and slowly shifted out through the half open glasses of the window like the scary ghosts in mild breeze. It seeped into all of Chetan's pores, travelling to his heart which beat more morosely. Even the owl shrieks came to him as if from a deep well rather than somewhere high up on the passing trees. On the rear seat, which by the way had no doors to enter, there sat a three feet tall cute pink teddy bear, smiling to the world like always.

Though the sound of changing of gears through the elongated shaft attached firmly to the gold plated steering, another masterpiece of engineering design from the history, was almost negligible, the rattling sound of reverberation had teamed up with the hiss of pneumatics and the grumble of the straining engine to overpower the song playing at a low volume on the contemporary audio system fitted right at the middle of the steering and the dashboard.

Whereas the music is always expected to soar through the air like an eagle on an up-draft, taking with it the very souls of the listening audience, stealing away their breaths from their tangible bodies, but the song that played was one of the saddest classic from the early part of the twentieth century. The lyrics were something like this, *"Soon there will be candles and prayers that are sad I know* but *let them not weep, let them know that I am glad to go."*

Chetan was clearly not impressed by that dull, tedious and repetitious music. The depressing tune of that sorrowful ditty irritated him so much that he turned the out of place music system off by long pressing its power button. In order to pass time, he began tapping the dashboard with the irregular fingers of both his hands as if he was an expert Tabla player. Unable to kill the boredom, he stared out of the window, maybe wishing he was anywhere but there.

Monty was unaffected by these petty and abstract things as he was just trying hard to concentrate on the driving, which by the way appeared a herculean task after those pegs of wickedly strong whiskey. For reasons best known to him, his focus was in simply not there. His shoulders slumped uncharacteristically with every passing minute and even his unblinking beady black eyes were losing it out to some random thoughts in his otherwise thoughtful and well regulated mind. His brain tingled like a hand that has been sat on for too long. In order to feel something out of the ordinary, there has to be a positive or negative event, but Monty's feelings at that time were absolutely neutral.

"Bear with me Chetan, as I am going to share with you the most traumatic experience I have faced in the thirty one years of my apathetic yet venturesome life." Monty said this in low spirits as if he had lost all hope and courage. These were clearly not the words of an indefatigable investigator, but those of a preoccupied obsessed theorist. Though they were heavy, his voice was still as deep and as pleasant to the ears of the listener as it was before. Maybe being normal was just not his forte.

Chetan already felt a bit relaxed after turning off the song and on the pure leather coated brown cushioned seat, he leaned back momentarily, pulling up the sleeves of his shriveled grey shirt, already dry from sweat after the entire day's laborious toil. His exposed forearms were streaked with green veins that sat comfortably within his oily light brown skin. Crossing his arms against each other, he nodded to the statement made by his chief.

"Just a few days back, I met an old lady begging at the side of the busy street near Naveen Market. She must have been a real fearless tough woman throughout her meager life, as she looked comfortable in a rugged cloth that contained all colors from the spectrum." As Monty said these words, the cigarette in his wet and strangely hard lips burnt out completely and he threw the filter right outside the window. He then continued with his poignant story, "She would have been much fairer if all those confluent dark spots were not there on her triangular face. So many of them on her little plump face with small brown pale spaces here and there, like the tips of grass struggling to show through the golden-brown leaves of fall."

Chetan slowly uncrossed his grotesquely long and thin arms as he turned more and more attentive with each pithy but needlessly formal sentence of the speech of his boss, just like how attentive a front row seated scholarly student gets when the lecturer describes a new chapter of her preferred subject.

"As I offered her a ten rupee coin," asserted Monty as he leaned just a bit forward but maintaining the erect structure of his back, "she uttered the most contemplative words about family."

"What were those words, Sir", asked Chetan turning his observant head slightly towards his muscular chief who was now occupied in the shifting the antique gears, but his facial expressions still comparable to a blank sheet of paper.

Perhaps years of smoking and alcohol abuse had made Chetan's voice sound like it traveled via rough vocal chords of heavy sandpaper into the outside world with a lot of force, or maybe some long or unrecognized illness had done it. No doubt once it would have been a pleasing deep and grave voice but now it confused the listener to differentiate the pronunciation of certain words as they literally sounded the same, example words and wards.

Shifting quickly to the third gear and stepping leisurely at the gigantic accelerator, and without even looking towards his co-driver, Monty repeated the few but impactful words of the feeble lady, "Memories made with family are everything in your life. May God bless you dear son, with the most unforgettable ones."

Chetan's eyebrows furrowed a little in an expression indicating displeasure. "Boring story again," he thought but had no valor to stop the chief, so he responded half heartedly. His nose widened as he said, "She was cent percent correct sir, and that is precisely why I always take leaves from work every now and then. Even my goal is to create memories with my loved ones."

There was a minute of silence as the theorist went into some intense deep process of thinking. There was silence to his soul. He felt the chill in his blood, coldness bringing the synapses of his brain to a standstill. Part of it was pain, yet the one he could endure, one he could sleep through night after night without the anesthesia of false hope.

Meanwhile, the deputy took this opportunity to withdraw another cylindrical and overlong cigarette from his pocket and offered it to the boss, who accepted it instantly, like a starving man stuck in the middle of the ocean on a deserted island snatches the packet of refreshments when the help arrives. He once again lighted it up for the commander, this time using a matchstick and then threw the remains of the stick through the window, straight on the dusty road.

The mud caked street by the way, was barren with a couple of hungry but unthreatening stray sober dogs roaming here and there, mainly near the dustbins that were brimful of stinking garbage, especially the plastic domestic refuse, and near the wastes of the shut food joints, struggling to find some nourishment for their budding little ones, right below the monumental hoarding that stated, "Save cows, save humanity," a convincing message by a couple of renowned local social and political workers of the compassionate and concerned society.

Despite no traffic, Monty was driving at a slow speed. Perhaps he loved the respectable tortoise from the famous childhood story of race of the hare and the tortoise or maybe when one is lost in a series of actions of considering or reasoning about some past experiences, he loses his usual momentum of the current progress. After a saintly short and explosive burst of breath, he continued, "This little episode at the apartment of Rajendra Mehrotra sir before sometime, reminded me of my superfluous family, my mom and my dad."

And then, there was that deafening loud noise due to sudden application of brakes. It was intense but incoherent. Following the horrible disturbance, there were a couple of seconds of complete absence of sound, sight and sense. Half of a meter was perhaps the only distance which saved their sharp ears from getting filled from the sound of crushing of glass mixed with the distinct crackles of their bones.

"Oh sir, please be careful when you drive. I know you have taken a couple of extra pegs of the free whiskey but we nearly drove over that protruding divider in the middle of the road," exclaimed Chetan, frightened from the fact that their centuries old car could have just overturned, had Monty not applied brakes and turned the steering wheel towards the left with his full strength at the precise time.

Thanks to the municipal organization's tireless efforts, it was a tricky road in the first place to drive on, full of revolting potholes and poking speed breakers along with the curvy divider extending above the surface in the middle of the narrow driveway. Secondly the thinker who was driving the vehicle was distinctly drunk. It does not matter anyway how skilful the Captain of the Ship is, if he is affected by alcohol to the extent of losing control of his own behavior, the ship is bound to sink taking everyone on it deep below the surface, maybe to rest in peace.

Though the application of brakes failed to put the smile off the pink teddy bear's cute face at the rare, the pleasant and comfortable co-driver's seat, despite its covering of buffalo leather, was not as cozy and enjoyable for the young man now as it had become a few minutes ago. The brown lips which now appeared like coffee without sugar, uttered, "Sir, I think we must discuss the ineffaceable memories first and then drive. Please stop the car. We can have the full conversation and then I will take a rickshaw to my residence and you can drive to yours." Surprisingly, all his words were now as clear as the facts after a replay is seen during a wicket on a no ball in a cricket match.

For the first time during this weird drive, Monty turned his perfectly black eyeballs towards his lieutenant and with a contemptuous wry smile on his muddled face, somehow still maintaining the grace in his comfortable full bodied posture. He took a left turn into a narrow lane and parked the car at the side of a comparatively insignificant pothole. The tail lights of the car perfectly reflected in the turbid water that lay there, maybe, due to the washing of someone's bicycle from the hand pump that was shying away in the dark on the opposite side of the road.

The presence of electric poles proved that there used to be street-lamps years ago in that lane, but they had all been sabotaged for their solar triggers. Maybe, that's how the local gangs arm their weaponry. The authorities too rig things up with dirt over the sensor and then after some days whatever they have rigged up explodes.

Without wasting a single second of time, Chetan unlocked and opened the door and immediately got down from the car. After leaving that warm and restful seat, he appeared as relived as a severely constipated man is while exiting the washroom. They say it takes just a few moments to reduce the measure of towering blood pressure, provided there are no more occurrences that make it rise again. The tension and stress from his face faded out and he could now afford to take a couple relaxing breaths.

Monty got down leisurely from his side of the car, the burning cigarette still in between the fingers of his overly assertive masculine left hand and moved towards the wooden bench by the side of a closed tea shop. The bench was built of several planks of wood crudely nailed together and looked like a middle school project gone badly wrong. The closed shutter of the tea shop in the background, a crooked bench and a hand pump on the opposite side of the pot hole on the filthy road appeared a perfect setting for Chetan and Monty to continue their dismal conversation.

"So what I was saying is that today's episode reminded me of my father and mother", Monty continued from where he had left, taking small, slow draws of the cigarette as he sat on the right side of the bench, followed by his deputy who had no option but to sit on the left, keeping a close eye on the high power car which Monty had not bothered to lock.

Chetan could see the dejection in Monty's eyes, his movements and his drooping posture. However, he dared mention it to him. On the other hand, Monty felt that he hid his emotions from the world and his position as ruler of the synagogue demanded a look of complete confidence and control. That was indeed strange because his body language sent clear vibes of inward weeping.

"My parents, dear Chetan, were pragmatic people who always taught me to deal with things sensibly and realistically in a way that was based on practical rather than theoretical considerations", said Monty with his eyes closed in remembrance but the burning cigarette still in his left hand and keeping left leg over the right thigh like a proud king sitting on his conquered throne after a fierce battle.

Chetan sat like any Minister would in the King's court. His legs were straight down with respect and shoulders bent slightly forward to show how attentive he was. He was indeed quick to respond, "In the last six years of our professional relationship, you have never mentioned about your parents and never have you taken a leave to visit them. Who are they and where do they live now?"

"Well, well, as you know my surname is Dhingra which makes me son of a Punjabi dad."

"Yes. That is so obvious, sir."

"My dad was a combative and loud renowned advocate, who practiced in the district court of Sitapur. He was much famous and respected within the lawyer community and had good contacts with the top officials of the town including some noted bureaucrats of the country."

"No wonder you are wearing this black radiating classically simple tuxedo now sir, maybe the notable style in you is just genetic," said Chetan rubbing the thin lining of facial hair on his cheeks with the uncut nails of his left hand.

"Yes Chetan, I am fashionably elegant and sophisticated because I try to copy my father's style from whatever I remember of him," said Monty raising his head just a little bit as the gel of his curly black hair shined jubilantly in the peaceful moonlight.

"Where is he sir nowadays?" reiterated Chetan, who was now completely attentive to each and every word and his eyes had almost turned into square shaped face of the dice.

The ash sprinkled across the wood of the crooked bench when Monty flicked the filter, as if each floating piece were a moment of his life sheared away. He inhaled deeply, letting the smoke seep into each of his living cells. Not bothering to listen to his lieutenant, he moved on with his story, "My mother was a mushy and soft spoken Bengali housewife."

"Oh, so theirs was a love marriage," exclaimed the lean deputy, Chetan. Normally, he was the one who hid all his emotions, but that was not the time to hide anything. The thought of the romantic story he was just about to hear, seemed to pour excitement in him, like the sunshine into white linen curtain in the morning.

"Yes, it was. But perhaps, that was also the biggest mistake of their life."

Alas, the lively excitement that had taken so long to build up, died with just one sentence, and Chetan went back to his seriously inscrutable mode as his eyes turned motionless and fixed on Monty's polished black shoes. Still, trying to maintain some positivity, he slowly raised his head and said, "Sir, nobody made a bigger mistake than he who did not do anything."

"Agree Chetan, but mistakes are your real teachers. And the most respected teacher is your latest mistake," replied Monty staring at the gold watch on his wrist, next to the fingers that held the special cigarette.

"Sorry to interrupt sir, but why was their marriage a mistake in your opinion?"

"Because of the daily arguments between them, and of course, the manner in which my father resorted to arguing with his fists after his words had already packed a powerful punch everyday on my mother was just beyond a normal man's imagination. Carefully spoken, without drama, his words had an air of finality to them and no matter how hard she railed against them, nothing would change his mind."

"So sorry to know that sir, but when the tension is so high, I believe that there should be an injection of love from either side instead of anger. Gift an idol of Lord Krishna instead of enmity."

"Sometimes, it is not that easy dear. I have witnessed as a kid my inviolable mother suppressing her violent impulses, maybe for my sake, and maybe for her own sake too, at times when my father was all up in her face, wanting a fight, forgetting that this was home, not court and she was his wife, not the opposite attorney or someone accused of murder."

"Misunderstandings are so disappointing. But where are they now?"

"Innocent misunderstandings are disappointing. Arbitrary events are also disappointing. The stories that actually grab all the attention are the ones that do not involve accidents, but people doing things on purpose, maybe to get the things they actually want, done under every circumstance, with a peculiar sense of desperation."

"Don't mind sir, but are they now separated?"

"The worst day of my life dear Chetan was not when I was almost killed by the open fire from that cheating mad woman last year, but the day when I lost my parents forever," said Monty referring perhaps to a life threatening event that was too hard for both of them to forget.

"Lost them forever, how sir? You have never told me about this," screamed Chetan, stunned by the fact that Monty's parents were no longer alive.

"Today I will share with you my story and how I came to this position sitting here at this very bench with you. But, let me go back several years and begin with an extremely short history of my story as it is important to understand it."

"You have all my time, Sir. I also have a couple of these special cigarettes left for you as you narrate the incidents from your mysterious life," said Chetan, checking the two long cigarettes in his wrinkled grey shirt's pocket.

Monty had all the emotion of wet concrete, his facial expressions just as loose. There was no anger, no joy, no sadness and no resentment. With the expression of a corner mannequin at a lavish cloth store, he began the crucial narration,

"As a kid, I used to sleep with my grandfather, in his room, adjacent to my parents' room in our dual room flat. There were nights I lay stock-still in the bed listening to the harsh sound of fighting and sometimes even of assault, overpowering the discourteous monotonous sound of snoring. My grandfather would snore all night long and my mother would shout, my father would begin laying into her and then the screaming would start. She cried, he seethed, he snored and I pushed my face into the cute pink teddy bear my six year old body was wrapped around in fetal position. I would think to myself whenever my mother left that sick place, I would leave with her, flee the unendurable violence."

"Intolerable," said Chetan with his equilateral dark mouth wide open in an expression of heavy shock.

When Monty spoke, his words were clear, clearer than water in the middle of the Arabian Sea. They seemed to echo from somewhere in the sky and the heavy accent and deep voice made him set apart from normal men, and made him seem as different as he was, in a good way.

"That night, my grandfather was not feeling well. The viral fever was burning him up, his aged and feeble body and lethargic spirit. He just lay still on his side of the bed as his skin radiated the heat of his blood. Frightened as you would expect a six year old to be in such a situation, I went to inform my parents. When I was about to enter their spine chilling and blood curdling room through the door which they never locked, I stopped and my feet froze exactly at the point where I was standing. Though I was right at the door and could see both, my dad and mom, I was too scared to enter that room. It was full of negativity."

"What was so bizarre there?"

"When the love between any couple dies, the trust also dies and what is born is the love for power. The usual argument between my dad and mom had crossed all the previous limits of endurance. That night, my dad was accusing my mom of adultery and she obviously was in tears. As a kid, I knew she was innocent and the cobbler had come just to repair my grandfather's old pair of shoes, but as an adult now, I do sometimes think that why the same cobbler used to visit our residence almost every second day."

"You can't be serious," Chetan turned as white as chalk. His eyes and mouth were frozen wide open in an expression of stunned surprise, and although he still managed to stare straight at Monty, he appeared as shocked as Julius Caesar when stabbed by the most trusted credible friend Brutus. The only difference here was that there was no Brutus, there was just the senior advocate Mr. Dhingra.

Monty had learned through experience, the importance of staying calm and maintaining composure in the worst situations. They say calm mind brings inner strength and self confidence, so that's very important for good health. Therefore, not melting like the wax in the burning candle of emotions was paramount for him as he continued the narration of this unforgettable memory, taking in lengthy draws of the cigarette.

"Then my respected dad moved towards the dark old unlocked wooden cupboard at the corner of his bedroom and from the top most drawer on the right side, took out his ancestral old fashioned gun. It was small, discreet, loaded and as deadly as it can get."

Chetan Prasad covered his sufficiently rueful face with the sweaty palm of his left hand as if someone was going deliver the final blow to him. His eyes turned wide and a gaggle of goose pimples laminated his frigid brown skin. Despite the fact that Monty knew that what was about to follow was something scary, difficult and dangerous, perhaps thanks to the whiskey and cigarette, he was brave enough to continue,

"At first the metal was cold in my dad's hands, icy perhaps, yet after just half a minute with his hand wrapped around it, the metal seemed ambient, feeling more like a part of his hand than a spooky tool of death. All of a sudden, the bullet spat out of his hand, red in the darkness. The sound was loud but I did not bother about it. The bullet hit my tender hearted mother who was only crying and pleading for mercy at that moment. It struck the broad forehead, next to her circular shaped red bindi and just below her saffron sindoor."

"Once in my childhood, while trying to climb a tree at school, I slipped and fell twelve feet to the ground, landing on my back. The impact knocked every wisp of air out of my lungs and I lay there struggling to inhale, to exhale or to do anything. The unbearable sensation of tingling pain of the current that passed through my nerves then is exactly how I feel now sir, trying to remember how to breathe, unable to speak, totally stunned as this scene bounces inside my little skull," said Chetan, still covering his furrowed face with his left palm and touching his consciously straight back with the right hand.

"Even the passage of the light slowed and the sounds became as if they were underwater. Aside from the rapid beat of my little heart, no muscle would move. The bullet entered as if she was nothing, just meat, blood, bones, blasting a cavity in her pious skull. Her face, so beautiful, so lovable in life was frozen, her big warm eyes wide open and her straight thin lipped mouth slack, as she was propelled backward with the plain white wall in the backdrop. Her eyes held mine and in those fractions of seconds she was there and then gone, the warmth of the ages that had been her love simply vanished with every drop of blood that turned her already red saree into darkest shade of crimson. Never till I breathe my last can I ever forget her final fall on the hard floor, exactly next to her soft bed.

The carnage did not end there, Chetan. After the brutal murder, the lethal eyeballs of the cold blooded killer turned towards the open door where he saw his son, that is, me, standing still and as emotionless as I am today, perhaps too young then to realize that humans even have the ability to react.

The pragmatic advocate may have realized at that very moment that he may not be punished for his anger, but the concerned family man had already been punished by his own anger. Perhaps he felt that he betrayed himself because of his hatred. The guilt made him ask for forgiveness. His exact words in the deepest masculine voice possible were, 'Sorry, but I have no other option.' Then he shot himself, the bullet hitting him straight on his own hair covered expansive forehead, using the same already loaded gun and with a splash of red color all over the spectrum of my little eyes, I lost him on spot, my feet still cemented at the open door and the tender voice box in my dry throat not able to produce any noise whatsoever.

The sick old man heard the two successive emphatic sounds and somehow managed to crawl into the room on all fours. He saw the scene, the two dead bodies and then he saw me. Words left him too. 'Answer me,' he roared with anger looking up as if someone was sitting above the ceiling and then he burst into the most hysterical crying you would ever see, into the screaming sobs only interrupted by the need to draw breath."

Monty may have been too young at the time of this terrorizing experience, but his mannequin reaction from that moment was exactly the same even on the present night, probably because of the years of hard work and practice of acting stone hearted, or maybe all his tears had just dried up, who knows? Maybe if he was an actor, he would already have respectfully won over the golden curvaceous lady. Even Chetan's brain stuttered for a moment, his eyes taking in more light than expected. Every part of him went into a pause mode until a few thoughts caught up.

"Though words have left me too sir, I would still say it will get easier to erase this ugly chapter of catastrophe from your resilient memory every time you try. If you don't mind sir, I would like to know how and where is your able grandfather now, the one who withstood the toughest test of life with such reliance on destiny." Chetan tried his best to continue the conversation even though he was tongue tied to speak many words.

"That was a night of no emotion in my life and today is another one. Ah, good question Chetan. My grandfather and I left that flat and moved to Kanpur forever, away from the staring eyes of the relatives and pinching mouths of the social circles of Sitapur, to start a completely new life here. He did not bring anything from the old residence, no furniture, no electronic equipment, no old clothes, not even his old spectacles, as he feared that those items would someday come back to haunt our memories.

What he did bring with him though, apart from me, was this Challenger and the three feet tall teddy who sits inside it. Despite his humungous efforts to totally eradicate all memories from my mind, which you know refuses to forget even the most negligible points about any incident, even an experienced man like him made a mistake.

Not sure I should call that a mistake, but this car was the one he gifted to his son, my father, on his eighteenth birthday, so he himself never wanted to empty his brain with his own memories. This car was a souvenir of the past, for my grandfather, and is certainly the most prized possession for me now as he gifted it to me with his eyes full of heavenly water on my eighteenth.

Coming to your question, Chetan, I lost him six years ago, on the twenty sixth day of December, due to old age and incurable neural disorders. That was the time when my career had just begun. He was the one who gave me all the confidence in the world and the push to achieve whatever I wanted to in my life. He was the one who taught me that whatever I get by achieving my goals is not important, rather what I become in trying to achieve has much higher value in life. He was also the one who made me learn how to forget the past but some scenes just could not wash away from my earthly brain."

"Sorry to hear that he is no more. What a strong man he must have been mentally and overly brave in his actions, to move on in life after seeing the death of his own child from his mature eyes which I am sure must have radiated a positive way out of even in the worst scenarios of existence. May the pure soul of the respectable man and your hero, rest in peace."

The grief surged into Chetan with every expelled breath, always reaching higher peaks, never sufficiently soothed by his long intakes of the adulterated surrounding air, full of smoke of cigarettes that burnt, one after the other like the remains of the departing souls at any burning ghat by the side of the holy Ganges. Missing only was a couple of tears that had subconsciously made way to the corner of his helpless eyes but some invisible force of the Nature had prevented them from spilling onto the materialistic wooden bench.

"What a cruel thing lack of trust is! It fills our hearts with hatred instead of love for our very own people." Monty said, surprisingly with a face of categorical nonchalance, like a teenager waiting on a long sunny day for a bus at the bus stop with a mobile in his hands and ear phones inserted completely in both his ears. The pain he hid behind that unconcerned look was like the fear of guilt in the barbaric red eyes of a bloodthirsty terrorist, randomly throwing out grenades, lonely, desperate and who knows, scared of his own life from deep within.

"I can't heal you sir but I assure you I will always provide you the support you need to heal yourself. I know that you have already learnt that past cannot be changed, while the present and future still remain in your own control. Your mind is supremely powerful and has already devoted itself to move forward in the way that works best for you."

"You are my apprentice Chetan, but today I proclaim that you are also my best friend. And friendship my dear, is precious, not only in the shade, but also in the sunshine of life. And I do believe that greater part of life is sunshine."

"Oh Monty Sir, I am an ordinary man with average looks. Neither do I have an ambitious attitude nor an energetic persona. I am content being an assistant of a detective and friend like you. Money making is never my goal of being attached with you, not even of my life. I see in you a true friend and robbing a true friend from life is like robbing the world of the Sun," Chetan replied, getting as much philosophical as his friend.

"And I am into this obscure profession, a personal investigator during the day of petty crimes like frivolous thefts, and an impeccable ladies' man by night. Because of my virile nature and robust personality accompanied with a flirty at times attitude, I am occasionally hired by middle aged men to spy on their otherwise credible wives on even miniscule suspicions of adultery. It has always been a one man show run by me with you as my backbone. I hope my dear Chetan, you can relate to the thought process behind my career choice."

"Yes, of course Monty, and as the legendary Ruskin once mentioned, little thought and little kindness are worth more than a great deal of money!" Quoting the famous words of John Ruskin, Chetan got up on his feet. He had been sitting for too much time and this perhaps was the test of his ability to sit and chat.

Following Chetan, Monty also stood up, throwing the filter of the finished cigarette away, snuggled in, "You are the only person I know Chetan who gives indefinite hugs!"

Chetan wrapped his right arm around the shoulders of his true friend and pulled him close, gently rubbing his arm. Despite the heaviness in his stomach, it fluttered at the feeling of his body press against his. Highly appreciative of this simple gesture, both the buddies sunk into the warmth of the tight hug. Some seconds after they separated, Monty's right hand went into the inner pocket of his tuxedo and out came the hard earned pile of cash.

"Money is my military, each note of this fresh currency a soldier. I never send my soldiers into the battle unprepared and undefended. I send them to conquer, to take some prisoners and bring them back to me." Monty said as he took out some notes from the bundle and offered them to Chetan, who accepted it with the characteristic devious smile, now back on his emotionless face.

Friendship is another scene after all, required to be adhered to in daily life, while professional relation is something else. The wise men advise, never merge business ethics with personal ethics even if your wife is your boss at the office! In this case, however, these two were just good friends.

Chetan gifted Monty the two remaining cigarettes from his pocket and Monty took them in a blink of an eye, as quickly from his hands into his as a wrestler from Haryana manages to backdrop his or her opponent.

"I will take a rickshaw or a cab from this place, you can drive to your residence, Monty, but be careful" said Chetan, looking here and there for some means of transport to reach his home.

Going back to his original Oscar award winning body language and facial expressions, Monty sat into his esteemed possession like a mythological king on the royal throne of his golden horse chariot and drove away into the threateningly inauspicious night, through the mud covered pot holes of the fractured road.

Chetan stood there, as still as the electric pole next to him, near the bench, waiting for a rickshaw, or maybe for a cab, who knows, he now had the money for it anyway. His motionless eyes meticulously watched the red tail lights of the eternal Challenger move further and further away, observing every minute visual detail as it faded away into nothing just like memories of an old man at death's door, fade away slowly and steadily.

Chapter III

Aim big, small aims are a crime

The night indeed was dangerously dark as if to protect a gloomy secret. Once waxing, the moon was now in the waning phase and had tapered into a perfect hemisphere of mute and mystic light. The irregular main streets as well as the narrowest and impassable lanes continued to remain devoid of humans but not without the company of dead and grim silence. Not considering the possibly deranged and murderous warning of the vigilant moon, and the obvious one that smoking is a slow method of suicide, Monty took out one of the two extra special cigarettes that Chetan had gifted him from his pocket and lighted it up using the lighter attached to the dashboard of the Challenger.

Just as he finished the first draw and removed the insolent roll from his silent but tremulous lips, he blew the smoke in the air carefully, as if he was the last pathetic straggler lost in a desert managing his limited items of food. "Till when Mr. Monty will you keep solving these miniscule messes?" were the exact words that seemed to echo into his quite slim and silky but highly apprehensive ears. Even the respectful and rigid fingers of his right hand, wrapped around the cigarette began to tremble with every passing breath. The smell and the taste were as bitter as his mood, but perhaps that was what gave him a faint hope that by the time he finished the entire cigarette, all his sadness and guilt would come to an end.

"After committing earthly sins and unknown mistakes, the place where we are sent is surrounded by strange doors on all sides, each one leading to a particular human fear. One and only one sound plays in a loop there and that is run! Run! Run for your life because the true headless ghost is here..." screamed a bloodthirsty ghost's shrill but distinct voice with a background score that was nothing but the sound of long iron nails being scratched over a jagged rock.

Despite the cigarette still in the middle of his lips, Monty could taste the saliva thickening in his mouth and a couple of beads of sweat trickling down slowly near his left brow. He immediately turned off the music system of the Challenger by long pressing its power button. "What on earth do they air so late at night? The day these FM stations are sued is not far," thought Monty in his head, slightly scared by the late night radio program. Even before he could take a deep breath, there was a loud striking noise, "Dhaad Dhaad," near the door of the Challenger next to his seat, as if someone just ungallantly kicked the ponderous door with full force, not once but twice.

"Woof, woof," imperishably barked a couple of street canines, who were as large as wolves, as they attempted to attack the Challenger that perhaps came in the way of their attempts to search food. One of them was white and the other brown, but both had almost no fur on their rather heavily built bodies. Monty turned his eyes towards them and then straight. He knew that the time had come to step a little harder at the giant accelerator. Though the two dogs chased the outlandish car, running in the middle of the road till the end of the lane, they did not step beyond it, allowing Monty to calm down just a bit.

The cigarette helped Monty cope up with the tension in his mind, making him feel lighter. He drove slowly between twenty and thirty kilometers per hour, sitting back on the leather coated comfortable seat, his back resting against its flattish cushion, as relaxed as one would be during his holiday on a beach. Disappointed as he was with the radio, he decided to sing a few lines of his favorite Punjabi song himself, "Hundred of them love me madly, they are all chasing me but I hide away from each one of them, only for you my love. If you say no to me, I am going to commit suicide in front of you!" The combination of the song and cigarette, perhaps aided by those pegs of whiskey, brought a genuine and comfortable smile on his face, taking away all the somber stress.

As the Challenger made its way into another posh locality of the town, Monty stared at the cigarette between his fingers. It had turned short enough to burn his skin. With a lazy effort, he leaned forward to throw the remaining filter out of the window. It was precisely then that he noticed a disgruntled black and white cat crossing the road with the stiffness of age. Its fur was dull and thin, unwashed and bare. Perhaps it once jumped from one roof top to the other with as much ease as it did from tree to tree but now it knew that age had taken its toll on her as it hesitated to even cross a barren road. Nevertheless, Monty applied brakes by pressing his shoe against the unimaginably tall pedal. Although the magnitude of deceleration was not much, the odd noise they made to completely bring the Challenger to a halt, was an indication of their age too.

Throwing the filter out of the window, Monty leaned back a bit on his serene and balanced seat, surprisingly still managing to keep his backbone erect and waited for the old cat to cross the road comfortably, which she did probably in less than ten seconds. As per Kanpur's tradition, when a cat crosses your way it is considered a bad omen and you have to compulsorily wait till someone else passes by. The bad omen then strikes that unassuming fellow, keeping you as safe as pure gold in a bank's locker. Though Monty did not believe much in these vague superstitions, he still was hesitant to drive forward. The only thing that stopped him was a dim thought at the back of his temporarily indescribable mind that if something bad happens to him, he would have to curse himself for not waiting after the cat had crossed his way.

Though he was neither myopic nor hyperopic, he furrowed his brows and shortened his eyes with a distinct facial expression of intense concentration, to see the exact time by the fascinating gold watch on his wrist. It was almost half past two and obviously there was no visible sign of the rising sun. The pure and long-lasting alcohol and those unusually long villainous cigarettes had begun to take their toll on the husky private investigator. Waiting for an unassuming fellow, he drifted into a practically instantaneous sleep and then came back within a minute. The drowsiness in his eyes and body was indeed unconquerable but he had to somehow keep his senses and limbs going in order to reach his home.

Somehow his sensitive ears heard the sound of approaching slow moving human footsteps. The bafflingly disordered sound was of someone walking on the grass, someone who had never learnt the art of walking quietly. Each footfall was chaotically spaced without any rhythm but that was not what concerned

Monty. He turned his diamond shaped head with the newfound energy towards the direction of the sound, which got more and more clamorous with every stomp.

There was a medium sized and middle aged perfectly bald man coming out of an open low wrought iron gate of a small one storey and old-fashioned bungalow. Though the bungalow was small, it was attractive. It resembled the one of those that the infamous rich men build for their tipsy pleasure nights while it stays unoccupied on all other occasions. The dark skin toned man did not exactly look stinking rich but the shine on the luxurious car parked on the neatly trimmed grass lawn inside the gate, seemed to speak volumes of the wealth of the dweller. He carefully closed the gate on his exit and walked towards the stationary Challenger.

Although Monty was feeling much drowsy from inside, the enigmatic investigator's persistent spirit took control of his physical senses as he attentively watched the undistinguished man. What struck his eyes the most was the pair of white artificial leather and moderately low heeled shoes that the unassuming man was wearing below his purple track pants. Apart from the green and brown hue near the thin sole of those fashionably clunky shoes, there was also a patch of crimson, perhaps as small as a USB port, and that was exactly what excited Monty. He observed the smile on the face of the man, the quirky smile that is automatically earned after accomplishing a sensitive mission. Judging by the saffron thread tied on his right wrist, visible clearly as he had rolled up the sleeves of his wrinkled white shirt till the elbows, Monty realized that the man was deeply religious.

As the man came near, Monty had a brief eye contact with him, but the stranger, who now appeared taller than before, remained indifferent. He had a thin but dark moustache below his swollen nose and was murmuring something that Monty failed to understand primarily due to his unclear words. The man walked away, disappearing into the lane on the left, passing through the imaginary line that defined the path taken the old cat to cross the Challenger's way, giving green signal to Monty to drive forward safely.

As Monty's head fell backwards to take the support of the seat's headrest, his eyelids slipped closed for a few seconds. The impatient wait for the man to pass had made him drowsier than he was before the aged cat had appeared. Gathering all of whatever energy was remaining in the various parts of his anatomy, he somehow managed to open his eyes but the rest of his body went absolutely limp. His breaths turned uneven in an attempt to start the engine as he seemed to appear unaware of what was going on around him. It was like a war against the sleep that tried its best to engulf him but he in return did all he could to resist it. He wanted water to splash over his face to keep him awake till he reached his home, but there was no bottle in the car. Probably staring right into bright light for a minute would help him defeat sleep he thought. He immediately pulled the key out of the self, opened the door of the car and tried to look straight into the white LED light that was diverging out evenly on the street, with its source lying somewhere behind one of the two trapezoidal windows of the compact bungalow, the one from where the supposedly affluent man had just departed.

"Bhoom," a single, loud and deafening gunshot sound and its multiple echoes that resembled the hostility of a thunder but without the raw power of a storm, were heard from somewhere that was not too distant. The sound was similar if not exactly the same as the one when advocate Dhingra shot his wife. The ear splitting noise could have been mistaken for the elliptical cracks of an oncoming squall by some inexperienced ears but there was not even a single cloud in the dark sky to back their logic. Monty had been in his obscure profession long enough to even guess the type of gun that was used for the supposed murder. "A 12 bore French rifle!" he said to himself as his eyes opened completely and the drowsiness left for eternity.

His blood seemed to awaken his brain and his body was now ready for the outcome. As he turned his head towards the glorious east window, from where the soothing light as well as the lethal sound originated even a large and sensuous mouth like his trapped between those muscular jaws froze wide open. It was exactly at the time of gunshot that the white LED light radiating from the weird window had been switched off, spreading peculiar darkness all around the street.

The only way a normal individual would have reacted to the threatening situation is by running away from there, not to be seen anywhere near at least for the next few days. But, Monty was not ordinary. "The ignorant buffoons will have no more digs at me!" recovering quickly from the shock, his lips whispered in a volume so low that it was not even audible to his own utterly sensitive ears. He perhaps took the needless remark made by the narrow minded security guard of the posh apartment way more seriously than it should have been taken.

He opened the door of the Challenger with a totally guileless grin on his face that exposed almost every tooth, all as white as the color of chalk. The extreme reaction indicated that something really bad was about to happen, or perhaps something immensely good as per Monty's unique perspective. He opened the dashboard, pulling the elongated handle with the bare thumb of his right hand. Inserting his left hand in, the suave investigator pulled out a semi automatic, short recoil 9mm pistol, preloaded with cartridge. The cold metal was as black as a ferocious bat and maybe three times more deadly than a hungry wild panther. It was perhaps one of those used by competent naval officers to kill the unknown and hostile attackers. He carefully hid the eminently serviceable pistol in the capacious inner pocket of his infernal streamlined tuxedo. Monty saw the gentle smile on the pink teddy bear's cute face and that smile assured him that what he was going to do was worth being done. He came out of the car, closing its heavy door with a loud thud. He did not lock the car but made sure that the keys were in the six inch right side pocket of his sober, businesslike trouser. With the expectant smile of happiness growing, much as the one on a devotee's face as he opens the lotus for Goddess Laxmi during Diwali Pooja, Monty moved towards the low wrought iron gate of the small old-fashioned bungalow that housed the mysterious window.

The tremendously spiked grilled rectangular gate, made of wrought iron, was incredibly low compared to those of the other structures in the locality, none the less, tall enough to reach till Monty's waist. Its width was perfectly adequate to allow the metallic grey colored luxury car parked inside, to pass in and out of it. Strangely, there was no board near the gate indicating the name of the owner of that bungalow and that stopped Monty from getting in. The excitement had transpired to the eyes and the complete body of the investigator and he began to search for the owner's name but could not see any text anywhere on the wall or the gate. Though the front cemented walls of the bungalow were definitely taller than the gate in the middle but not as tall as those in the neighborhood. They seemed as though they were once white in color but weather and age had turned them almost yellow.

Monty saw the two storey, conveniently big house towards the left, which was approximately three times larger in area than the mystified one and had a prominent name plate near its spotless gate that stated, 'The Shukla Paradise, 25/7, Tilak Nagar'. On the right, there was another spectacular building that seemed pretty modern judging by its architectural excellence. It was not as large in area as the one belonging to the Shuklas, but its three storey structure and the delightful three car parking made sure that three families could easily reside there. There were no individual names on that building too but there was a board near its entry. It read 'Santusht, 23/7, Tilak Nagar', indicating the apartment's name, which translates to being satisfied, along with its address. Both the buildings had something of the personality of the owners in it, a hint of the people behind the design. Opposite to the mysterious bungalow, on the other side of the road, there was a large children's park with several swings and a couple of old mango trees but enough empty space to play cricket. It was surrounded by narrow lanes on both sides.

"Bungalow number 24/7," said Monty to himself as he opened the short gate which the bald man had closed on his exit. Years of experience had polished Monty's skill of opening even the most irregular and unstable gates and doors to such an extent that there was literally no sound when he pushed that spiked gate. Strangely, the gate was not locked from inside or outside and that helped him to maintain the pin drop silence. He opened it exactly that much as was required for his entry into the premises, with all his five senses now completely active despite those cigarettes and alcohol.

The first and foremost thing he did was to cautiously look for any CCTV cameras monitoring the entry of the bungalow. Though it was exceptionally dark inside, Monty did not want himself to be captured by the infrared vision of those closed circuit television cameras. In the dim moonlight, he saw towards the top, to the left and to the right, towards the back and even across the walls but let aside any camera, there was not even many wires, apart from the electric cables and the DTH cable that originated from the receiving dish placed right at the middle of the roof, going into the house through the closed inexplicable window. It was fair to assume that the house had no monitoring devices because if there was not even one outside, then surely there cannot be any inside.

There was a 30ft wide and approximately 40ft long empty area between the actual structure and its gate with a covering of well maintained grass that may have been lush green during the day but appeared like a black carpet during the night. Around one-thirds of it was occupied by a steel grey luxurious car which perhaps only the wealthiest residents of Tilak Nagar deserved. More than the brand value, what Monty was concerned about was that there could be an intruder hiding below or behind that splendid vehicle. He bent at an angle of 45 degrees and rotated his head 90 degrees to each side to have 360 degree view around the vehicle. Content that there was nobody, alive or dead, in that fairly small lawn, Monty proceeded towards the wooden door which was located right in the middle of the 30ft wide bungalow.

The house looked like a cut out from a famous architecture magazine. Though there was nothing so weird in the bungalow by the local standards, it looked too spooky in some strange way. "Looks like the local kids during the day time rumor this to be a secret government base," thought Monty as he observed the private house which stood still at the end of the lawn, as if beamed there rather than constructed. It was as if it had rolled off a production line, but they had forgotten to build an entire floor, let alone a second coat of the brownish paint on the cemented walls. The roof line did not peak in the centre as was the fashion a couple of decades ago, but instead it sloped to the left, peaking at a couple of meters from the edge. There definitely was no visible chimney. Though both the trapezoidal windows were fairly large to let in maximum sunlight, but they were fashioned so well that the house must have stayed warm in the winter days.

As Monty took baby steps towards the square shaped wooden door of the house, he heard the sound of crushing grass behind him. It was not a continuous noise one would imagine from a garden roller but the defined short crunch that originates from a footstep. The darkness pressed on Monty and his left hand went to his tuxedo, searching for his tool of death. Though the urge to turn around was a desperate one, he fought against it till there was another crunch. This time it was lighter and slower as if the maker of the noise was trying his best to be quieter. Everything he examined showed that all will be okay but somehow there was an intrusion, but whatever that was, it failed to scare Monty. He was the one who once on a mission, would stop only when it was accomplished.

Using a strategy which had once worked very well, Monty pulled out the pistol in his left hand as slowly and gently as any mother would handle her new born child but making sure of hiding it from the view of the person behind, and ran forward all of a sudden. Without any pause, after completing ten steps, he turned around full 360 degrees, with his left arm in forward extension position and the index finger on the trigger with the pistol pointing to where the intruder's head would have been. It takes a second or two for any information to sink in even if it is a spectacle right in front of one's eyes. Monty's lips stretched wide in a manic grin and his eyebrows arched for the cloudless sky. It was the same old cat who had crossed his way earlier and was now tress passing the property at its lethargic pace, unconcerned of the imminent danger. Without wasting many seconds, Monty sent his pistol back, next to his heavily beating heart and took the remaining four or five steps to the wooden door.

Though the square shaped door was enormous in size, it looked perfectly ordinary with its lock and key system instead of the modern biometric scanners. There was no doorbell, but even if it was there, Monty would have not pressed it. The understandable and rightful dread crept over Monty like an icy chill, numbing his brain. In that frozen state, his mind offered him just one thought. "This is it," he said to himself and it meant that there was no avoiding the danger. He was like a chicken being packed into a cage in a truck leaving for the slaughter house, only difference being that no chicken ever knows where it is heading towards but Monty knew it.

With a rapid push of the brawny left shoulder, Monty was able to open that door without touching its gold plated handle. Surprisingly, it was not locked and opened inward easier than Monty had anticipated, only because of its light weight. There was no light switched on inside. It was as dark as a cinema theatre but there too is some visibility due to the movie running on the giant screen, and here it was almost zero. Though Monty could see absolutely nothing, he could smell the pleasantly bitter smoke that was filled in there. It was not as bad as the burning of coal itself, perhaps because of one of the exquisite flavors of the tobacco free hookah. Burning coal would mean conversion of chemical energy to light energy as well, thought Monty before realizing that someone was definitely smoking a hookah near the door before a few minutes but the fun was all over by that time.

A person who does wrong is taken captive and might be tortured by taking one or more of his senses away. Monty was not willing to be tortured as a captive as he had not done any wrong. Investigating a crime at an alien location where the killer and the victim might very well be hiding, would never be possible if vision is taken away. Proceeding as a captive rather than a soldier would be foolishness. And that was precisely the thought that made Monty take a U turn, as he ran back leaving the door open. Running over the black carpet like a deer being chased by a rampant lion, he jumped over the short gate and opened the door of his Challenger in a jiffy.

There are times when retreat from a war is termed as bravery and not cowardice. It takes a considerable amount of courage to backtrack, to let the enemy walk over, and to ultimately find another route around to eventual victory. Without entering the car, Monty bent over the front seat miraculously keeping his spine erect as his hand reached for the invariably smiling pink teddy bear. He picked up the soft toy and below it on the rare seat, there lay a battery operated flashlight which Monty grabbed and kept his buddy back. He closed the door of the Challenger, and once again walked into the house through its gate and straight towards the door with the portable light device in his right hand.

Monty desperately wanted the nicotine to sooth him but he had personally laid down specific rules and the first one of them was a total ban on cigarettes while at work. Sometimes those self imposed rules would come back to haunt him but he had learnt the art of postponing his urge, the one that mimicked a natural transmitter in his nerves and that accelerated the speed of his walk. With the flashlight now turned on,

Monty once again entered the smoke filled house through its open door.

Inside was minimalist. Since it was dark, Monty could only see things that fell into the parabola of the illumination generated by his flashlight. There was a narrow corridor, about 20meters in length and a door at its end, opposite and identical to the one he entered from. The walls on all sides were fashionable shades of white and the floor made of grey concrete. There was nothing at all on the walls, no paintings, no photographs, not even a hint of blood stains and that was astonishing. On either side however, there were two small doors near the entry door, which led to rooms as one could imagine.

With silence laying on his facial skin like a poison and following the scrupulous protocol, Monty reached the identical wooden door but it was locked, perhaps permanently as there was neither a handle nor a lock on the plain plywood jammed into the front side of the door. "Surely, nobody can escape from there," he said to himself as his lips converged into a pout, momentarily letting out a sigh. There were just two more mysterious doors where the criminal might be. Monty transferred the flashlight from his hand to his mouth, surprisingly holding it firmly even with his tremulous lips, helped of course by those muscular jaws. He pulled out his pearl handled pistol, ready to shoot even with the gentlest movement of the forefinger of his right hand.

Rigid anticipatory attention was the need of the hour and though his body begged for a brief and much needed rest, Monty's brain completely rejected his own body's plea. He walked with soft and noiseless footsteps towards the black oaken door on the left of the one from where he had entered and the one which was unexpectedly left half open. In spite of the fact that that door was only five steps away, before he could reach there, his left shoe caught in something and he stumbled, almost falling flat on his face but somehow managing to maintain his balance. In the process the flashlight fell on the floor from his mouth, making a vague, disastrous noise but by some means did not turn off. Though the event was petty and stupid, it momentarily maddened Monty as he did not want to in any manner alert the hiding criminal. Picking up the flashlight, he once again fixed it in the middle of his lips. Looking at what made him trip, he realized that it was just a pink colored Yoga matt, rolled up and kept near the door. It was strange that he did not notice it in the first place but his experience came handy as he did not waste much time thinking about things that did not matter.

A distinctive and equally unpleasant smell overpowered the smell of the hookah as he entered the door, which opened into to a square shaped, white walled dining room cum hall. Towards the left was a tall, glassed, built-in cupboard that had three shelves, each crammed up with different kinds of cutlery, including the gold plated one, which perhaps was used only for the special guests. Just below the cupboard and at the corner was a soft, expensive and plush couch, probably the one which only those debauched men could afford who were lucky enough to have stinking rich fathers. Examining it carefully with the entire focus of the flashlight on it, Monty observed that there were no wrinkles on the black leather signifying that nobody had sat on it for quite some time. He also noticed a single A4 sized paper lying on it. Thinking that it could be a clue, he picked it up and began to read. It was just a hard copy of a mutual fund investment document. Though it was merely of three lakh rupees, it had the investor's name printed in bold letters on it and that read Scarlett White.

That unusual name took Monty back to the moment when he had a downright vulgar brawl with a couple of hardy and nocturnal roadside Romeos. It was around three months back when he visited an out of the way bar with Chetan Prasad. There he had a casual encounter with a two time beauty pageant winner, the one who was probably the most pleasing woman to the senses and mind of any man of the city, Scarlett White. He turned the pistol in his hand over and over as if it was a magical wand, momentarily thinking about the scene when she sipped her cocktails one after the other without any worries, until a couple of damned rogues tried to intrusively touch her bare back. Though Monty and Chetan had no idea who she was at that time, being the gentlemen they were they came to the rescue of the diva in the black solid woven layered fit and flare one piece dress. Though the unfortunate drunken quarrel was obviously one sided, Monty remembered how Scarlett had introduced herself to him after his victory, in a weirdly cheerful voice that sounded similar to that of a famous Bollywood singer. The profound introduction was as brief as the vote of thanks that preceded it, following which she left the bar, perhaps half past eleven being too late for the delicate lady.

Life should be lived with a sense of urgency and therefore every minute was as precious as a solitaire. Monty followed the advice given to him by his grandfather in the good old days of his childhood, especially in a situation that was as threatening as the present one for him. He kept the document back on the couch and turned the flashlight towards his right. There was an old and rectangular dining table, about the length equal to Monty's height and width equal to the horizontal span of both his arms. Not caring for the smooth dark cherry wood and the lustrous quality of its well waxed wood, Monty observed that one of the four wooden and cushioned chairs was out of its place, proving that someone had used it recently. He immediately kneeled down on both his knees and examined what was on offer below the four legged table. There were no blood stains which he had anticipated, no pieces of stale food, no napkins, not even particles of dust, absolutely nothing on the grey floor. He got up on his legs and the next examination point was the table top.

It was evident that the one who organized that table was a master at arranging things as all the items were reachable quite easily for persons sitting on all the four unarmed chairs. The centre had cylindrical plastic stand containing clean knives, spoons and folks, all made of stainless steel. Just next to them, were three glassed bottles, all of different shapes and sizes; one each of expensive brands of whiskey, vodka and beer. The dining table must have looked really presentable when fresh and hot food was served in the elegant platter that lay at the corner of the table, near the out of place chair, with its beautiful blue print pattern further elevating the aesthetic appeal. As

Monty moved near the table, he observed that the platter was not washed. It contained marks left by oil of something that was served in it. Monty's left arm was free and he touched the platter with it on its side, to guess if it was recently used. It was indeed reasonably hot. Adjacent to the platter, there was a steel glass, filled half with water. Monty picked it up and inspected its rim using the focus of the flashlight to realize that it had been used by a female recently as it had prominent marks of a pink lipstick.

Before moving towards the other end of the room, Monty checked what was behind his back. Turning almost 360 degrees, he observed that there were a couple of rectangular papers lying on the space below the trapezoidal window. This was surely not the window which Monty had seen from the exterior as it was closed. A couple of spiders had made their webs near the old fashioned lock of the window, proving to the investigator that it had not been open from at least fifteen days. He rushed towards the couple of papers with careful footsteps that were not even audible to his own ears. They were fixed deposit receipts issued by ABC bank, worth rupees ten odd lakhs each, renewed at 7% annual interest just a day ago. The important find once again was the name of the account holder, Scarlett White, once again.

Time and memory always move in opposite directions. Although Monty's Moral Science teacher at school had taught this to him in a different sense, he realized its significance when he stood near the window with even the seconds-hand of his golden wrist watch refusing to stop. Keeping the receipts back as they were, he took out the flashlight from the clutches of his lips and moved towards the diagonal corner of the room with the light now in his left hand and pistol still in the right one.

There was an inverted mineral water can on a hot and cold water system kept on a high raised stool at the corner. Monty observed the copper jug with floral design that rested in the narrow empty space, next to the handle of the outlet of water. There was nothing significant there he thought and as he was about to turn away, his eyes got stuck on a tiny piece of paper on the floor, just below the water system. Thanks to his symmetrical bone structure and abundance of uric acid and vitamin D in his body, there was no noise whatsoever when Monty bent at almost 90 degrees to carefully pick up that little paper, keeping the flashlight on the floor, as he let out a sigh through his mouth.

It was a white visiting card, with all the details of someone named Master Shams-ud-din from The Powerful Horse Boutique imprinted on it with an image of a fiery black rearing horse next to it. While it may seem a normal visiting card, Monty knew it straightaway that he had found his first clue. The card had a cross marked on it, from corner to corner, with a brown sketch pen, or perhaps a permanent marker. This was obviously done by someone in intense anger, or an uncontrollable rage, who knows. Monty slipped the card into the six inch right side pocket of his trouser and moved towards the heavy wood paneled door, not the one from where he entered, but the one next to the water system.

It opened into the place that was the apparent origin of the stupefying and overpowering smell, the comfy and ultramodern kitchen. It was rectangular in shape, fractionally larger in area than the usual kitchens and had a trapezoidal window exactly opposite to the entry door, similar to the mysterious one but fitted with a white colored exhaust fan. The walls were superficially attractive and were decorated with stylish green tiles. All four sides had cemented shelves, topped with hardest black granite, with the bottom most ones around six inches above Monty's waist.

Monty flowed into the smelly kitchen as if uninterrupted flowing was the only way his body truly knew how to stay invisible. Towards the right of the grilled window, was an electric induction plate stove adjacent to the traditional stove connected to a gas cylinder kept at the floor just below it. There were no signs of anything cooked recently on any of those equipments. On the left of the window was a sink, made of steel with a couple of unwashed plates lying in it, perhaps to be washed in the morning. There were the normal utensils used for everyday cooking like the pressure cooker, the kadai, the kalchi etc kept neatly into their respective positions below the window and Monty did not waste time on looking at them as he knew that they had absolutely nothing to offer.

As Monty turned the flash to his right, he saw that there was a square shaped washing machine. What excited him was a faint shadow that appeared out of nowhere on the dark blue colored plastic body of the machine. Maybe this was his next clue about the crime. On his tiptoes he reached up to the washing machine, those black turned red eyes wide open, hoping to see the first signs of the gunshot. He kneeled over his right knee, looking for the object whose shadow was so evident in the middle of the blue box. Not only is expectation the mother, but even the grandmother of frustration. He gave that lacy black bra hanging from a little plastic stand hidden behind the big machine, a pointless stare as if his irritation could inflate it. Perplexed by the situation and also by the odd smell that did not refuse to fade away he quickly stood up and examined the opposite side of the kitchen, where there was a large sized refrigerator. Monty had seen in movies that how some killers hide the dead body even into hopelessly small refrigerators. He quickly opened it, pulling it using his left hand. Forget dead, there was not even a living body inside it apart from a two hundred gram chicken leg piece, a half filled tomato ketchup bottle, a couple of red Himachal apples, a large green cucumber and three bottles of beer. He closed it with a jerk, not caring for the safety of the items inside.

Moving to the last corner of the kitchen, he saw that there was an already switched off microwave oven. Next to it was a platter, similar to the one on the dining table and that was the reason of the foul smell. It had burnt chicken kept over it. Though some may call it overcooked, it was as black as coal and good enough to be thrown into the plastic dustbin that lay just below it on the floor. Perhaps someone was waiting for it to be cooked but his or her life ended before the wait was over. Frustrated by the lack of evidences, Monty, kept the flashlight on the oven for a second, picked that platter up and dumped the chicken into the bin as he moved out of the kitchen with the pistol still in his right hand and the flashlight in the left. Moving through the dining room cum hall, he took exit from the door into the corridor.

He looked at his wrist watch. It was exactly five minutes to three, neither morning nor night. Without any facial expression of sleepiness or of irritation, he moved into the black door on the other side of the corridor, this time careful as to not tumble over the out of place Yoga matt. The peace was shattered the moment he entered into the unlocked door, with Monty almost screaming with an expression that could be termed as a mix of stunned surprise and delight. That was it. It was the bedroom, the scene of crime and the victim's dead body not far from where he was standing.

They say three can keep a secret if two are dead. It was a case of emergency for Monty to save himself from a potential fire of another gunshot. His brain had restarted after being shut down for some time. His body turned unpleasantly damp and sticky as there was the glisten of cold sweat. His eyes, now as red as tomato soup, turned as wide as the National Highway, as he assumed that someone was coming to deliver the fatal shot. What he saw, no one else could see. Trapped in his own psychosis he realized that the flashlight would not be enough to be used in such a situation. Looking across the pink walls, he spotted the switch board, right next to where he was standing. Throwing the flashlight away to the side, he switched on all the switches with his sweaty left palm, falling to the floor in anticipation of a gunshot with his eyes closed for a second, but there was none. Rising up on his feet as quickly as the free fall of a man pushed from the terrace of a two floor building, he quickly locked the room from inside to avoid any potential threat from the outside.

In her early thirties, opulent, glamour girl, eye candy of the town, winner of two beauty pageants, who loved to dress in the most amazingly crafted chic dresses along with matching high heeled stilettos, Scarlett White may have been entertained by different disreputable men on many occasions, but this had surely topped the bill. The spectacle of a man driven insane by hatred is a rare sight to behold, and if it amounted to the destruction of lakhs of worshippers, so what! She lay on the grey floor, next to the comfy double bed, dead. Dead is permanent, dead is forever.

In life the eyes that possessed every shade of the sky from dawn to dusk, in death they were absolute black. The spark in them had completely extinguished, but unlike any enthusiastic fire, it was without any smoke. Standing still for a minute at his place, Monty stared at the lifeless body of the unfortunate diva that lay in a manner that could be confused with someone sleeping on the floor. Her distinctive, royal head was towards the end where the red colored alarm clock with a round dial, was kept on the bed while her neat bare feet were towards the door where Monty stood horrified.

She had opted to tie her silky black hair into a long braid for her last sober look. Though she had taken off her clothes for the bedtime, she still covered her voluptuous assets with a green and white bra that complimented her leaf like underwear. The rest of her body was pretty bare, exposing the soulless curves and bikini waxed smooth skin for one last time. There were at least half a dozen branded pairs of footwear, mostly high heeled stilettos, hidden below the bed, adjacent to her naked snow-white feet. Monty remembered that when he met her, how she moved with ever part of her being, with her fragile but wonderfully flexible limbs, her facial expressions which could kill any inexperienced man on spot, her never ending fidgeting no matter what. Now, she was still.

Monty had rehearsed house searching for quite some time but now a silence lay on his skin like a violent narcotic poison. It seeped into his blood, almost paralyzing his brain as his pupils became dilated and there was a tremor in his hands, especially the one holding the tool of death. His face was full of awkwardness, not even hurrying to save his feelings, to fill the void with a statement of appreciation for the deceased. He picked his eyes off the stationary body, raising his eyebrows, letting out a noiseless sigh and entrusted himself with a herculean task of finding out the man behind the most fortuitous murder. Without squandering any more time on emotional feelings, the investigator's brain guided him to find out some kind of evidences left behind by the triumphant murderer.

He looked around the handsomely paneled bedroom. There were no signs whatsoever of any scuffle. The double bed was undoubtedly an expensive one and not surprisingly, it was unoccupied by any human. All that it contained were the things that could not relate to the gunshot. There were four pillows covered by white covers with pink patterns to go with the slightly wrinkled white bed sheet. There was a closed laptop lying next to a photographic album. Monty did not want even the slightest of opportunity go unnoticed.

He grabbed the thick album and quickly went through its pages. It was a wedding album, of Hargurjeet Singh, the son of a former Member of Legislative Assembly, and the one who was a regular in the local news' happening parties section. Of course his bride had to be the most glamorous one in the town and Scarlett White indeed was. The news of their divorce was in the newspapers a few months ago, maybe a year or two ago, Monty could not remember when exactly had that happened.

The maroon carpets on the floor, made of furry and soft velvet were not ripped but wrinkled. Bills lied crumpled in the pile of papers to be shredded near the corner, where there lay a brown plastic stool. There was an ashtray on that stool that was full of haphazardly sprinkled ash and the remaining filters of at least half a dozen cigarettes. The smell of those filters was strangely foul but sweet, but Monty was not there to spend time on things that did not matter. Next to the stool was a single stemmed hookah with a glass based water jar at its base. The charcoal discs were visibly hot and the smell of the flavor had not yet subsided indicating that it had recently been used. "Someone was here less than ten minutes ago," said Monty to himself, tilting his heavy head towards the left to let the drop of sweat trickle away.

Behind the hookah, there was a large all purpose cabinet, maybe a wardrobe, similar to the one in most of the architectures across the country. It was locked and Monty knew finding the key would be a ridiculous thing to do as it would take hours. He observed the thin screened LED TV hanging on the wall, just opposite to the bed, next to a mammoth wall clock, above the set top box. The time by the analog clock was five minutes past three, as Monty turned around, 360 degrees to examine the other corner of the room.

There was a dainty and costly little dressing table, which Monty assumed was a new buy as it still had the sticker of a famous online furniture vendor. The chair kept opposite to the three set mirror was not like an ordinary one as it had cushions on all four sides. It could be termed as a mini sofa, though its dimensions were nowhere close to being one. There lay several make-up items, scattered like files on a judge's table at the district court. Monty took quick glance at all of them, the dozen shades of lipsticks, the eyeliners, the creams and brushes, hairclips, combs, hair straightening device, three expensive perfume bottles, a deodorant, a couple of share holding documents enclosed in envelopes posted to Scarlett White and female items which he had no idea about. At the corner lying all alone as if kept there without keeping the proper arrangement in mind, was a red and green colored empty pouch of Zuban pan masala. The solemnly inquisitive eyes paused at that unusual sight because as far as Monty was concerned, he knew for sure that this brand was not sold at any of the markets in Kanpur. He picked up the pouch and read that it was made in Rajasthan and then he kept it back. Maybe Scarlett was ardent fan of pan masala, he thought but did she have it sometime ago, was the question that came to his inquisitive mind. Anyway if she was a big fan, how come only one pouch was there, he thought. Perhaps the killer was an addict of the brand and that pouch was a clue.

Practically almost next to the dressing table, there was a single, unremarkable door that possibly led to the washroom. It was partly open but Monty decided to investigate it later as he saw another cabinet, near the one ton window air conditioner at the further corner of the room. There was nothing worth seeing there he thought as the cupboard was locked and the ac was already turned off. What attracted him though was a strip of certain medicine lying on the floor, on the other side of the bed. He moved swiftly towards it and grabbed it by his left hand. It was a full ten tablet strip of Levetiracetam, one of the salts used to control seizures caused by epilepsy. It was quite possible that the killer dropped his medicine while trying to escape after the murder, or perhaps Scarlett was suffering from epilepsy.

Finally he moved on to Scarlett White's lifeless body lying on the floor. There is no such thing as a beautiful body when death has already claimed the soul. There is no romantic corpse. Death is death. Although her flesh had not started to rot yet, her pliable lips were almost brown, even with the application of a pink lipstick at the night time. There was no foul smell near her body, instead the scent of the deodorant which she had applied, probably sometime before the gunshot, was like a freshly cut lemon. Monty's brain stuttered for a moment when he did not find the most obvious thing, the pool of blood. Forget pool, there was not even a drop anywhere near her motionless body. It should have flowed like a lazy river out of the limp body and splattered on to the floor, turning the grey to red. Monty's eyes turned wider to take in more light as they failed to spot any bullet wound all over her bare body. Every part of him went into a pause, waiting for his thoughts to catch up. He wanted to guess the exact distance and direction from where the shot was fired but how could he tell that without any blood or wound. If there was any bullet mark on any of the pink walls of the room, Monty would have assumed that the killer missed his target but here he was at the crime scene with the victim's dead body without any wound, after clearly hearing a gunshot and with a deadly pistol in his own hand. The obvious thought in his mind was that perhaps the bullet had entered her ear canal hiding the usual surface damage but no doubt it had the same impact as usual in the brain. The shooter must be highly skilled as targeting a moving ear canal from a distance is one of the most difficult things to do.

The silence of the murder room made Monty's blood cold, as did the steady but gentle August breeze that entered through the open trapezoidal mysterious window. The only sound he could hear apart from the continuous noise of the rotation of the ceiling fan's blades, was the sound of his own heart that began to beat faster than normal. As he sat next to the inert body engrossed in his own uncertain thoughts, there was a tiny but audible single sound of shutter, as if someone just clicked a picture using his mobile camera. There was no flash of light but it was not even required to get a descent capture as Monty had already switched on all the LED lights of the room.

"I know your heart died in your chest cavity long ago, show me your face if you still have any guts left," said Monty without any expression of fear on his face despite the fact that he was more than just a bit scared deep inside. Though he extended his right arm in the forward position, pulling the trigger of his pistol, ready to take an aim, he could not see any living creature in the entire room apart from the multiple images of himself in the three mirrors of the dressing table.

It was obvious that the picture was not taken by anyone outside the room as the glass of the window was heavily greased and the door locked. Perhaps somebody hid in the washroom, thought Monty as he made a bold but dangerous move towards the partly open door of the dark washroom. He kicked the wood violently and frantically entered the washroom, ready to shoot the intruder without a second thought. Apart from a long and narrow ceramic bathtub, a wash basin with a leaking tap and an old fashioned green colored Western flush commode, there was nothing notable in there, taking out the buckets and mugs of course. The cold look on his own face that reflected into the washroom mirror could give anyone shudders. His hands were tightly closed around the lethal pistol. Any outsider would think either he had no sense of humanity or his heart was made of stone. He came out of the washroom in a minute, his brain still confused about what was going on.

The investigator stared at the victim's body like a man with no morals, no manners and no knowledge of the Bhagwat Geeta, although that was not the case with him. Once again, there was that tiny but audible single sound of shutter, as if someone again clicked a picture using his mobile camera. Monty's eyes turned wide like a wild animal as they traveled undecidedly from wall to wall, ceiling to floor, window to door, of the room failing to locate any intruder. "There is nobody else here, surely," his lips murmured at a volume which even he could not hear.

With his free left hand going into the left side six inch pocket of his trouser, he took out his own mobile, not the most luxurious one but certainly not less in features. He walked towards the dead body with baby steps and observed that Scarlett had died with her mobile still in the clenched fist of her right hand. Maybe her breathlessly steep fingers were pressing against the buttons of her mobile, which in turn was taking pictures, obeying the commands like any good smart phone would.

What a joy it is using a smart phone. So soft and mellow, warming and goes to the core. It is perhaps the link between the body, soul and the society. It helps one to love more strongly, to feel connected and perhaps to do what is right. Keeping his own mobile on the maroon carpet, Monty kneeled to gently pull that phone out of her earthy and cold hand but a muscular guy like him struggled to get it. Though she was not breathing any more, her fist had clenched so tightly around the phone as if it was a part of her body and would go to the heaven above with her. Anyway, applying a bit of power, Monty managed to pull it away.

Surprisingly, it was not locked. Monty began to investigate the phone and like any nice, hard-boiled investigator would do, he first opened the call records. The moment his eyes struck the phone's screen, dread owned him, pushing against him like an invisible tempest, attempting to reverse his steps back to the Challenger. It had his teeth locked up tight, nothing getting in or out of his mouth, not even the breath he badly wanted. He could feel his heart thudding in his chest and the bile rising to his throat. The drops of sweat behind his ear now converted into what could be compared to water oozing out of a small hole in the garden hose. Scarlett had dialed 100 and surely she must have spoken to the officers for a minute before disconnecting. The call was made exactly thirteen minutes ago, around the time when Monty entered the house. Probably the police officers had already dozed off; otherwise they would have already arrived. In any case, Monty knew that they would obviously be on their way and could reach the crime scene any moment.

He did not want the pompous police to locate and prove the guilt of any accused killer before him. That would undo his unconquerable unstained valor and ordinary people like the security guard of that apartment would continue to take cynical jibes at him. He did not even want to work with the police as that was against his rigid protocol, being an independent private investigator. Like most of the humans, Monty was a more than just confident with his own opinions, impressions and judgments. It was exactly at that moment that he decided to take up the investigation of the murder all by himself. "What will be, will be," his mind said to itself. He knew that being a top ranked investigator did not give him the right to go about it all by himself, competing against the police and the investigation bureau and without any access to forensic science, but he had no other option. Though his face never showed it, deep within, he was deeply saddened by those infuriating taunts. The only aim he had was to shut all of them once and for all. Aiming big was his forte as he considered small aims equivalent to crime. The worst scenario would be his failure but his grandfather had taught him that failures are pillars of success. Anyway, nobody gets defeated all the time and nobody wins all the time but champions are invincible because they don't miss an opportunity to succeed.

The black gemstones of Onyx shined like pebbles washed by the ocean waves and a child like smile blossomed on his face that could ignite inner laughter in all who saw, but alas, there was just a lifeless body with him in the room. There was a sense of urgency in Monty as he wanted to escape the crime scene before the police officers reached there so that they don't have even the slightest of doubts about him investigating the murder. He knew that great things could be achieved by a series of small things done with greatness. Before he got up, he saw that just before dialing 100, Scarlett had called a particular number ten times on a trot. It was saved in her phonebook by the name of Sooraj Singh. Neither was there much time, nor was Monty in a position to memorize that number, so he picked up his mobile and instead of saving that number in his phone, he clicked a picture of her phone displaying that number clearly.

"Meow, meow" was the noise he heard all of a sudden but immediately he knew that it was that old black and white cat in the lawn. Perhaps it signaled Monty about the possible arrival of the police. He kept Scarlett's mobile next to her body and slipped his own mobile into his trouser's pocket. Telling him to stand there was like telling fire not to burn. Though he was visibly as tired as a laborer after an entire day's physical work, each of his muscle wanted to move, to jump.

Hiding his pistol into the inner pocket of his tuxedo as if it had a device that could prevent the weapon from detection even by a metal detector, he walked quietly towards the locked door with his heels raised and the entire weight of his body on the toes so as to not make any noise and obviously not leave any footmarks behind. He had obviously assumed that the remorseless killer had already escaped the premises. Though turning of heads was so natural when he walked, but at that time his walk was like an octopus, limbs moving in a childlike chaos rather than anything a body language expert could explain. The horrid, numb urgency had made him completely forget about the two sounds of the shutter. He picked his flashlight from below the dressing table and switched off all the LED lights of the room, turning it as dark as night in a jungle devoid of moonlight. Silence was absolute and that had a medicinal effect on the senses of the independent self-reliant investigator, reassuring him of no movement outside the door as he unlocked it slowly.

It was just plain dark and quite outside. Monty did not want to use the flashlight as that would mean letting the any potential police officers hiding there know about his exact location. Moving on the tip of his toes, he walked through the narrow corridor carefully, estimating the turn towards the main door, reaching there in less than ten steps. He had left it partly open when he entered and it seemed nobody used it since that time. He hid the flashlight, slipping it into the back pocket of his trouser, perhaps designed specifically for that purpose.

The lawn was silent like before as he walked pass the luxury car, parked as it was when he entered. Once again, jumping out of the open short heighted gate, he reached his esteemed Challenger quicker than what he had himself expected. As he sat on the comfortable buffalo leather seat, he let out a heavy sigh of relief. Nobody saw him at the crime scene and that meant half the battle was already won. Struggling to maintain the erect posture, partly because of the drowsiness and stress and partly because of the alcohol and cigarettes, he closed his eyes for a minute, resting his masculine little chin on the steering, and relaxed.

From behind, there was a sudden blast from a staggeringly loud siren that forced him to open his bloodshot eyes. In the rear view mirror, a dark blue colored police SUV appeared, the red and blue lights flashing brightly in the gloomy night. It was obviously the dial 100 squad. He could not believe his luck, he did not want to anyway. Without even wasting a second, he turned the key to start the engine. And then he saw something that his eyes did not want to see. The old cat was back and casually crossed the road at its lethargic pace, just a couple of meters away from the Challenger's front steeled bumper. The beady eyeballs moved from left to right following the cat, generating an uneasy feeling in Monty's mind. Going straight would go against the superstition, taking reverse would mean telling the police about his presence and standing still would definitely indirectly create a doubt in the officers' minds that Monty himself is the murderer.

The adrenalin flew over his veins like a carp through the river, but he could not move a single muscle, not even to scream. The absolute confusion completely paralyzed him, and the more he thought about running away, or simply moving forward a bit, the more he felt discouraged and utterly upset. His brain had given up and he looked towards his companion, the pink teddy bear who sat motionless at the rare seat. Its smile gave some courage to Monty and without caring about the bad omen he shifted to the first gear. Leaving the clutch slowly, he pressed his shoe against the giant accelerator. A simple smile actually has the power to do wonders. The Challenger moved forward and took a right turn into the empty lane, guided by the three headlights into the dark.

Chapter IV

<u>Do good</u>

<u>and</u>

<u>good will return</u>

The traditional mullioned window, strongly representing the architectural brilliance of the early 1990s, cast a checkerboard of the unclouded sun onto the clean tiled floor that itself contained black circles entangled with each other in a chaotic tumble of excellence, over a simple off white base. The dusty and translucent curtain that was folded halfway towards the left side of the closed window, added a speckled orange glow to the morning sunlight.

The uncontrollably exuberant and harsh sounding small and round alarm clock, sky blue in color, placed at the corner of the queen sized comfortable bed jarred the sleeping young detective out of his peaceful deep sleep and he jolted up, smashing the snooze button with his left hand as hard as he could. Not only did the nasty smash prove to be fatal to the assault over the impatient ears of Monty, it even proved to be catastrophic to the pleasant and much needed sleep he was in, especially after the incidents of the previous night.

With his black eyes, still half closed and resembling the dark side of the half moon, and his entire body apart from the left hand and the portion above the neck covered entirely by a crimson thin blanket, he saw towards the small clock next to his soft pillow. It was thirty minutes past nine in the morning and he had no other choice but to uncover his muscular body from the cozy quilt by kicking it away with as much force as he would kick an escaping burglar from his own house to break his bones. The quilt was thin and weak, it flew in the air for a moment, reaching almost up to the brown ceiling fan that was luckily switched off, and fell down on the bed itself but the time in between was sufficient for Monty to sit on crossed legs on his soft mattress on the cold metallic bed.

Monty sat in the Yoga pose of deep meditation, facing towards the window that was to the right of the bed, similar to that of a Yogi at the Himalayas. Perhaps this was the way he started his day every morning. His eyes were shut as he was lost in important thoughts and prayers. He was dressed in just his training pants, black in color and made of silky tricot with a tapered fit. It contained the badge of the famous brand near the hip and three white stripes on the legs to finish the decent look.

The upper part of his body was bare, making it clear that he did not get into that shape without spending a lot of time at the gym. There was nobody else in the room, otherwise that poor fellow would be shocked, stunned, amazed, flabbergasted, wonderstruck and mesmerized by the physique of Monty. His chest was well chiseled and abdominals sculptured to perfection exposing the six packs exactly like the model from those jeans photo shoots. His shoulders were round and protruding with a very limited percentage of fat while his biceps were the size of a monkey's head and triceps looked like perfect diamonds. The tattoo on his waxed muscular chest was a shining star in the dark sky and it also acted as one on his masterpiece brown skinned body.

After the two minute meditation got over, Monty lazily rolled open his eyes and rubbed them with the inside of his palms. Waking up can really be unpleasant, especially if the dreams are better than reality, which was indeed the case with Monty. Though, he was not fortunate enough to remember exactly what he dreamt about that night, a genuine smile appeared on his oily morning face. The thought behind it was an obvious one that even if he was lucky to remember his dream that remembrance would have eventually faded away with passage of time. So there was no point in wasting energy and time trying to recall that classic fragment of fiction and imagination.

His right hand reached for the remote control of the air conditioner kept on the blue colored plastic stool, just next to the black bed, accompanied by a plastic bottle, half full of drinking water, and Monty's mobile. He picked the remote up to turn the cooling machine off and what followed was a pin drop silence in the room. The ac was a 0.75 ton window ac, white in color, perfectly placed in the opening exactly of its own size, just below the mullioned window. Though its primary function was to chill the little room, it also allowed Monty not to feel lonely in there as it made as rumbling sound as the engine of a 1000cc motorbike.

Exactly next to the air conditioner, there was the switchboard, made of plastic that contained six switches and two sockets, the larger one hosting the ac plug and the smaller one had the charger of mobile fitted into it. The other switches were maybe for the fan, a tube light that was fitted at the corner of the ceiling above the window and a night lamp that was inside its designer case fitted right precisely behind the bed.

The other side of the bed had three wooden cupboards, fitted into the wall due to lack of space. The simple wooden handle of the rightmost cupboard acted as a support for the hanger that contained the macho infernal tuxedo, the distinctive uniform of the independent detective which was totally hiding the mirror fixed on the cupboard behind it. And that was all. The room was of the size of a small cherry on the top of the three scoops of ice cream in a giant cone. The empty space in the room was so less that it could safely be disregarded. Monty stood up, leaving the quilt and the pillow unarranged and carefully walked barefoot towards the wooden door of the room. He reached there in just a couple of steps and unlocked it. He did not push it to open it, instead turned towards the middle cupboard and slowly took out a red and white striped towel from it and then moved out of the room through the door, switching off the night light and the power switch of the ac on his way.

The exit to the bedroom was the entry to the hall of the 1BHK flat. The hall had the flooring same as that of the bedroom, although the color of the walls was just a shade lighter. It must be a square shaped area with each side measuring around 10 ft only. There was a small sized LED TV hanging on the wall perpendicular to the left of the main door, adjacent to the bedroom door. Exactly in front of that 15inch screened TV, was another set of mullioned windows and a couple of blue plastic chairs placed in an irregular manner in the middle of the compact hall. They were not expensive but appeared that they were cleaned properly every day. Next to the chairs, there was a circular plastic table of white color, standing firmly on just one stilt, giving it the appearance of an open umbrella. All it contained was the crossed visiting card of Master Shams-ud-din which Monty may have placed there on his return at night and an ashtray, made of glass, containing the remains of a filter of a cigarette that had totally been smoked. There was a shoe rack near the exit door that was house to the black detective shoes, his training shoes and a pair of home slippers. There was no ac in the hall and perhaps it was not even required if the bedroom door was left open and the ac inside was switched on. The ceiling fan on the top was completely satisfactory for the hall and one tube light, enough to light up the entire area.

Monty opened the window of the hall to allow fresh air. Accompanying the air, the dazzling sun rays streamed in too like a flamboyant guest, not waiting even for an invitation. Monty peeped out from the wide window but the scenery was not magnificent. It was easily perceived that he was just on the first floor and all he could see was his grey prized possession, the Challenger, parked in the parking at the ground floor between other cars below and a huge wall blocking the view of the busy street behind it. Only if he was somewhere above the first floor, he could have a clear visual perspective of the street whereas at the present he could only hear some of the mixed noises from there, especially of car horns and vegetable vendors.

Then he walked towards the washroom door to freshen up, which was opposite to the main door, pushing the kitchen door, next to the washroom, wide open on the way. The weird thing about the compact flat was that all the doors were exactly identical to each other and a new person coming there for the first time would get confused to identify which one leads where. Though there was nobody else in the entire flat, Monty still chose to lock the door of the washroom.

Time, as priceless as maternal love, kept passing and water, as invaluable as air to the breathing creatures, kept getting wasted as Monty was locked inside his washroom till he heard the repetitive sounds of the doorbell. Someone was at the door and Monty was still not ready. He finished his daily bath in a hurry and came out, wrapped in the red and white towel to open the door with his hair, body and feet still wet.

"How many times will I tell you to open the door after one ring of this faint electric doorbell?" screamed the lady who stood in justifiable anger at the main door in a voice that sounded like an eight year old kid yelling for her beloved stuffed toy. Though she sounded childish, her nervous, round and little face was young, and she maybe around twenty five. She wore a sweat stained white t-shirt above dusty blue shorts as if she had come running from the market. Her bare arms and legs were as pale and lean as her face, which of course had no sign of any makeup. The nails of her hands and legs were neatly trimmed without any color in them. The right leg just below the knee had a bruise as if she had fallen down on concrete and hurt it real bad. Her hair was combed back into a messy ponytail. Her nose was oily, perhaps more than her sunken cheeks and broad forehead. The slippers she wore were full of dust as if she just walked out from a desert. She was not any princess. She was merely a domestic helper.

She entered the flat in a hurry, closing the main door with a thud and with a folded newspaper in her right hand. She did not feel awkward or shy at all on seeing her employer wrapped in just a towel; instead she continued screaming at him as she removed her dirty rubber slippers, placing them on the shoe rack just next to the polished black shoes. "Here is today's newspaper. It is above ten and you have not picked it yet." She continued to express her anger as she moved towards the kitchen, almost colliding with the boss, who moved quickly out of her way without uttering a word in his defense. As she entered the kitchen, Monty entered the bedroom to cover his body with the black uniform.

As he came out of the bedroom dressed in the macho infernal tuxedo over plain black cotton socks, he wore a puzzled expression on his handsome face but his hair was nicely combed and gelled with the shining cream. His brain was a void, a dark void that consumed all the events of the previous night with each and every detail and was left with nothing. There had been a pre-mediated cold-blooded murder and there were exactly three prime suspects of the crime. The little glimmer of hope that radiated into him to soothe his blood was the certainty in his mind that one of the three – Sooraj Singh, Master Shams-ud-din and Hargurjeet Singh, was the actual culprit. He wanted to independently solve the mystery as soon as possible, even before the police could actually begin their investigation. Cynical jibes were not something he could tolerate anymore.

Chetan Prasad was on a leave that day as he had gone to his paternal village to meet his family. "Should I call him and discuss the entire matter or should I not disturb him as he must be busy creating unforgettable memories with his family, something that only lucky people like him get to do" was the question that bounced inside the enclosed, round and strong skull of the perplexed investigator. He finally decided not to call Chetan. He would be there the next day anyway. "I must start the investigation today myself and he will join me later" was the final decision made by Monty, realizing the fact that he was the chief and Chetan was just an ordinary apprentice.

"Take your ten boiled eggs," screamed the lady, bringing a hot bowl full of boiled eggs from the kitchen and keeping it on the table next to the crossed visiting card. "My head is paining very much and I am not feeling well. My body is not allowing me to put the broom and wipe the floor today, but I will do it otherwise you will cut my salary. I request you to order your lunch from the hotel today as I cannot cook it. I am sorry and please, please don't cut my salary. This is the irony of the poor in this country." She yelled at the top of her voice looking straight on Monty's forehead. However, he did not bother to respond. He was lost in his own conflicting thoughts but the screams seemed to annoy him and being a human, he reacted.

"I am thinking about something Rita, so I request you not to disturb me. If you are not feeling well, you may leave. Take rest at your home and come back to work when you feel better," said Monty taking the first bite of the boiled egg.

"Where is Chetan Prasad sir? He gives me a pill to swallow every time my head pains and it gets all right within five minutes. If you can provide me that pill, I will cook the lunch too."

"He has gone to his village today, and I don't have any medicine for headache."

"Please call him and ask for the name of the pill. I am dying of this pain."

"I told you not to disturb me. You are making me lose my temper. Go back to your home. Let me do my work." His voice got louder and his irritation got evident. The beady eyes turned from those eggs towards the tiny eyes of the screaming lady and the brows tilted slightly but after completing his statement, he turned back to eating the boiled eggs.

"I cannot go back as my uncle will shout at me for skipping work. You don't know what a strict man he is." Her tantrums began turning her breath from regular and quiet to a panting gasp, the one that leads to hysterical crying if not comforted at the correct time.

Monty wanted to chalk out a plan for interrogating the three suspects and Rita Mishra's emotional outbursts were creating a lot of hindrance to his thoughts and planning. Just before he could say a word in reply, she started crying. It was more than normal crying, it was the kind of sobbing of a desolate person, drained of all hopes. She sank to her knees on the tiled floor, not caring for the dust below or the pain from pressing the bruise on her right leg against the floor while the tears flowed out from her little eyes like a stream of water from a garden hose.

Surely this sudden release of strong emotion was a result of the haunted thought of her strict uncle and not only because of the pain in her little head. Monty, being the lady's man he was, quickly realized the need to comfort the young woman. He wrapped his heavy left arm around her narrow shoulders and pulled her close, gently rubbing her pale arms. She sunk to the warmth of his side, appreciative of the simple gesture from her boss. Her crying stopped and she looked at Monty right into his black eyes as if looking for some more consolation.

"I will go back to my home after two hours," she continued in a normal tone, "as my brothers will also be there then and in their presence, my uncle is not that strict."

The intellectual capacity of Monty's brain was caught between two opposing needs. On one side, he knew that there was something seriously wrong between Rita and her uncle and looking at the bruise on her leg and the pain in her head, it could also be physical abuse. She was screaming for no proper reason and this was the proof that there were definite traumas, both physical and mental, she was going through. Maybe, the loud shouts were just a weapon used by her to fight her own fear and not feel abandoned. On the other side, he wanted to begin his investigation and interrogate the three suspects without any delay. The latter seemed a wiser decision than spending time on helping the lady in distress. Being selfish is sometimes the need of the hour and that thought was exactly what made Monty arrive at a final decision. He concluded quickly that he would first shut the mouths that mocked him and later he would help the distressed lady.

"You are such a sweet girl Rita. Go in the bedroom and sleep for some time. Let me do my work while you take rest. That way you will not have to go to home early to your uncle and even I will not get angry and will also be able to do my work. Possibly, a short nap might even make you feel better," Monty explained his physically and mentally weak domestic helper like a true gentleman.

She quickly realized that what he said made a lot of sense. The weight lifted off her narrow shoulders as if a heavy child had just leapt off after a long piggy back ride. She walked taller straight into the bedroom without saying anything with a lighter and carefree stride. She noticed how the light, straight out of the sun, streamed in the room through the mullioned window. Arranging the pillow and folding the quilt on the bed, she sat on crossed legs on the floor of the warm and cozy gap between the window and the bed, lost in thoughts of her own and slowly fell asleep in that very position, taking support of the wall and not occupying much space, next to the stool containing Monty's mobile and the bottle of drinking water.

Meanwhile, Monty continued eating his breakfast of ten boiled eggs sitting on the chair in the hall. If he could have opened his mouth any wider, he could have swallowed an entire water melon in one go. His eating style was similar to a caveman, taking massive bites rather than cutting the eggs, stuffing his mouth too full. There was no water to end the healthy breakfast.

He stood up steadily and walked into the bedroom to reach the plastic bottle kept on the stool. As he took hushed steps on the glossy tiles, much smaller than normal, towards the blue stool, his eyes were fixed at his own feet. The gentleman was extra careful so as to not make even the softest noise of any type that would disturb the fragile lady in deep sleep near the stool. He picked up the bottle, and along with it his own mobile, and moved out of the room, checking his own appearance through a glance at the mirror on the cupboard, feeling superior and insecure, both at the same time.

Monty would never admit his fear. The tension in his brain could be at a level that would induce numbness in others but he would carry on as if nothing ever went wrong. Not a man in a thousand could spot his stress. He was like the duck, which kept swimming over the lake with a smile and never quickened its pace even if a great monster came on its way with his ghostly mouth wide open and sharp teeth protruding out of it.

Scarlett White was the glamour girl of the town. When a well known celebrity like her is ferociously murdered, the first ones to reach the spot of the crime, after the police officials of course, are the media personals. They try to cover every aspect of the story even if the investigating authorities do not wish to reveal many details for obvious reasons. With this thought, Monty switched on the TV and browsed through the news channels, both English and Hindi, spending more time on the local ones.

The news flashes on various channels became the markers of time, not that Monty minded. He stood watching all the news headlines and details hoping the big one would come sooner rather than later. With his mobile held in the tight grip of his left hand and TV remote in his right hand, he kept his vigil like a surfer observing the high waves before entering the sea. He was dreaming with his eyes wide open, he was hoping to complete the investigation before the police could start it, albeit in his own head. The music of the breaking news on the TV became the music of his dream, magnified, sending his spirit soaring but not finding the anticipated news anywhere made him come back to the reality.

Though the sun streamed right on his head, his mind was clouded with grey. His face shrunk and the broad shoulders slumped but not much as he sat on the blue plastic chair, next to the table, thinking why the media was not covering such a big story; maybe the police or the investigation bureau did not permit them to. As his mouth set into a semi-pout, he switched the TV off and started flipping the pages of the newspaper. His black eyeballs moved quickly from left to right and top to bottom through all the pages of the English daily, taking more time on the local news section, but to no avail. There was absolutely no mention of the murder or perhaps the newspaper was printed at midnight before the big news spread.

Monty sighed. His suppressed sigh was similar to release of air by an inflated balloon that slowly deflates due to a microscopic hole somewhere on its smooth surface. The tension in his head did not lift entirely and what filled his mind was a state of confusion instead of relief. He made one final attempt to find the news of the murder and that was through the news mobile application on his smart phone, but once again, to no avail. The confusion only increased but one thing was clear now and that was that the media was barred from covering the story of this vicious murder. Monty had no idea why but in a way he felt that this would give him a better chance to start his investigation from scratch and do it all by himself, with help from Chetan and that too if need be.

Monty kept the mobile on the side of the table, shut his eyes and bent forward touching his head gently over the even white surface of the plastic table, trying to remember something. He was all illogical thus far and feigned isolation, but not anymore as the reassuring words of his beloved late grandfather came to his rescue. He remembered the smile with which the departed soul held his hand into his twenty years ago and each and every expression of confidence the old man had on his plump and wrinkled face.

The words that gave a push to Monty away from isolation were, "Nothing is impossible in this world if you have the confidence to do it. Roads have been built cutting the immense mountains made of rock, green trees other than the prickly cactus have been grown by sheer hard work in the barren deserts, the muddy soil has been turned to glittering gold and special humans have stepped on the moon which is so far away for the ordinary." And then he imagined an abstract figure of his grandfather asking the younger form of him, "Do you know dear Monty, how was this made possible?" All of a sudden he shouted out loud just like he used to as a kid, "Only because of confidence and hard work. Self belief is the biggest virtue of humans." The abstract figure's smile widened as he explained to his little grandson, "Correct. Life is full of miseries and not just physical, but mental as well. Only the ones, who have sufficient confidence and self belief, are the ones who conquer all barriers to reach their goal. You, Monty, are a confident boy and will always achieve whatever you desire but never lose self belief in your life. God bless you."

"Thank you Grandfather!" shouted Monty as the abstract figure slowly faded out of his imagination, patting the young version of his dear grandson, exactly like the cloud of smoke that Monty was so used to see flying away into the sky above his head every time he smoked a cigarette. Not quickly, but steadily he raised his head up and sat straight, his shoulders turning back to their broad position but his eyes still closed, maybe to wait for the last bit of the figure to fade away. His pristine lips that had gone straight a while ago now widened and folded up towards his aptly placed nose from both sides, raising his prominent cheek bones in the process with a smile radiating confidence. After taking an unusually long breath of air in, filling his lungs to their maximum capacity, he exhaled it in one go, opening his eyes, this time full of light and inspiration; the smile still intact.

Monty was not a coward, for only a coward would sacrifice emotional death to save physical self. He was willing to be the champion who was pushed into the ocean and told to swim. The unassuming casual taunts, like that of the security guard had turned him into a hungry vulture tossed up in the air to capture its prey. Hope decorated each and every pore of his skin like the droplets of dew on a green leaf in the early winter morning. His eyes demonstrated the state of his mind which clearly knew that today will be better than tomorrow. Remembering Lord Ganesha, he declared open his mission to solve the murder mystery with the words, "Ganapati Bappa Maurya, Mangal Murti Maurya."

The first suspect indeed was the mysterious man named Sooraj Singh, the guy whom Scarlett had called ten times, one after the other, only minutes before her murder. Monty had the image of Sooraj's mobile number saved on the cloud for extra precaution and quickly browsed to it to see the number. He did not hesitate to call Sooraj from his own mobile knowing that noon was absolutely the perfect time to call someone who was a complete stranger.

"Hello... hello... Is it Sooraj Singh..." were the words that Monty spoke in his deep and pleasant sounding voice as the call was received but there was as much silence on the other side, as any teacher would expect from the obedient students of her class after shouting, "Pin drop Silence," a couple of times. Whoever had received the call seemed to be a rude person as he disconnected the call as if it was not Monty, but an ad agency this side trying hard to promote an impractical product.

Meanwhile, Rita woke up from her nap and had already come till the table adjacent to Monty's chair. She observed the disappointment registered on her boss' face before he could hide it. A sarcastic smile that played on Monty's dry lips and a shake of the head were enough signs for Rita to understand that something had gone wrong. She tried to help. "Sir, maybe the mobile number tracking app informs the people about a detective's call in advance, and as Chetan sir is absent today, why don't you try calling from my mobile?"

Quickly realizing that Rita was just standing next to him, Monty replied, "It is also possible that there was an issue with the other guy's network. They don't have proper network coverage in all areas. Anyway, how is the pain in your head now?"

"Less. I will put the broom and wipe the floor but that pill which Chetan sir gives me would have helped a lot. I am of the opinion that you should try my mobile once. My heart says it will help you." She sounded as innocent as the most mischievous student in front of the Principal of the school.

This statement brought a small smile on Monty's face as he realized that Rita was trying her best to get her mobile recharged by him. "All right, I will call using your mobile and in return I will get it recharged by fifty rupees."

Happiness is what she felt after listening about the fifty rupees recharge of her mobile, although the joy was short lived due to ongoing slight pain in her head. She quickly took out her mobile from the inner pocket of her shorts using her right hand and offered it to her boss. It was not a smart phone, rather an old fashioned mobile of grey color, weighing as heavy as the obsolete landline telephones.

"Thank you Rita," said Monty as he started dialing Sooraj's number pressing the number buttons, each making its own loud and annoying beep like sound, "but I want you to say hello first and after the response from the other side, introduce me to him and I will continue the conversation." Rita agreed and Monty pressed the big green button. Once again, the call was received and Rita said loudly, "Hello." This time there was a response and that too an unexpected once.

"Hello," said the female voice on the receiver's end. Judging by the name, Sooraj Singh was surely not a woman and this is what surprised Monty and he prompted Rita to continue the conversation. Rita repeated what she heard from her boss, "Madam, may I speak to Sooraj Singh?"

"No, he is not at home. If you have any message then, give that to me." The voice of the woman indicated that she must be a mother of two and hailed from a remote village. She sounded exactly like the female teller of a branch of any government bank in a village, rude and ill mannered. Her tone was that of a fish seller in a crowded evening fish market and she stressed a lot on the vowels. Even a hello from her mouth sounded like halo.

"Talk to my boss Monty C Dhingra ji," said Rita as she handed over her mobile to Monty who continued the conversation with the offensively impolite lady.

"I am Monty, the famous investigator of Kanpur and I want to meet Sooraj Singh urgently."

"He is not at home."

"Who are you?"

"I am the mother of Babita and Rinku."

"Do you know Sooraj Singh?" Monty tried to confirm as the lady was taking names that were out of the context.

"Yes. I am his wife."

After getting the confirmation, Monty tried to fix a meeting with the first suspect, saying, "When can I meet your husband?"

"Come to our home within an hour. He is a very busy man. I will tell him to wait if you confirm that you are coming here."

"Where is your house? Can you tell me your address?"

And she dictated the address of her residence but Monty did not write it down. He was so much into the mission that he would not forget it even it was as long as Kanpur's telephone directory.

"Thank you, I will be there in…"

And she disconnected the call even before Monty could complete his statement. He turned towards Rita briskly and returned the mobile to her, saying, "Thanks." Without wasting any more time, he stood up on his muscular legs and proceeded towards the shoe rack to pick up his already polished black shoes. Perhaps they were polished in the night itself, for saving time every morning.

As he wore those shoes containing a designer lining of silver on the top, over his plain black cotton socks, he said to Rita, "I am going Rita. I have urgent work to do.

I will leave one key of the flat on the table. After you finish your work, lock the door from out and leave. I will get late. Do not cook lunch for me. Along with the keys, I am also leaving a currency note of fifty rupees which you can use for recharge of your mobile."

Rita's pale face lightened up, evidently because of the gift of fifty rupees. The pain in her head seemed to have disappeared completely as had the pain in the bruise of her leg. She ran into the kitchen, as fast as leopard on the hunt, only to return with a broom in her hand and a broad and grateful smile on her slender face while her lips were as muted as a television when it is switched off.

Abiding by his promise, Monty kept a crisp currency note of fifty rupees on the table along with a key of the main door and in the process he picked up the crossed visiting card of Master Shams-ud-din and carried it with him in the safe custody of his left palm. He had complete faith on his employee exactly like the trees have on Mother Earth. He knew that she won't touch any valuable and that after the broom and wiping work would get over, she would carefully lock the flat from outside and would also bring the key back the next day safely. By the looks of it, it appeared that he had trusted her several times previously too and every time she had proved herself trustworthy.

As he left the flat through its main door, Monty realized that he had forgotten to wear his branded and expensive gold plated watch. It was certainly not a necessity with the smart phones taking over the modern lifestyle and Monty had no time to go back inside for accessories. He walked swiftly towards the staircase and down to the parking, which was visible from the window of his flat and where the Challenger was quietly parked. Quickly he unlocked it using the special elongated key and sat on the leather coated comfortable seat with a thud due to the haste. He kept the visiting card inside the dashboard, without wasting time in trying to adjust it properly among other stuff in there. He looked towards the music system from the corner of his eye but decided not to play the music for this short drive and immediately drove away towards the address he remembered very well in his brain.

Chapter V

Is the road to success same as the road to failure?

The particular locality of the residential address as dictated by the impolite and presumably ill-bred lady over the call was not much far from the apartment where Monty lived. Although the distance between the two would hardly be over three kilometers, there was a huge divide between the two neighborhoods, quite like the difference that exists between the people on two sides of an international border. The cosmopolitan culture had opened the considerate minds of the rational individuals from Monty's fairly opulent vicinity, while the former still was the home to mostly those who not only lacked sufficient money, but also had no great deal of worldly knowledge. People without distinctive qualities classified the modest residents of those two neighborhoods as rich and poor, or as educated and not so educated and also according to their caste and occupation, but what they never understood was the reason behind the drastic difference in the thought process of the two vicinities.

Maybe the elaborate structure and rigid mindset of patriarchy under which the diffident woman must have been raised in, forced her to disconnect the call on hearing a stranger male's voice, thought Monty as he shifted the long gear shaft on the big steering wheel of his esteemed Challenger, taking a left turn towards the main road, having reached there in just a few seconds of driving straight out from his apartment's galvanized iron gate. It could also be possible that she read the name and designation of the caller on her mobile number recognition application and decided not to answer it. The fact that he was going there only to interrogate the first suspect of the horrible crime and not to challenge any existing norms of the society, helped him realize that anything of much relevance could not be inferred from such doubts in his cultivated mind. He continued driving even as the hot sun rays attacked his handsome face, falling perpendicularly but refracting at a small angle through the slightly slanted windscreen, fitted perfectly into the grey metal of his car.

The afternoon sun was as deadly as a recently erupted volcano. The rays were as hot as the molten lava, the only distinction being the absence of fumes. Conceivably the total non-existence of the clouds was one of the reasons why the boiling rays fell directly on the surface of the Earth. What a challenge it would be for anyone other than Monty himself to wear a black tuxedo in that heat. Perhaps that coat gave him confidence and a feeling of superiority as he showed no visible sign of being uncomfortable, apart from a couple of obvious drops of sweat wetting his hair near the wide forehead. Anyway, a wise man once said that if any man can practice the same thing for over twenty hours, he can be perfect at it, and the private investigator had been wearing tuxedos almost every day since a decade or so.

No matter how perfect a man makes himself in his respective field, he can never compete against Mother Nature. The rays of the sun created nuisance for the beady eyes of Monty as he had a tough time keeping them fully open due to the refracting rays directed right into them, despite them being as black and unreflective as the stones of Onyx. To protect himself, Monty slowed down the car in the middle of the street and turned back so that his left hand could reach the cute pink teddy bear in black shades sitting at the rear seat. He pulled the black shades. They were branded ones and he put them on, enhancing his handsomeness by more than just a fraction. The shades were round in shape and large in size, with the diameter of both glasses about 5cm and the frame containing a blue lining along its black surface. Not only did it provide much relief to Monty against the penetrating sunlight, it also forced most teenage girls and even the gossiping aunties, passing by the street near the moving Challenger, peep into it until it went away from their sharp eyesight.

Monty was not driving fast but at an average speed of 25kmph on the crowded two way street. He would have loved to reach the residence of Sooraj Singh as soon as possible but he did not want to reach there with an unpleasant dent on the already rough surface of the body of his treasure. What was annoying him though was the ridiculous driving of the blue car he was following. The road was comparatively wider than other roads of the city but not wide enough to let Monty overtake the car ahead him due to the continuous traffic coming from the opposite side. The car ahead him was being driven by a driver who seemed to have an illegally acquired driving license as it was so obvious that such people who clearly lacked the skill required for driving, could never pass a proper driving test.

The irritating driver slowed down his blue car to about 5kmph, or maybe even slower than that and on the top of his maddening driving, he was not giving away any space for the vehicles behind to overtake his car. All of a sudden between a child specialist doctor's clinic on one side of the road and a wine shop on the other, he turned slightly towards the right and slowed down even more, almost coming to a stop, forcing Monty to blow the loud horn ten times. Even the drivers of the cars following Monty's Challenger seemed to be out of patience as they joined in the honking spree, but there was no effect whatsoever on the absurd leader.

When a flash of annoyance comes into even the sanest of all minds, it is always accompanied with a faulty idea. As Monty's face flushed red with anger over the mindless driver and the frustrating thought of getting late to meet the first suspect, Monty decided to overtake without bothering about the traffic that came from the other side. As he was overtaking, the foolish driver opened the door of his car with a sudden jerk, forcing Monty to apply brakes with all his power, bringing the Challenger to a stop at the right time to avoid any type of accident. Not even realizing what had just happened, the dolt took out his head, covered with a layer of thick black hair resembling a bush, and tilted it to a small degree towards the road, spitted pan masala straight on the concrete of the street, with the masala coming out of his mouth following a parabolic path like red colored water from a water gun which kids play with during the colorful festival of Holi. For some, it might be strange that a man could fill such huge quantity of pan masala into his small mouth. However, it was not something unique for Monty and the drivers behind him. In fact, they were all used to such characters on the roads of Kanpur.

They say even if Yoga and meditation fail to give one the much craved peace of mind, driving in Kanpur without uttering a foul word from his mouth would certainly convert his troubled mind to that of a meditating saint on the Himalayas. Monty waited for the driver to close his door and overtook the blue car, stepping with nearly full power on the large accelerator as soon as he got the space to do so. The anger disappeared in a flash of seconds and he continued his drive towards his destination, taking a right turn into the desired locality.

The locality was an overly crowded one and made of a mesh like framework of narrow lanes with a main road in the centre. The mesh of concrete held the British era structures with almost all of them going up to the two floors each. If someone took a picture of the vicinity using a camera fitted on a high flying drone, it would appear as a perfect fishing net, wrapped around a pile of numerous unlucky fish, all approximately of the same size and arranged in square shaped divisions of roughly the same color separated only by the thin thread of the net. Only on 10x zoom, the threads would be seen laden with freely roaming ants in huge numbers, which in reality were the people in those narrow lanes.

It was obvious that the Challenger would not be able to enter any lane, not due to its class, but due to its width. He decided to park it in the only available paid parking at the main road of the locality. The parking fees was a mere forty rupees and it was prepaid. The men, who guided Monty as he parked the Challenger, stared at him as if they had never seen such a good looking man before in their lives, causing an unpleasant feeling in the detective's focused mind. Monty took out his wallet from the back pocket of his trouser and paid the fees to one of the rogues and got down from his car, collecting the parking receipt and keeping it in his wallet which he then slipped back to its safe place. He locked the car carefully and keeping the keys in the side pocket of his black trouser, he walked towards the left.

Not only were the lanes as narrow as the corridor between the rooms in a good hotel, they were also half occupied at several places by the shopkeepers who kept their top selling items on the road for easy display to their prospective customers. Those items included almost everything from lifeless mannequins dressed mainly in colorful polyester clothing to locally made ladies purses and duplicate copies of branded sunglasses. The range was wide from low priced leather shoes and belts to plastic and stuffed toys that attracted kids quite like ivy flower attracts the honey bees. Even the regular customers had to purchase their required articles spending more time on bargaining than on selecting what to buy.

The number of cows, buffaloes and bulls was very nearly same as the number of humans in the crowded lanes. Monty had to be extra careful so as to not step on the dung that the broken pavements were full of. There were also a considerable number of food joints, especially those that offered Chinese food and Chats as their specialty. People ate the delicious food but paid scant attention to the hygiene. In fact, the road was full of disposed plates, spoons and left over food and even glass bottles of cold drink. Monty did not want to dirty his expensive and polished shoes, so he walked slowly with measured steps towards his destination until he reached the famous Kallu Pan Shop.

This shop had grown as a brand over the years in Kanpur and now had more than ten branches all over the city. Monty was standing at the place from where it all started. Passing through a group of four men who were busy smoking and chatting with each other about the confusing political combinations, he went near the person who was engrossed completely in making Pan while sitting on a mattress placed at a height of around four feet on an elongated wooden base inside the 4ft x 5ft shop. He must have been thirty five years old and was dressed in a simple white kurta pajama and had a long moustache on his brown but chubby face which also supported a long tilak on his forehead.

"Sir, can you please guide me to Sooraj Singh's residence?"

The man looked up. His experienced eyes were dark brown in color and he appeared annoyed with something. In his loud voice and rude tone, he replied, "Sooraj Singh lives in fourth house, next to the temple and in the lane opposite to my shop," and he pointed towards the lane he was mentioning.

"Thank you. Is he a regular to your shop?" Monty began his investigation by trying to gather as much information as he could about the suspect before physically meeting him for the first time.

The man left making pan and keeping the katha and chuna away on their respective stands, he turned towards Monty saying, "Yes, he is. If you meet him, tell him to return my four hundred rupees. I had lent it to him last month for a day or two."

"Yes, sure, I will say that to him. Does he usually borrow money or this was the first time?"

"He borrows from me every now and then but always returns it before the due date of the loan. This time he has not given it back."

"What kind of a man is he? I am asking you this because I am going to meet him for the first time and that too with something very significant." And as Monty was saying, he took out a currency note of two thousand and offered it to the pan maker, who pulled it towards himself like a starving hawk pulls an unaware rat.

"He is a good man who works as an honest taxi driver. He appears deeply religious and performs Pooja at the temple every morning but I doubt that all of that is just a show off. His talks and actions do not suggest his inclination towards God. I am telling you all this because you look like an educated man and we rarely have such people visiting our place," replied the man whose body language did not change even a bit even after receiving a handsome tip.

"Thanks, but what kind of actions and talks he indulges in?" Monty eagerly asked the pan maker who was providing appreciable information about Sooraj Singh as he wiped the sweat off his forehead from the knuckles of the loosely clenched fist of his left hand.

"He loses his cool and gets a little vulgar at times which I don't think God fearing people do, and if you ask any random girl of this locality, she will tell you that he is one of the biggest eve teaser here, despite his age and him being a married man. And Sir, please don't ask much about my customer to me. Go and meet him directly at his house."

"Thanks Sir. I will let you continue making these delicious pans and I hope one thousand six hundred is good enough interest on your loan."

And the two men smiled at each other, folded hands and lowered their eyes, bidding goodbye like typical Indian gentlemen. Monty turned towards the desired lane and the informer started making pans as he was before meeting the detective. The steps that Monty took towards his destination through the red brick covered pavement were similar to those that he would take to glide over the shining floor of marble like a slinking leopard.

As Monty entered the lane, he saw people walking roughly in one direction and that was out of the lane, some of them chatting with each other with their heads down as if their minds were lost in some important thoughts and they did not want to be disturbed by any kind of eye contact with the ones coming from the front. Monty could easily distinguish between them as Hindus and Muslims from the way they were dressed. As Monty moved further, he observed that the followers of the two religions were in almost equal numbers until he reached the temple of Lord Shiva, which was exactly the third building on the right side in the lane.

The temple was not a huge one but sufficient for accommodating ten devotees at a time but there were just two of them and the priest at that moment. It was indeed a clean and very well maintained temple containing one huge shrine of Lord Shiva and several paintings of His family including his son Lord Ganesha and wife Goddess Parvati. On the ground floor of the building, exactly opposite to the temple, was a community hall where an Islamic scholar had just finished his religious speech and some of the listeners were still sitting and chatting while the others had left. Monty was amazed to see the cultural cohesiveness in the people and realized the fact that no matter how hard the politicians and media try, they cannot separate the people based on their religion. He joined his robust hands to take the blessings of Lord Shiva and rang the big temple bell to mark his presence before entering the house next to it which was indeed his destination to meet the first suspect of the first degree murder.

The fourth house of the lane by the way was perhaps the smallest structure in the entire locality. It contained just a ground floor with no upper floors. The grey colored house was rectangular in shape with its width comparatively more than its depth into the lane. It was made of four walls and a roof that was covered with blue colored plastic covering hanging till the entrance door and windows, maybe to protect rain water from dripping down into the rooms. The width of the entire house must be around 20ft if not less and the depth was about 10ft only, making it an extremely small building for human habitation. It was quite possible that it was once a shop that was at present being used for residential purpose. On one side it had the Lord Shiva temple while on the other side there was a huge three floored building that must have at least ten flats accommodating a family each. Staring with his eyes wide open at the shabby walls, Monty feared that those shivering walls would not last more than a year or two against the beckoning call of gravity but once again, the feeling of selfishness crawled into his mind. He was there to begin his investigation, not to help others or sympathize with them. He proceeded towards the door of the miniscule feeble structure.

It was a door that was perhaps in place to safeguard against the worst weather conditions and stray domestic animals rather than any undesirable intruders. Maybe the neighborhood was safe or maybe there was nothing inside that the intruders would be interested in, thought Monty as he observed that the weak door was framed with unevenly cut planks of wood around the outside edges and one across the middle to give it strength to stand straight in its place, while the lower portion was just a plywood nailed in there to cover the entire opening. There was a brass colored handle on the left side that had totally dulled with age and greasy marks of the fingers. Surprisingly, the door had no hole apart from the keyhole carved in the handle itself for the people inside to see who was at the door. There was no sign of CCTV cameras installed anywhere near the residence as well and visibly, there was no doorbell anywhere near the door.

As Monty stood still, just three inches away from the door with his eyes fixed at it as if they were blessed with x-ray vision to scan the area behind the door, he raised his left hand with the bare knuckles of the loosely clenched fist facing the wood and knocked thrice. He had over a hundred butterflies in his stomach while his strong head buzzed with all kinds of possibilities. The muscle near the corner of his right eye, below the round shades, twitched involuntarily as he began tapping his left foot on the bricked pavement waiting impatiently for the door to open.

Hardly had five seconds passed since the knock when the wooden door opened outwards surprisingly without any noise, forcing Monty to take a step back to allow it to open in its full swing. The lady who opened the door was perhaps the one he spoke to on call. Her skin tone was that of dark walnut and she wore no makeup apart from the surplus application of ruby red lipstick on her lips which were not thick or thin but medium in size. The lower lip of the lady, visibly in her early thirties, however appeared fuller than the upper one as if injected and wanting to be pampered.

She was dressed in a pale green saree, covering her round shaped head with it like several other Indian housewives take pride in doing. The color of her saree was as green as the freshly made mango pickle while it was not exactly matching with her blouse, which was navy blue in color, similar to the Indian cricket team's uniform for limited overs international matches. The blouse exposed her navel which was exactly in the centre of her slim belly, proportionate to her lean arms, both covered with red glass bangles till almost the elbows. She was wearing a thin silver coated anklet on her bare feet. That was perhaps the only piece of jewel she wore as there was no necklace round her neck, no rings on any of the ten ladyfinger shaped fingers and no earrings on her small yet pierced ears.

There was something in the way she held herself, maybe diffidence, so much that she looked confused as to where her slender limbs should be in order to appear naturally placed. Her forehead was wide and glistened with cold sweat but the wine red circular bindi with a circumference of less than 2cm which she decorated herself with was fixed in the middle of it as if it was painted right there. Her button shaped nose was somewhat large but not plump or bony and had no bump on the bridge, in contrast to her flat and hollow cheekbones, perhaps due to stress caused by her emotions or overwork.

Due to the covering of saree on her head, the length of her black hair beyond the orange sindoor was not completely visible but what Monty focused on was her brown eyes, which were darting back and forth, shining a little due to the sunlight that fell directly on them. Her eyes held secrets for sure, the same way an old pot keeps several layers of brown soil essential to keep the green plant safe with its roots held as firmly in the soil as the secrets in those brown eyes. She was indeed a next door Indian housewife.

"Hello Ma'am. Sorry to disturb you. I am Monty C Dhingra, the detective and I have come here to meet

Mr. Sooraj Singh for an important discussion. I had spoken to his wife over the phone and fixed my appointment with him," said Monty trying to make an eye contact with the lady from behind the shades but failed as she lowered her gaze to his black shoes, as if they were the only ones visiting her house.

"Welcome inside. Yes, you spoke to me over the phone. I am Babita and Rinku's mother." Her loud and rude tone coupled with sharp and unpleasant voice served as a proof of what she said. Monty entered the little structure on her invitation as she moved sideways to allow him to enter into a surprisingly dark house, dark enough to force Monty to take off his shades and fix them in the pocket of his shirt.

The room where Monty just got into was exceptionally compact, may well be less than 8ft in length and 10ft in breadth. The cemented interior walls were creamy white in color and it was visibly clear that they had been painted decades ago as they were full of marks of trickling water, which in turn indicated that there were several definite leakages from the ceiling. The first thought that came into Monty's sensible brain was that had Chetan Prasad been there, he would have surely raised a question or two about why the walls were totally bare with no framed pictures, no paintings, nothing. As Monty turned his observant head up with an expression of innocence masking his true intentions, he observed that the ceiling was deep black in color, not that it was painted such but because of the stifling smoke that stuck on it like magnetic stickers of Monty's favorite cartoons that he used to stick so fondly on the refrigerator in his childhood days; the only difference being that insolent vapor blatantly refused to leave.

The ceiling was black and there were no windows to allow complete penetration of sunlight into the room and on top of that the lights in there were switched off, making it feel like it was late in the evening instead of noon. Only the fan was on but it hardly made any noise apart from the faint sound of rotating blades. There was no other sound from the outside world, not even a bird or engine noise.

The room also served as a parking for a lightweight bicycle which was right in the left corner, apart from being the makeshift kitchen for the family. The utensils, mainly made of steel, and gas cylinder were kept on the floor of the right hand side near the school bag sized stove, occupying almost half of the area, while there were two plastic chairs that looked as if they would break anytime, kept on top of each other on the other side. That was all about the typical poor man's house.

The fact that there were no windows surprised Monty but he observed that there was a doorstep without a door leading maybe to another room, which he guessed would be of approximately the same size of the room he was standing in. Only a thin sheet of plastic that acted like an opaque curtain was hanging there to act like a door between the two chambers.

"Rinku's father has gone to the market and will return in five minutes," said the lady as her tone turned dull and even the volume of her distressing voice decreased almost three times. "Babita, come here, we have a guest at home; offer a chair to uncle," she tried hard to be loud while calling her daughter but her voice was breaking, unlike the way it was a few seconds ago.

From behind the curtain of plastic entered into the room Babita, a ten year old gracefully thin girl with willowy arms and legs as thin as pencils, neatly dressed in a sleeveless pink top and a red skirt that reached down till her knees. Her hair that might reach till her waist if let open, was properly combed, oiled and tied into a well made ponytail. She had a black thread tied to her neck and carried it like the sophisticated ladies carry their costly necklaces in kitty parties. Her little face was exactly like what her mother's would have been a couple of decades ago. She seemed a pretty shy girl and covered her mouth with the back of her left hand, sucking in the knuckles of a couple of fingers and did not dare to say a word.

She went straight towards the plastic chairs kept opposite to the bicycle and picked up one chair and offered it to Monty, who being the gentleman he was, told her to leave it as he would arrange it himself and went on to ask her, observing the bruise on her right foot, "Thank you for the chair little one, how did you hurt that foot?" She remained silent, maybe due to her shy nature or maybe she did not want to talk to a stranger.

In the meantime, there came running barefoot her younger brother Rinku through the same curtain from the other room. He was around six years old and though his face was small in size, it clearly carried an expression of innocent naughtiness. He was humorously smiling with his little mouth wide open, the corner of his lips reaching almost till his flat nose, revealing that his front upper tooth had just broken and a new one was about to come out. He was modestly dressed in a half sleeved red t-shirt that appeared to be of a size apt for a twelve year old and a white colored half pant that belonged to a five year old. He came near his unaware sister as quickly as a cheetah and pulled her ponytail. She reciprocated with a scream and then the two kids ran inside, the elder one chasing the younger sibling behind the mysterious curtain.

Before Monty could sit on the chair that was arranged for him, Sooraj Singh's wife offered him a glass of drinking water. Monty saw the steel glass kept in a steel tray held firmly in the lean hands of the lady and then he raised his head and eyes towards her face to thank her for her kind hospitality. His face turned as white as chalk in an expression of sudden shock and his mouth opened wide and froze there.

The lady was staring right at his forehead, almost one and a half feet above her normal gaze, with her brown eyes too stationary to even blink. Slowly her eyeballs went up towards the root of the eyelashes making only the white portion of her eyes visible. Even prior to any reaction by Monty, her hands trembled with a bizarre continuous sound of the red glass bangles hitting each other and her brown skin, dropping the glass and the tray right on the floor below, next to the black shoes, missing them by a whisker but making a noise loud enough for the two kids to run out from the peculiar room to see what had happened.

The slim body of the lady in green stiffened and her svelte limbs continued the uncanny jerking movements, as if she was not a human but a phantom which haunts lonely roads at night; only waiting for the soulless body to levitate. Monty could see clearly that her tongue was pressed hard by her own teeth as her mouth was left open during the uncontrollable rage. The sudden twitching movements of her muscles seemed involuntary and the kids began to shout on the top of their voice, "Spirit has again come inside her," hugging each other as tight as they would if the end of the world was near. It was that suffocating hug which had stopped Rinku from getting into fetal position on the floor due to sheer fear.

And when Babita's scream converted into suppressed crying with her cheeks trembling and tears bursting forth as water released from a dam, even Monty's heart started pounding so hard that he could feel pulse pressing out of his ribcage from the jerking veins within. His body shook from inside as his breaths came in short pants but he tried to take control by trying to hold the lady to prevent her from falling backwards and breaking her own skull in the process.

Her saree had fallen off her head due to continuous movement exposing her deep black hair which reached till her waist. The hairclip had fallen off in the commotion, leaving her hair unevenly open, with some portion of it covering half of her voiceless face.

The panic and anxiety attack flowed away within a minute or so as the lady turned normal, her eyes coming back to their original place and her tongue set free by her own tooth and the jerking of her muscles also came to a complete standstill. She felt embarrassed to see her saree off her head and her hair open and quickly ran behind the curtain as the kids followed her. Even their crying seemed to stop but Monty still preferred to stand rather than sit on that chair, waiting for his breath to come back to normal till the lady returned in her customary look.

"Are you fine?" enquired Monty observing the lady from head to toe as she appeared absolutely fine.

"Yes I am, actually I have not taken my medicine today, so the evil spirit returned to punish me. I am sorry I dropped the glass." She went towards the utensils and picked up a cloth hidden below the steel plates. Going down on her haunches, she started wiping the floor where she had dropped water. The area was so less that it hardly took ten seconds for her to finish the wiping as she kept the wet cloth in the corner.

Although the answer she gave was not the one Monty expected, he decided not to continue the conversation about her health, keeping in mind the mentality and education level of the woman. Focusing only on the mission, he attempted to begin his interrogation.

"Ma'am, can you tell me where your husband Sooraj Singh was yesterday night?"

She smiled and lowered her gaze to the floor. She felt as shy on listening to the question as the touch me not plant when someone actually goes near it. She covered the left half of her round face with the saree and replied, "He was out, driving his taxi." The volume of her voice was so low that Monty had to literally guess half of the words she said as they were not clearly audible. And then a blush seared through her right cheek for no reason whatsoever as she attempted to hide her full face except the lowered eyes with her saree.

And then Monty heard gentle footsteps of someone entering into the house through the dilapidated door, with its sound echoing all over the settlement due to its compact structure. What would once have been white, the canvas shoes of the six feet tall gentleman were now rusty brown with the soles worn out and demanding a change. The inky black laces trailed on the floor, overlong as they were, fraying like a neglected horse tether. Even if a student left his answer sheet blank during the examination, she would score more marks than what Monty deserved in guessing who that man was.

Sooraj Singh was wearing a dark blue polyester track pant, visibly crafted with cheap quality fabric which may not last long but was the big and tall man looked somewhat comfortable in it. Although the lower did not appear to belong to a very fashionable person's wardrobe, but perhaps offered a sufficient deal of flexibility as well as breathability around his approximately 34 inch waist. A pure white crew neck t-shirt surprisingly with no design printed on it, hugged his bare 44 inch chest giving it an appearance as though it was stuck there using a good quality glue instead of being worn as part of his attire. The neck size would be around 16 inch but his shoulders were broader than the average forcing him to wear an extra large t-shirt. Though he was dressed like those who are young at heart, the red colored cotton napkin that he hung at the back of his neck, resting on his massive shoulders on both sides was a spoiled sport.

Though his clothing was western and not so expensive, his caramel brown skin tone and facial features were a hundred percent Indian. His powerful jaw, fitted at the perfect angle to his wide chin, lifted his heavily built and slightly pudgy face accompanied by a sarcastic smile on the large mouth just below his sword shaped moustaches. Monty could distinctly imagine that the suspect must be devoting several minutes daily to oil his belligerent moustaches, while his cheeks were clean shaven revealing a few brown spots on them on both sides, similar to the tiny chocolate chips in a chocolate ice cream. His pitch black hair was brushed neatly backwards, reaching till his shoulders and stood there unmoved, not because of any hair spray but coconut oil.

His eyes were a mixture of blue and green, perhaps a shade which is as tough to describe as it is to solve a fuzzy puzzle in seconds. Though the color was between blue and green, even yellow crept in around the edges, trying hard to take over but was not successful. The forehead was as wide and big as the flat sole of a ten year old kid's foot, with as many as six wrinkles on it. It was decorated with a colossal Tilak and a couple of uncooked rice stuck firmly on it, displaying the religious inclination of the accused. His fore limbs were longer than they should be according to his height, and the arms were covered with a thick layer of impenetrable hair. He was carrying a giant pale green bottle gourd in his left hand, as Monty observed a thin gold ring on one of his fingers.

"Pushpa, make this gourd today for lunch," he said to his wife in a voice similar to that of a brave commander of a battalion in a war ordering his troops attack the enemy; only a bit more harsh and authoritative. He appeared to be a man who could never whisper as his voice was made such by God that he would always be audible to the people ten yards away from him. That was precisely the reason his children heard him and came out running through the plastic curtain.

"I don't want to eat gourd. We had it yesterday and two days back too," screamed Babita seeing her father with a gourd in his hand.

"Come here," said Sooraj in an even more authoritative manner and as Babita went near him he hit her with the gourd right across her little face and she fell backwards, almost falling flat on the floor with the force of it. "Have you been appointed as the District Collector that you dare to demand food of your choice?" said the angry man in his unreasonable and overpowering rage. The poor little girl had not expected her dad to react so strongly but the weight of the vegetable and the strength with which it hit her stunned her so much that she could not even cry. Her mother came to her rescue, helping her to get back to her normal posture and then took her away with the gourd in her hand, walking slowly out of the room with Monty shell shocked with what he just witnessed.

"Dad, I eat gourd every day," said Rinku, "I don't want to eat it today." Before Sooraj could assault his son, Monty jumped in between the two of them. Using his shrewd eyes, Sooraj stared straight at Rinku's cheeks and simultaneously shouted out loud, "Pushpa, give Rinku the noodles which I bought yesterday. Our little boy is bored of gourd." Rinku smiled and went running inside through the greasy curtain.

"You must be Monty, the person my wife told me about. I heard you called today and are looking forward to meet me," said Sooraj, maintaining his tone of authority as he turned towards the thinking guest standing as close to him as two ferocious boxers before the bout starts. The look that Sooraj Singh used to observe Monty from head to toe was similar to the one that a vicious and slightly insane villain of an old time Tollywood movie gives to the undisputedly beautiful heroine.

"You should not have hit the girl like that," realizing the mindset of patriarchy and violence in the first accused man.

"You look educated Mr. Monty. You must be capable enough to understand that you are nobody to comment on my personal issues. She is my daughter and I can do whatever I want to do inside my own house. And I believe that this is not the reason that has dragged you out of your comfort zone to a poor man's house here," replied Sooraj with his unblinking eyes staring right into the two black gemstones of Onyx, leaving Monty with no other option but to turn a bit defensive, especially after observing the aggressive nature of the taxi driver.

"I came here with a purpose but standing here I observed that your wife is suffering from epilepsy. You must consult a neurologist for her treatment."

"Yes, I know that she is suffering from Juvenile Myoclonic Epilepsy. She has consulted a neurologist who suggested her to have her medicines daily. She eats those tablets of Levetiracetam without any gap in the dosage. Yesterday, after I purchased that bloody strip, I mistakenly dropped it somewhere on my way back to home. I am a poor man so I cannot afford to buy two strips at the same time. Maybe she suffered an attack today in front of you, but it is not something to worry about as it is genetic. Instead of talking about things that make fun of my economic conditions, can you please come on the main agenda of our meeting?" There was no expression other than that of dominance on his masculine face and his charging eyes did not blink even once even when he narrated the medical condition of his wife. An image of the full strip of Levetiracetam near Scarlett's bed flashed into Monty's imaginative brain but he decided not to mention it to the suspect.

"Does she have 750mg of Levetiracetam daily?" Monty tried to fix the pieces of the puzzle as much as he could.

"I can't afford so many medicines, so she breaks one tablet into two. I save half of my money in this way. Come to the point."

"That is sad. Do you think we should talk about Scarlett White here in this room?" the self seeking investigator asked Sooraj in as clear words as possible, noticing the change in the body language of the suspect. He could visibly spot the acceleration in Sooraj's heart rate and that his mind was playing certain past stories which only he knew about and that too in a loop. Sooraj could not maintain eye contact with his guest any longer as his eyes were now captivated by some kind of blank space with his mouth opening a little, providing an entry passage for extra air straight into his lungs and what followed was complete silence for almost a minute.

"I am a poor man who leads a substandard life, but Monty Sahib I do care for my despondent family. They are my own people. Let us not pollute the air of this pure house with the conversation you demand," Sooraj's tone changed from that of power and influence to that of the typical man of a closely knit family as he turned towards the main door of his house with a simple hand gesture towards Monty, requesting him not to start the interrogation within those scruffy walls. Monty, with all his experiences coming handy to him during such exchanges, immediately walked out of the door, followed by the suspect, who carried the two plastic chairs out and arranged them on the pavement between the temple and his house.

As Monty stepped out, he could feel the difference in the sunlight and the lack of it inside the dark room forcing him to take out his black round shades from the pocket of his shirt and putting them back on once again, taking his handsomeness and style to another level. He sat on one of the chairs facing the wooden door, while Sooraj sat just opposite to him facing the boundary wall of the temple. Unexpectedly, Sooraj took out a box of cigarettes from the side pocket of his track pant and pulled out one for him while offering one to his guest.

"I don't smoke this brand," said Monty as he effortlessly refused to accept the offer.

Taking out a lighter from the other pocket and lighting up his cigarette and feeling a bit more confident than he was inside the house, Sooraj replied, "I am not rich, I have just this one."

"It's alright. I smoke only the tobacco free smuggled cigarettes from Italy, which my friend arranges for me. If he was here, I would have surely given you a fantastic company."

There was no expression on Sooraj's face as he was lost in sniffing the injurious roll of paper, trying his best to appear normal and not scared of the situation.

"So how do you know Scarlett White?"

Sniffing stopped and the bluish green eyes turned up, giving an expression of nervousness, but the quality of his voice still remained normal as he said, "300 bucks is what I make per hour from my taxi. This is my time of work but I am sitting here with you."

Monty realized that the time of this meeting overlapped with the working hours of the suspect, so he had no other choice but to make a deal. "I will pay you two thousand for this meeting, which might end much before sixty minutes if we can be precise with our words." The sarcastic smile reappeared on the wide mouth of the pudgy faced accused as he nodded in approval of the deal.

"Now tell me what the link between Scarlett White and you is?" Monty's feet tapped on the floor in a loop, not because of a melodious tune, but because of impatience.

Sooraj's backbone seemed to have the power of a rod of iron, as straight as it can ever be even while he was smoking with the cigarette held firmly between the fingers of his left hand. His right leg was kept on the top of his left thigh with an oval shaped hole peeping through the uneven surface of the dusty sneakers of the right foot. With another sniff going straight into his lungs to fill them with the black smoke, he began his story, the one which Monty waited to hear since he fled from the crime scene.

"I wanted to permanently delete this chapter out of my memory but the severe tantrums of Scarlett White just don't permit me to. Go and tell her that I don't want to meet her anymore."

"Obviously she will never meet you again and by the way, I am not her messenger, I am investigating her murder. Kindly cooperate with me if you don't want me to use other methods." Monty sounded like a strict headmaster.

The bluish green eyes of the taxi driver widened and grief surged with every expelled breath reaching the peaks but not coming down to the normal, not even after the soothing effect of the August breeze. Tears filled into his eyes that now appeared helpless but something held them from spilling over the grass that was trying to grow in the gap between the bricks on the pavement. Forgetting that almost the full cigarette was left to be smoked, he dropped it right on the ground below as his left hand folded completely into a punch to support his head which drooped down like that of a traitor who had just been declared guilty. "Om Shanti, May her soul rest in God's lotus feet. It is very shocking to hear this," were the exact words that came out of his mouth after a silence of a couple of minutes.

Monty sat still observing the reaction of the suspect, capturing every moment and word into his mind like a videographer on a wedding shoot. When he realized that Sooraj had come back to normality, he said, "Were you not aware of the murder?"

"No. I met her a few days back but then it was all normal."

"How do you know her?"

Sooraj Singh was sitting near the doorstep of his own house in the warm breeze of August, yet his limbs began to shake with the bones rattling, perhaps with the fear of the future that loomed before him if he got exposed. As Monty observed the building anxiety of the first suspect, Sooraj seemed to be ready to begin his elaborate rationalizations of the past but maybe with a nagging voice at the back of his mind reminding him of the doom ahead if he made any mistake. Looking towards the investigator, he began the narration of his story with Monty listening to it attentively and without interrupting in between.

"Fire has an uncontrolled aggression. It does not care whether it burns wood, meat or any part of the flesh of a bubbly human. Similar to the hostility of any disastrous fire, was the nature of Scarlett's ex-husband, the respected Hargurjeet Singh Ji. Though theirs was a love marriage, it was more of a mismatch than a match and when they separated, over a year ago, Scarlett received the little house in Tilak Nagar as alimony. That was the house where she dwelled till I last met her.

Bigger the brand more is the value on its tags. Judging by its construction, I am of the opinion that that house was a secret place of adultery for her husband during his bachelor days, but alas, he was left with no other option but to let it go, along with the luxurious metallic grey colored car which Scarlett was so fond of, perhaps because of its spacious rear seat. But, what many people don't know is that she never learnt driving, possibly due to the lack of time in her busy schedule.

The house had no quarters for the helpers although she had a couple of part time housemaids and a chef who came, performed their duties and returned to their own homes before sunset. None of them had the key of the main door and if Scarlett had to go somewhere during their work time, she would inform them in advance and they would not come that day.

She shared a cordial relation with all of them and they had great respect for their employer. I worked as her personal driver and was forced to work at odd hours based on her plans, most of them being made at the last minute.

Scarlett was an alcoholic. Perhaps after her divorce, she turned to drinking more heavily than before as there was no one to tell her to stop, to say she had had enough. Expensive bottles of whiskey, vodka and beer were her only friends. She would feel lonely if there were less than four full bottles in the house. That was her emergency alert and she immediately went shopping if it reached that level, even if it was two in the night.

Hardly did the bottles reach that count as every other day she attended the late night parties at various clubs and lounges all over the city, choosing them not on the basis of their offers but their crowd. She was fond of loud music, the one which was louder than thunder and the one which made even the heaviest cutlery on top of the tables rattle like a shivering beggar sleeping on the side of the road in late December. She preferred neon lights that flashed everywhere like the police sirens albeit ten times more colorful.

I think, and you may agree with me, that the foremost point of concern when you need to go to these trendy parties is the portraying of substantial variety in design of your attire. And especially for someone who had been the winner of a couple of state level beauty pageants, being richly decorated was an obligation. Though she mostly opted for lively prints on luxurious silk, she would never pay any attention to the weather while choosing her dress for the night.

Never did she like to repeat any attire or its accessories. It was always a new combination, something that always kept her a cut above the others. She was not hesitant to wear provocative dresses even among a crowd of teenagers, perhaps the new fans and their comments made her feel satisfied about herself. Although she was not a regular to the gym, she picked figure flattering outfits over the noble and simple ones.

All her dresses were masterfully tailored by Master Shams-ud-din, the middle aged deviant tailor and the owner of The Powerful Horse Boutique. Never did she share a harmonious relationship with that double dealing sly character. Matters between the two got worse with time to the extent of physical blows on his terribly out of shape body by her refined punches. Becoming more and more intense with time, the need for revenge for the wily Master was like a septic wound with its only effective antibiotic being harsh retaliation. In my opinion, if you go to him and tell about this murder, instead of expressing sincere regret, he would burst out into hysterical laughing to the extent of spraining the muscles of his own chest.

It was a chilling night and probably the date was the twenty sixth of December, when she went for a party to one of the most expensive lounges of the city. It was not her birthday that day. In fact, it happened to be the day that marked one complete year of her divorce. As usual, I was waiting for her to come out till five in the morning just like my wife waited for me to reach home before she could doze off. Money is essential and makes a family man work overtime without much fuss. The company of my brand of cigarettes and some sleep deprived yet jolly drivers and guards helped me stay awake as she danced inside with the VIPs.

Late at night or early in the morning as some would call it, when the dance floor had already converted into an abused chess board, with the black and white squares spilled with drinks and broken glasses, the VIP dance stopped. With the lights up for the cleanup of the whole mess, that seemed exciting just a while ago, Scarlett, along with other girls and guys could barely walk out without support.

All our cigarettes were over but the wait was worth it for all of us, the poor men. Though the testosterones in our bodies had prepared us thoroughly for the fashion parade, we were not quite ready for the beauties that came out from the door one after the other. Some of them had blue eyes, some as black as you but all of them had loads of makeup on their tempting faces. All the sober eyeballs turned towards Scarlett when she made her way out, looking for support to walk till the car. Kangaroos of Australia would feel ashamed when they see real Indian men like me jump so swiftly to guide the lady in red towards her luxury car.

Four inch pencil heels might hurt after several hours of continuous and intense dance so Scarlett had to let those black stilettos off but did not want to walk barefoot as it would mean that her long gown from the back would rub against the dirt on the sidewalk. Also, her feet were too clean I guess to be stepping over the ground. Perhaps the rich are built delicate. So, on her orders, I lifted her up in the strong arms of my poor self. Her weight was not too much but her red gown and black jacket were as heavy and rich as her, making me move slowly towards the car.

My companions were now jealous of me. I could feel it in their eyes even though they kept silent, helping their ladies and gents towards their cars but keeping full attention on me. I was tiring as I was sleep deprived but I did not want to show to anyone that I was tired. With my chest pumping out and measuring four inches more than what it would normally do, I walked towards the car as Scarlett held my shoulders as firm as the hands of a butcher while cutting a goat into pieces.

The hangover did not allow her to sit straight on the spacious rear seat of the car, so she preferred to lie down on her back with her curvy legs bent in the shape of a diamond, peeping out sensuously through the silk with her delicate feet glued together horizontally. I drove speedily towards her house, observing through the rear view mirror, the shaking of her knees as her palm played with the irresistible area between her legs resulting in a whooshing sound of her breath.

When we reached her house, even before I could turn the car's engine off, she got down and ran towards the door, barefoot and without caring for her gown which unfortunately got dragged over the wet grass. This came to me as a surprise with a subsequent thought that maybe she had gained some energy from her raunchy deed in the car. I had the keys anyway, so hurried up. Carrying her stilettos in my left hand I quickly opened the lock using my right hand and as it was unlocked, she ran in, straight into the washroom. I followed to keep the footwear and the car and door keys in their respective place before I could leave to attend my waiting wife, the poor lady.

Just as I was about to exit her bedroom, the washroom door opened and Scarlett came out, wearing a black shining leather sleeveless crop top with a keyhole design in the front. The top covered her assets somewhat perfectly but did not extend beyond that, exposing her navel brilliantly like some of our Bhojpuri cinema actresses. Below that she wore black high waist shorts which were of the same material as her top but hugged her bottom as tight as the stiff leather saddle on a rambunctious pony's bare back. Her curvy legs were once again exposed and this time the three line tattoo on her right thigh was clearly visible but unfortunately I am not educated enough to read Greek script. She was still barefoot but not for long as she wore her dancing stilettos in a flash which I had already kept next to her unpolished dressing table.

Her hair flowed down her back meandering around her pulpy shoulders, resembling the black ink leaking from a tilted inkpot making sure to create shadows down her red cheeks. Her eyes were like those of a heavily drunk fox having an icy grayish green hue of the lens like the first sprouts of plants after the end of a new year's snowfall in Nainital. Though all of us, including the poor men like me, know that she was an epitome of beauty, the one whose social media images made almost all boys drool, but I was exceptionally lucky to observe that she was much more pleasing to the senses in a private room. If she was a loaded gun in her public attire, she was a deadly nuclear bomb in her privates. I was tired and sore, but I did not care. I did not want to sleep anymore, and I completely forgot about my poor wife. That was the moment when I felt some tingling in my pants and immediately I knew that I had to hit a six at the no ball delivered to me. Remembering all the warnings my companions had given me a while ago but caring for none, I stopped inside her bedroom, closing the door for privacy but what followed was highly unexpected.

She offered me a deal. I had to act as her submissive for about an hour and would have to do whatever she commanded. It was the beginning of a dark secret relationship between the two of us, a dreadful relationship that nobody on this planet would ever be aware of till one or both of us breathed our last, which unfortunately happened sooner than expected. I entered that unholy romance not only for the sake of my entertainment, but also for the sake of three thousand rupees which she offered me for her complete satisfaction. Three thousand as you know is a big amount for a poor man like me.

Her beauty had gained my trust and I was bound so deep that I could never run away even after the monster in her appeared. She was a psychopath, a lunatic, a sadist. She had a couple of leather belts which she used for whipping my bare back, some strokes giving more pleasure than pain as she went on to handcuff my large rough hands using her pink plastic cuffs decorated with a real pigeon's feather, which I could have broken anytime I wanted to but was bound morally and financially not to do so. Whenever I pretended to break free, she would slap my cheeks to remind me where I belonged. She seemed to love it if I screamed like a tortured soul and when I barked like a street dog but I made sure of not overdoing that kind of drama. She never allowed me to look at her face during the play, but I believe it was totally red and furious like a true sadist's should be. Her domination intoxicated me and I wished that those moments would never ever end. Unfortunately, she never allowed me to touch any part of her other than those mushy toes peeping from the shining black stilettos. Both of us never undressed completely and that obviously served like as a reminder of the class divide between the two.

That was not the only day she completed her fantasies. The dramatic relationship between that rich lady and this poor man continued for several months. Whenever she desired, we would spend an hour or two, mostly enacting simple scenarios but sometimes she would want special costumes and even an illogical script. During the initial days, it was something very new for me, but gradually I started enjoying those salacious sessions. I felt more at inner peace when I served her in that way. Sometimes, she would pass a sarcastic smile and that elevated me to a new degree of masochistic pleasure.

As the days turned into weeks and weeks into months, I gradually realized that the dark relationship between Scarlett and me was not only damn difficult to understand, but also the one that none of us could ever name. We were not friends, not lovers and not at all belonged to the same class but we turned so close to each other's heart and life that we could not spend many days without a random session. Though the extra rupees I made were spent on my family's needs, this was a relationship which my wife, a simple housewife as you have already seen, would never understand. Being completely aware of each and every detail of her medical condition, I knew the day she comes to know about it, she would be in an incurable mess. My children are young and if something happened to their loving mother, who would take care of them?

My love for my little ones is precisely the reason that led to my resignation from the job four months ago. I fabricated an untrue story about how my wife had come to know about my affair with my boss and that she had requested me to quit with immediate effect. As I narrated this false tale with as much confidence as an ambitious lawyer during a hearing at the court, Scarlett believed it and accepted my resignation without much fuss.

The very next week, she hired someone else as her new driver but as I had expected, the new man refused to serve her in the way I was doing it. He would just drive and clean her car but never work overtime. She used cabs for late night parties as there was no one to drive her car at odd hours. Isn't it ironical that despite being so rich, she never learnt driving? She called me back, not as a motorist but as her comfort slave, once a week for sessions that lasted around a couple of hours, in exchange of the usual three thousand rupees. A poor man like me had no other option but to agree to serve her. We continued those sessions till about ten days back but then I decided to back out completely and that is why I stopped receiving her phone calls and answering her text messages. She called me ten times yesterday night as well but I am a family man who sticks to my decisions. I did not know that yesterday night would be her last one otherwise I would have surely paid her a visit for one last time. Though I am poor, I am a man full of heart and courage. Perhaps if I was with her, I could have even saved her from the murderer's vicious attack."

As Sooraj ended his narration on a sad note, his eyes were almost full of desolate droplets that come from a person drained of all hope. Leaving the chair, he stood up for a second and then sank to his knees, not caring for the mud on the pavement that dirtied his track pant. His hands went up to his head for support as he opened his mouth wide for proper inhalation of air as his throat and nose had choked up. Monty, on the other hand, sat as still as a deer's gaze into the headlights of a jeep in the middle of a dense forest, quite possibly trying to figure out whether Sooraj Singh was a good orator or a good actor.

It took under three minutes of absolute silence for Sooraj to catch back his normal breath and sit straight on the chair, but this time his body leaned forward and the shoulders had dropped significantly. Monty waited for this moment as patiently as a couch potato on his couch at midnight. He was not done yet as Sooraj had left a few key points unanswered. So, he asked, "How much wealth do you think Scarlett left back?"

Sooraj lifted his eyes and making a contact with Monty's, he answered as quickly as humanly possible, "The bungalow in posh Tilak Nagar that she had received as alimony, worth around two crores and a luxury car worth fifty lakhs. Apart from that she had fixed deposits in ABC bank with their net worth around fifty lakhs and investments in mutual funds and bonds with their net worth approximately forty lakhs. She also had investments in shares of several companies with a net investment around fifteen lakhs."

"That was precise Sooraj, who is her heir?" said Monty, trying his best to hide the expression of shock from his face as Sooraj had mentioned the exact amounts of Scarlett's wealth distribution without any pause.

"Well, I am a poor man and when poor men see multiple digit figures on documents, we too dream about having those documents in our name. I was close to her. I was the one who used to take print outs of her investments and other important papers, so I knew about her worth since a long time. She was an orphan and divorced lady. I don't think there was any legal heir to her assets. Maybe she wrote a will and if you can access that will, you can come to know what she has left for whom."

"Who do you think would be behind her murder?"

"Though she was full of tantrums, she was a sweet person at heart and had no real enemies. The only guy other than her ex-husband who hated her was her tailor, Master Shams-ud-din, the man who was looking to take revenge of his insult, especially after Scarlett had given a tight slap right across his bearded face and that too publically, due to his unprofessional behavior on her birthday. Now Monty Sir, the onus is on the police and you to find out the truth and severely punish the culprit."

"It is always the court that decides the punishment Sooraj Singh, not the police and never the investigator."

"Justice is always delayed Monty Sir and though we boast of an honest judiciary that treats people equally without favoritism or discrimination, in my personal opinion, that is not the reality. A political party or a man with power or authority can knock at the door of the courts at the middle of the night for an urgent hearing but a common man or a poor man like me even after he is drained of all resources, might not get any dates for years as he helplessly sees his case pass from him to his successors over the years."

"Maybe you are right but this is a topic of debate that we will engage in some other day, as today I have lack of time. The court needs evidence and it is up to me to present it in an impartial manner to give pace to the judicial procedure."

"Do remember the history Monty Sir. There have been several cases where a cold blooded murderer has never been proven guilty just because there were no evidences found against him. In such cases, I think there are two possibilities; either the criminal is such a mastermind that he leaves absolutely no evidences behind or the investigator gets his share to cover any traces of evidence left behind."

"Did you just offer me a deal?"

"No, why would I? In fact you are the one who has informed me about this heinous crime, otherwise I don't think I would have ever come to know about it," said Sooraj Singh, the guy who had been as serious as a dead man thus far. Till now it seemed to Monty that even if Sooraj was happy, his face would remain immobile, sunken into the kind of grimness an average person would have before a job's interview. All that changed in a flash as Sooraj positively howled, slapping his hand up and down almost involuntarily and could barely breathe due to his own laughter.

"Please find out the truth as quickly as you can. If you need any support from me, I am always there at your service," he concluded after getting normal following the strange amusement he had a moment ago.

Monty nodded as his hands reached his wallet kept in the rear pocket of his trouser. He took out a currency note of two thousand and then another of five hundred rupees and offered it to Sooraj Singh with the latter pulling it from the former's hand like a frog grabs an insect with his tongue. With his black eyes fixed at Sooraj's forehead, Monty said, "You are a seriously funny man. Here is what I promised; the extra five hundred is for your wife's medicine. Take care of her. If police comes around, be careful and don't offer as much details to them as you have done to me. Remember, I am closer than them in finding out the truth."

"Om Namah Shivaya" exclaimed Sooraj Singh folding his hands and joining the palms against each other to form a Namaste, as Monty and he got up from their respective chairs, "and you also remember Sir that I am a Mahakaal bhakt. I am a devotee of Gods and Goddesses. I will never kill anyone as that is not what the Gods demand from their devotees. The wish for her to be here fills me with such rage and bitterness that I think I will explode. One day I will sit alone and grieve for her, but first I would have to accept the fact that she has really gone. Though a genuine man like you brought this disheartening news to me, there is still a part of me that holds the memory back. There is still a part of me that will never believe she won't come bouncing around some corner to control me, to make me serve her in the most reprehensible way possible. Although the news which you brought to me was possibly the worst one I got to hear in several years, it was my pleasure meeting you as you look determined towards your goal and I like determined men."

"I will not be a hero until the real criminal is behind the bars. Till that time, it is war. Someone crossed the line and I will never forget that. I cannot rest until he is beaten, and I don't mean just beaten down. I mean dead. There is no place he can hide, I will find him, destroy him," said Monty as he corrected his shades which had slipped a little over his nose.

"And I don't much care how it happens, I don't need him to suffer, I just need his cold dark eyes extinguished from this universe. You may think it an overreaction, but you underestimated how much I will miss her. Don't think I will play by the rules either, real pleasure and the passion within me allows me to exterminate the rodent that attacked my Mistress. I am always here to support you Monty Sir, not for you but for her. Just know it," said Sooraj as the two men bid goodbye to each other.

Monty walked on the bricked pavement, crossing the temple and out of the lane with some questions still unanswered and categorizing into his mind all that Sooraj Singh had said. Sooraj on the other hand, entered the temple to offer prayers to the Gods above, perhaps praying for the peace of the departed soul. Passing by the famous Kallu Pan shop, Monty did have an eye to shade contact with his content informer on the way, who was busy in making the pans for his chit chatting customers. The two nodded at each other as Monty kept walking through the crowded lanes, with his eyes pointing downwards to avoid the dung and dirt on the road, but his mind was engrossed in the plans ahead.

As he reached his car, he unlocked it and sat on the driver's seat. He was confused about Sooraj Singh. He could feel that his brain cells had been randomized. At one moment, the first suspect had said something really important but at the very next minute, he was manipulating the facts. There were more paths than clues. For the first time since this mission started, Monty's face was completely fallen, no mask of coping left. It was certain that Sooraj tried to hide something. Anyway, Monty opened his shades and threw them towards the back seat, where the cute and smiling pink teddy bear sat all alone. The shades landed exactly at the proper place above the nose and in between the ears of the teddy, enhancing its grace to a new level.

The addiction of smoking special cigarettes haunted the individuality of the otherwise confident investigator. After a couple of puffs, he was not Monty C Dhingra, but Monty C Dhingra plus someone else, the latter taking dictatorial control of the former. He needed it and it was there in the dashboard but the rules that he had laid down himself prevented him to take a few puffs in the middle of his work. After a long while, he found himself alone and desperate. Even Chetan Prasad was not there to soothe him and provide those divine cigarettes if the lone one burnt out. He laid his head gently over the soft surface of the leather cover of the massive steering of his Challenger as puffs of warm breath threaded out of his lips. His eyelids shut for a couple of seconds and then opened, accompanied with a quick sarcastic smile up his lips. A smile of determination it was, determination to find the truth and he decided to meet the next suspect, Master Shams-ud-din without taking any break in between.

Chapter VI

Can someone blaze inside with outer ease?

Convenient to all its users and expedient to the enterprising team of its creative developers, the utility mobile application ingeniously directed Monty perfectly towards his next destination, the lucrative workplace of one of the most experienced and competent dressmaker of the town, Master Shams-ud-din, who was presumed to be nothing more than a mere suspect by the astute private investigator. The apparent movement of the luxurious and sleek Challenger as a result of combustion of fuel in its bulky and resonating engine was exactly like the measured walk of a hardworking, fiery and confident horse, back to its peaceful and modest stable after a long day of tiring work and a good amount of fresh grass in its rumbling tummy.

Speed was not a major concern as Monty concentrated precisely on driving cautiously his right hand driven luxury car, with all his thoughts and attention directed only towards making sure of avoiding any potential mishap exactly like a perfect horse whisperer, full of patience, love and kindness towards his horse but not the mission of course. Even his analytical mind at that time was as empty as the wallet of a typical salaried individual at the end of the month.

They proclaim that a horse's wide range of monocular vision has two blind spots, the first one in front of the vertical face making a cone similar in shape to the one they serve ice cream in and second right behind its head which extends over the back and behind the tail when standing with the head facing straight forward. Therefore, as a horse jumps an obstacle, no matter how huge the hurdle is, it still briefly disappears from its sight right before the horse takes off. The regulars on the streets of Kanpur, like Monty himself, had an eyesight similar to a horse's vision but for any inquisitive tourist who was out for a perpetual vacation, the various glorious hues on the way leading to Master Shams-ud-din's The Powerful Horse boutique, were much inviting and would definitely catch the profound attention of the holidaymaker's curious eyeballs.

The main road stretched onward hugging the brown flatland and bisecting the concrete jungle, taking sharp and sudden turns here and there unlike the purposeful shifts of the golden gear of the extravagant Challenger. It was once indeed a smooth new tarmac that had totally bleached to grey due to the welcome of numerous suns, like the hot and relentless one on that particular unpleasantly warm and a bit humid afternoon.

The street was a monochrome patchwork, each one lined with a shiny border of tar. Those boastful fixtures were in their place maybe only for a public display of accomplishments of the enormous cash flow. Despite that hotchpotch framework of concrete, there were still wide cracks and deep potholes to be careful of while driving. Adding to the chaos were some broken and unplanned speed breakers, of course apart from the regular ones that seemed to be there merely to act as fun filled swings for little children traveling in any vehicle and a nightmare for the expecting mothers.

The green trees and their asymmetrical brown branches, which would have once been the saplings of the highest quality, were now lumpy and bumpy resentful trees, growing tall but without any strength, competing unnaturally against the towering and pre-eminent apartment blocks they were planted too close to. Larger parts of the protective outer sheaths of the trunks, branches and twigs of the woody shrubs failed to fulfill their intended purpose due to being exposed constantly to the life threatening air pollution, mainly from automobiles and money minting factories.

The sidewalk for the most part was a combination of red bricks, smooth concrete and open scary manholes, albeit scattered with litter and the fallen brown leaves of the aging trees. It was almost one in the afternoon but there were some skinny men still sleeping soundly on those dirty pavements as if they got an opportunity to rest after several days of severe back breaking tasks. Most of them had extra large clothes of different shades, no matter what their actual sizes were. They had great company though in bare dogs, cows, pigs, squirrels, rats and cats. Appallingly some of them even chose to rest in secluded areas like the protruding and narrow dividers in the middle of the crowded streets.

Electricity wires strung from rusted brown electric posts decorated with stickers of local leaders and used primarily by the stray dogs to relieve themselves. The wires, both of electricity supplies and telephones and also of the infinite TV and internet connections, dangled at about one and a half storey height. Most of the frightful connections were made by unbelievably entangling those wires challenging all the theoretical concepts of Physics, if only Gustav Kirchhoff was still alive. Even the live wire was plugged in by some small time power thieves.

But all this was beyond the daily regard of the pedestrians who either walked or rode those black and white bicycles, made of iron, heads down to their respective destinations. Maybe if they removed their watchful eyes off their beloved shoe, they would directly step on or ride their bicycles over the feces of stray canines or the sacred but practically useful cow dung.

Buses, cars, trucks, scooters, motorbikes, cycle-rickshaws, multiple colored e-rickshaws, green and yellow auto-rickshaws, green tempos, bicycles, pedestrians and animals shared the driveway, paying scant attention to traffic rules. There were some traffic signals that still functioned, but they acted as mere show pieces, just like the decorative sparkling Diwali lights of red, yellow and green colors, outside every home during the festive season. The combined air pollution caused by all the vehicles seemed to be more though, than what is caused by the burning of numerous fire crackers on Diwali.

Some buses ran with their doors missing but most passengers were comfortable holding on to the so called rod at the door as there were no vacant seats available. Auto-rickshaws were packed with passengers too, not just inside, but also on their roofs. Many chose to stand on the rear bumper of the moving green Tempos. They maintained their balance like an expert juggler who juggles several balls together and quickly. Trucks seemed to take a more polite approach, with each of them carrying catchy slogans on their rear bumpers, like, "Blow Horn," "If you have evil eyes, your face will turn black" and "You will be allowed to overtake only when there is space," which was never the case. Scant attention was paid to the pollution aspect of the trucks as most of them exhaled black and deadly carbon monoxide straight into the atmosphere without any concern.

The affluent, on the other hand, obviously used only their personal air conditioned luxury cars as their preferred means of transport, and indeed, there was a lot of money in the town of Kanpur. Anyway, in the Indian towns, unlike the metro cities, people opt to use their personal vehicles more than public transportation as it is more convenient and effective with regard to time and parking.

There were no traffic rules. Every vehicle and every pedestrian was responsible for its own safety. Anyone could take a sudden turn any side at any speed, anyone could park anywhere he wished to even if it led to a traffic jam. Nobody had the time to bother about these petty issues and neither did anyone have so much patience to put them in order.

On both sides of the street, there were monstrous hoardings, some periodically paid ones, and some just made to stand tall illegally on bamboo sticks dug deep into the ground. Approximately thirty percent of them contained commercial ads of local and national firms and their products or services, while the remaining seventy percent depicted giant sized photographs of local politicians, lawyers and other prominent people of the town, expressing good wishes to each other and perhaps to the ordinary citizens as well.

Just below one of those giant posters, there was a left turn into a narrow lane, with no traffic. Though initially doubtful about entering such a small living street, Monty had no other option but to follow the map under the direction of the mobile application as it could obviously never go wrong. Though his eyes were black and dark, they had too much light in them; light that flashed itself towards the road to the fulfillment of his mission. "Your destination is on your left," were the words of the digital assistant when Monty realized that he had actually reached Master Shams-ud-din's The Powerful Horse Boutique, surprisingly and thanks to good luck, with no new dent on the rough and tough body of his grey Challenger.

There were a few medium sized affordable cars parked on the side of the left side of the living street that itself was small in width, half on the pavement and half on the patchwork, but there was not enough space for parking the big Challenger. Monty turned his watchful eyes towards the left, towards the right and on the rearview mirror, to find a perfect spot to park his possession. His observant eyes did not blink even once but slowed, yet the effect was soft and inviting, instead of harsh. Perhaps his wet lips, not smiling, but tilting in weird angle, gave an impression of how eager he was to meet the unsuspecting suspect.

And then the black stony eyes came to a rest as they spotted a cycle rickshaw parked leisurely between two medium sized affordable cars, one white and the other grey. The middle aged rickshaw puller with untidy windblown white hair, dressed in a checked and faded blue lungi and a white vest with a couple of holes for extra comfort, was barefoot. Maybe he was a lazy fellow or perhaps the afternoon sun had completely taken over him, anyway, he was lying down unaware of the surroundings but not sleeping, on the passenger seat of his own rickshaw, absolutely relaxed and comfortable in that little space and weird position.

Perhaps that was the only space available for parking the big car but the forlorn man with a disheveled appearance neither looked towards the approaching car, nor seemed to have any intention of doing so. Annoyed by unresponsive behavior of the ordinary rickshaw puller, the loud horn was blown sheepishly by Monty on a rather empty street. On listening to the unpleasant noise of the horn, the scruffy character turned his vulnerable face towards the Challenger. His point blank eyes were narrowed, rigid, cold and hard. And when those red eyes met the two gemstones of Onyx, Monty tilted his right eye slightly, raising his right eyebrow just a little and then returned it back to where it belonged. This gesture and the look of unassailable confidence in those expressive eyes was enough for the drab eyed to leave his warm resting space and quickly stand up on his thin yet powerful legs, which were perhaps as lean as those of a catwalk model but surprisingly had the strength of cycling whole day long. Without wasting any time, he walked away, pulling his traditional cycle rickshaw out of there, allowing Monty to easily park his car in that space and proving the fact that sometimes words are not required to achieve a goal as body language and class do all the talking.

After turning the sturdy engine off and pulling the long key out of the self, Monty closed his eyes for a couple of seconds and took a deep breath. The sigh that came before opening his eyes was a signal, not of his resolve leaving but of the level his tension had reached. He was more like an old fashioned kettle, still full even when some steam forced its way out. His left hand reached the dashboard, which contained the expired registration and insurance papers of the car, an elongated cigarette, the one gifted by his dear apprentice Chetan, the deadly pistol which he hardly used and obviously Master Shams-ud-din's fancy white visiting card that had been marked with a cross using a brown sketch pen.

He was tempted to take out the cigarette. In fact, he even picked it up from the filter using his left thumb and index finger but once again the protocol overpowered his urge. Perhaps, through a long and painful process, he had learned that satisfaction was inside the job, not based on materialistic things of the outer world. He left the tobacco free non-injurious roll, in the dashboard itself and picked up the crossed visiting card. With one final vigilant look, Monty left it upside down in the car's co driver seat, closed the dashboard from his left hand, got down from the car but did not lock it as usual. The expression on his ruddy face was that of a tortured soul and the pain disguised as an angel. He turned his titular head towards the building that contained his destination.

It was two floored old grey structure with a rounded vault forming the roof of it. The entire building, which was more in width than in length, contained three different shops – Mishraji ki Mithai, the authentic Indian sweets shop on the left, general physician Dr. Ram Agarwal's clinic in the middle and The Powerful Horse Boutique towards the right. The architecture seemed of the British era and the first thing that Monty thought on seeing them was that these three were surely tenants under the then popular Rent Control Act.

All the three shops had identical sized white tin boards with red boundaries and black text painted on them above their doors, which themselves hung on their hinges at a jaunty angle. There was a small open window on the left of each door but it was nothing else apart from a gaping hole for the wind to rush in and out at its own will.

They say if you pray for rain, you got to deal with mud too. People who choose to spend time in praying for good health, skipping their regular exercise are usually the ones that end up at a doctor's clinic more often than not. Dr. Ram Agarwal was a just a general physician but the number of patients waiting for their turn was easily in double digits. They were all stuffed inside like a pack of cards, not on the playing table, but into the card box.

Mishra ji however, was not as lucky as Dr. Ram Agarwal. His sweets shop had no customer at that time, though the aroma that was coming out from the door of the authentic Indian sweets shop was enough to invite any passer by inside. From the trademark Desi Ghee boondi laddoos topped with freshly cut dry fruits, to the rich Kajoo Barfis with a silver covering over them, there was something for almost everyone inside, but not for a determined man on mission.

Neither flooded with customers, nor sending out any sensory invitations, at the extreme right of the building, The Powerful Horse Boutique, was in fact the destination where Monty was looking to encounter the second suspect. The white board on the top was exactly the same like the back side of the visiting card, just a different size. The formidable horse in the logo on the board was indeed black and rearing with its front legs in the air and the rear ones grounded. "Why is this horse in this logo rearing? Maybe it signifies aggression, maybe fright or may even portray pain and disobedience. Surely this is a sign of someone burning within himself, looking for some kind of revenge," thought Monty.

The muscular and broad shouldered detective in black tuxedo was right in front of the open brown wooden door of Master Shams-ud-din's big on moneymaking yet not much ornamented from the exterior, The Powerful Horse Boutique. The anticipation in him of meeting the next suspect was a nervous kind of energy. It tickled through him like electrical current, starting from his head and ending at the ground below his toes. That little thought about the horse on the strange board was enough for him to walk inside without wasting any time.

A welcome rug greeted Monty as he walked into the door. It was a filthy old rug, maybe once of the color of fresh cherries, but soiled by the daily rough rubs of mud caked shoes, slippers and sandals. As the investigator rubbed his rather clean and well polished black leather shoes, carrying a silver metallic design on the upper surface, on the earthly rug, his vigilant eyes went straight into the interior of the prestigious boutique, looking mainly for the prime suspect.

Unlike one would imagine it after reading its name, the boutique was not enormous. Its shape resembled that of a giant cardboard shoebox, albeit it was made of concrete. It must be around 10ft wide and 20ft in length. Surrounded by three white walls on three sides, there was a 2ft narrow wooden table which served as the partition between the customer and the tailors as it covered around three fourths of the width of the entire shop, leaving little space for the tailors to come out or go in comfortably, one at a time. Around 4ft of length were left for the customers to stand, talk to the tailors, place orders and receive their clothes and there was no chair or for that matter any furniture for the customers to sit on.

On the top of the partitioning table, there were a couple of different cloth pieces, one red and the other blue, three scissors, two large and one small, a couple of inch tapes used for body measurements and a notebook along with a use and throw blue ball pen. The lower portion of that table was covered with a thin lining of low quality plywood, just to make it opaque.

The walls were white and at some points, the paint had started to chip off over the years. Even the most competent, efficient and accomplished warhorses require some kind of process to preserve them, food being the most minimalistic demand. According to that inductive logic, those gloomy walls obviously needed a compulsive whitewash. Mostly blank, the wall on the left of the customer in his normal stance contained two calendars, one Islamic and the other English, hung on a couple of hooks, less than a foot away from each other and at a height equivalent to the height of the shoulder of an average person. The English calendar had several marks that were mostly irregular circles made with ball point pens. Perhaps those blue and red marks represented the due dates of the orders, or maybe they were for some kind of bulk purchasing deals of buttons, zips and the other stuff.

Dressed in sparkling white well stitched kurta pajamas and each one of them wearing a white, short and round skullcap, similar to a glorious king wearing his Royal crown while presiding over the proceedings of his court, three tailors were performing the obligatory Namaz, the physical, mental and spiritual act of worship, facing towards the end opposite to the customers' space. Monty was quick to realize that he was standing, facing towards the direction of the Mecca. He stood still, thinking which one among them was Master Shams-ud-din, and continued observing the compact and small scale boutique a little more. The dutiful tailors were occupied with great deal of concentration in reciting prayers as they stood, bowed and prostrated themselves. Apart from the sound of their prayers and the fan adding a sort of background tune to it, there was profound silence in the boutique.

The observant black eyes of the sturdy lad, comparable to the keen eyes of a hungry hawk, noticed that there was no chair even for the tailors to sit, in the entire boutique. There were just white sheets of cloth, covering the entire portion of the cemented floor behind the table, acting as a perfect carpet and all the work on those three sewing machines, cutting and tailoring, was done sitting on them. It was indeed littered with bits and pieces of cloths of all colors, giving it the look and feel of a perfect workplace.

There were no air conditioners to battle the heat and humidity, only one ceiling fan and that too was working at an awful slow speed, as if the motor in its wretched condition was too tired to rotate its blades. If the two tube lights located at the right and left of the ceiling fan were not switched on, the workplace would have been as dark and dull as a loathsome prison in the basement, despite the scorching sun outside.

On the wall towards the right of the customer, there were numerous ladies dresses, from fashionable attire stitched elegantly to alluring night gowns, from fancy salwar suits to bridal lehengas, hanging there, each one on its own personal hanger. There were some plain, some striped but mostly checked male shirts and trousers too but their poor modest and limited section was not much exciting to eyeballs of most men and was completely over shadowed by the colorful and vibrant outfits of the females.

The fact that surprised Monty the most was that there were no CCTV cameras anywhere in the workplace of those skilled and hard working workers. "Are they not bothered about the safety of their own boutique, or are they trying to tamper with some kind of proof?" were just some of the questions that bounced into the loaded skull of the keen eyed detective, especially after noticing some bare holes at good heights on all walls. Nothing was placed there but those holes seemed like tiny eyes staring right at the customer and the tailors from all four directions, maybe to get the best view possible. Surely, Monty thought while quickly imagining the views from all angles through those forlorn holes, there has been some kind of tampering with the security system of the shop. What added to his suspicion was that there were absolutely no gadgets, no laptop or computer, not even a printer or a credit/debit card machine. "Are these guys really decades behind, or are they into some kind of suspicious activity?" were the other queries that needed to be answered by the hawk eyed and personable man on mission to investigate and solve the murder mystery.

On the wall opposite to him, there was a small wooden door that was not locked, but just closed. "Where does this open? Maybe it is the washroom, or maybe it is trial room," Monty was still thinking as the tailors sat to conclude their prayers. He quickly exhaled an air of excitement as now he was going to continue his investigation. The feeling of anticipation once again tickled through his body, head to toe, like an electrical spark.

Two tailors ignored the presence of a potential customer despite an eye contact with him and went straight towards their sewing machines, just a step away from where they were praying and sitting on crossed legs, started their routine work of cutting and stitching lifeless cloth pieces and crafting them into fashionable and ceremonial outfits which would go on to make priceless memories for their occasional as well as regular customers.

The third one was more courteous than his inattentive colleagues as he came towards the detective, waiting there alone from sometime. He was barely a twenty something youth, the facial hair made him look like his actual age. Had he been a clean shaved lad, people would not have taken more than a couple of seconds to think of child labor being employed in the boutique and complained to the concerned authorities against it. His eyes were pure and friendly while his face was of the size of a ball, not a football but a leather cricket ball, possibly a little lighter than that. In one of the most polite tones, raising his right hand to his thin and narrow chest between his sagging shoulders, he said to Monty, "Adaab Bhaijaan."

Raising his strong masculine right hand to his muscular and well built chest, Monty said in his soft and deep voice, "Adaab. I am Monty C Dhingra." And after an odd pause and still with all the seriousness embedded deep into his handsome face, even before the young tailor could react, he continued, "You may not know me but I want to urgently meet Master Shams-ud-din."

Words are not a human's only means of communication. The look from Monty while introducing himself said it more than anything else. His black gemstone eyes pointed straight at the forehead of the young tailor, and this authoritative look of dominance, coupled with an erect backbone and a just a slight bend of the broad shoulders towards the listener were enough to put the craftsman on the defensive. "Please wait Sir, I will inform him about your visit," were the only words he could manage to say in a nervous voice and a jerky tone, lowering his eyes to avoid any kind of an eye contact. After receiving a serious and unhurried nod of approval from the unexpected guest with a perfectly explicit body language, the edgy tailor walked away towards the closed wooden door and quickly pulled its handle to open it and enter inside, only to return in less than a quarter of a minute.

"Come in Sir, but please take off your shoes. We don't wear any footwear beyond this table. You may keep your shoes on the shoe rack here," the tensed man said in his jerky tone, pointing towards a blue colored dirty plastic shoe rack with three shelves, hidden just behind the table and holding three pairs of blue rubber slippers and one pair of men's leather sandal. The electrical current had disappeared from his body and Monty seemed much more confident. They say anyway that the body language of the person in front of you might define yours too.

Precisely following the instructions of the tailor, he took off his branded and well polished matte black shoes, ten in size, without any haste and placed them watchfully on the top shelf of the rack. As he turned towards the garment maker, the highly strung boy quickly lowered his gaze, demonstrating not with any argument, but with strong evidence, the fact that even if the brand is removed and people are made to stand at the same level, the body language still sets them far apart. The barefoot tailor guided him towards the door, and on his plain black socks below the black trouser and black infernal tuxedo, Monty walked towards having a strong belief in self and assurance of solving the enigmatic mystery as soon as possible.

As the suspicious door was pulled by the young man, Monty's eyes straight away entered it, followed by his well built and broad shouldered body. It led to a room that was small and quiet. If the workplace outside was of the size of an atom of hydrogen, this room was not larger than a single electron. Such a tiny room it was that there was no empty space in it whatsoever. It was square in shape and surrounded by green walls on the left and back while there were white walls on the right and front of the door. All the walls of this storeroom turned into office, were nicely painted and no color was chipping off from anywhere as was the case outside the door. There were no paintings, no CCTV cameras, not even any calendar, absolutely nothing on those smooth walls. The only thing present on the left wall was a wooden switchboard with half a dozen circular black colored switches and a metallic large size regulator for fan. These were the priceless things which were obsolete in other buildings but still being used in the not so well maintained pre-independence era structures.

There was small rectangular table, made of teakwood, standing as upright as a sergeant and it occupied almost full width of the compact room. It maybe 5ft in length and 3ft in width and was definitely not made to be used as work desk, but some circumstances must have forced it to act as one. A closed laptop, couple of books written in Urdu, a pen stand, a few blank A4 sized papers were kept in the most unsorted manner on that work desk which itself had a significantly uneven surface, possibly due to its age, along with a couple of pouches of a well known brand of pan masala. Those pouches were shining even more due to the reflection of white light, falling straight on them from a thick fluorescent tube light, fitted on the white ceiling at the top of the table. There was one table fan fitted at the left corner of the table. It was a unique fan, possibly an antique. It had just two blades inside a steel cage, but the noise it made was a proof of how the aged and experienced tend to proclaim themselves as the de facto boss of their relative fields. This fan was indeed old but the breeze it created would set the young ones pondering. There were a couple of empty wooden arm chairs for the guests, similar to the ones available for the students in Government high school classrooms but without any form of art or text inscribed on them, almost touching the door behind them. Opposite to them, on the other side of the teakwood table, on a cushioned presidential desk swivel chair on set of wheels, adjusted at the highest possible height, there sat Master Shams-ud-din.

The suspect had the appearance of relentlessly strong man who once had muscles, broad over the back and thick in the neck. Now, he was an ordinary man, albeit one with some extra kilos to carry around as those once honed limbs, now were mostly fat. He was majestically dressed in shining white Bhopali kurta that flowed like a skirt, reaching midway between his knees even when he was sitting with his legs crossed. It must have been specially left a bit loose to hide the fat around his belly, but had carefully crafted pleats at the waist. The kurta was mainly plain but the collar was made of golden cloth with Lucknowi Chikan embroidery on it. Same cloth was used at the cuffs not just to protect the garment from fraying, but also to enhance its elegant look. Only a stylish man with a cultured sense of fashion could have carried that outfit containing a creative blend of Bhopali and Lucknowi traditions with each one, acting as an amplifier to the magnificence of the other while refusing to leave its own hallmark. Though the pajama below the champion was a straight and plain white, it did not matter as much as the green turban on the top of his almost square shaped big skull, hiding his hair completely quite like the way people hide their cash when commuting in a public bus.

The question that remained unanswered was that whether he was bald or he had grey hair? In fact, the locks visible on the side of his brown rough face were showing signs of aging. Monty guessed that the suspect may be in his late forties and that he must be very particular about his salt and pepper beard. The hair it contained was thick and impenetrable, a perfect adoption of the Sunnah. There was no moustache though to complement the profuse growth of hair on the flat chin and the lower portion of the round shaped cheeks of the man, keeping the area under the long nose and above the lips totally bare.

His eyes were tiny and when a person has such small eyes, the first thing that people generally observe is its shape. There was no fault with their shape, but they were set much deeper than normal into the skull, giving an illusion of a more prominent brow bone below those thick and untidy eyebrows, with the left one almost touching the right one. The eyes however were covered under a circular pair of spectacles, similar in shape to the one Mahatama Gandhi used to wear during the Indian freedom struggle against the British. The round glasses were fitted firmly into a metallic frame with silver polish on it to give it a smooth appearance. The lenses contained in that silverware were thick and bifocal proving that the power of the eyes must have been high enough and with such a high power of the eye, escaping so quickly in the dark would not have been easy, imagined Monty. The weight of the spectacles coupled with the oil on the long nose, covered with blackheads, was enough to drag it out of its place to a much lower height, sliding towards the wide nostrils.

"These eyes have a long story to tell," realized Monty as he entered the compact room behind the jerky tailor, who chose to leave immediately, not even having the patience or the nerves to introduce the two strangers meeting for the first time. Monty stood opposite to the Master with his muscular arms bent from the elbows and palms resting on one of the two armchairs. The look on his face was as serious as that of a bowler who is entrusted to bowl the final over of an innings with seven runs to defend and two wickets left.

Master Shams-ud-din was engrossed in his mobile, holding it in his left hand and operating it with the thumb and index finger of the right hand. He was as serious as the batsman on strike in the above scenario. "What exactly is this man doing?" questioned Monty in his own mind while observing the Master's lips. They were red, not naturally red like the sweet cherries from Turkey, but carmine like the orange bellied skimmer from South America. The color though, was just a mask on the original shade created by the regular chewing of the tantalizingly flavored pan masala of his favorite brands. This common practice of keeping his mouth full of the pan masala was a substantial proof of the man being a common resident of Kanpur. Just as Monty tried to peep into the mobile screen of the suspect, Master Shams-ud-din partially closed his eyes and slightly tilted his square head, straightening it through the neck and raising both his hands up with the mobile still in the left hand and then bent over to spit the chewed masala from his mouth straight into a plastic dustbin kept just below the table, near his legs. The dustbin was blue in color but heavily decorated with carmine red masala spits, both dry and wet.

Simultaneously, he exclaimed, "Oh No! I can't curse that player as I pray not to be deprived of the mercy of Allah but I don't like losing an online game." His voice was as gentle and pleasing to the ears as a cuckoo singing its melody in the morning. The pause with which he completed his speech was an indication of the man's mechanical cleverness. And then, his eyeballs turned towards the handsome man standing in front of him, inhaling the air of confidence and exhaling positive vibes along with the company of a smile that one can never forget.

"Salam Sahib, please have a seat," said the suspect, smiling back at his well bred guest. His tone was rich, luxurious and warm. Perhaps his deep voice was one of the additional business tools he used to get new clients and to make sure that the existing ones come to him again and again.

"Which game was it sir?" questioned Monty as he pulled the armchair and sat on it with his black hawk eyes fixed at the unsuspecting eyes of the suspect to observe even the minute details of his body language.

"It was an online game of 8 ball pool. I was on a streak of 12 wins and then I made a mistake. The shot I played was a wrong one and I gave a sniff to my opponent. He managed to win it from there. I lost more than half of my hard earned virtual coins." Master Shams-ud-din was so direct and precise that he reminded Monty of his lecturer of Chemistry who declared confidently that the weight an atom remains the same even if the electrons' weight is not taken into consideration.

"That is sad sir. I can sense you hate losing."

The round eyeballs embedded into the tiny eyes behind the thick lens fitted firmly in that old fashioned silver frame froze on meeting the two gemstones opposite to them and the Master replied, keeping the mobile on the table and next to the closed laptop, "The best part about losing in a two player game is that there is always a human who wins, therefore, I am not that sad as there is someone who is happy because of my loss."

"That Sir is a noble thought indeed but would not be applicable in case of gambling and betting." Monty said as his right hand reached the inner pocket of the infernal tuxedo and out came his own visiting card. Offering it to the green turbaned man sitting opposite to him, he continued, "I am Monty C Dhingra, a private investigator and I am here for an important conversation with you."

Master Shams-ud-din accepted the visiting card but did not bother to view the details with much attention. Still with his eyes in direct contact with Monty's, he said, "In your black eyes, lays your humanity Sahib. They convey the person you are and this visiting card you offer to me is just an explicit text of your contact information, which I will use later to get in touch with you."

And then the craftsman shouted loudly in a dominating tone, "Sarfaraz, get two glasses of cold drink, one for me and one for my personable guest." This was probably his way of treating his important visitors. But, Monty refused to have it by saying no loudly and raising his hand in denial, and that made Master Shams-ud-din shout once again, "Sarfaraz, leave it. Don't get any beverage; my guest is not here for that." Sarfaraz was probably the nervous young tailor who had guided the investigator into that small office, and he would now be a relieved man, presumed Monty.

"I am here for an indispensable conversation, sir we can have cold drink some other time."

"Monty Sahib, as you must be aware, this boutique of mine, The Powerful Horse Boutique, is one of the most fancy and famous boutiques in Kanpur. I am Master Shams-ud-din, the owner of this place. My father started this venture in his young days and I have successfully managed to continue this profitable business, all thanks to the Almighty Allah. It is only because of the hard work done by me and my team and blessings of Allah, that today we have reached such a position that all the important, influential and reputable personalities of Kanpur come to us for their tailoring needs. Approximately every rich man's daughter or wife in this city has something in her wardrobe, stitched by us. The males also come to us but we specialize in ladies' attire. I welcome you and look forward to serving you in the best way possible."

Monty carefully heard to each and every word the suspect said, trying to market his boutique using his secondary tool of business in the best way possible and when the Master paused for a couple of breaths, he sneaked in, "Sorry Sir, but I am not here for any tailoring need. Maybe I will come again for that in the future. I am here to talk about Scarlett White."

The pocket sized eyes of Master Shams-ud-din, which had so much compassion before hearing the name of Scarlett White, now had emptiness. The anger that boiled up into the square shaped skull, fumed from his eyes. Those eyes turned into a knife on Monty's ribs, the sharp point digging deeper. Uncomfortable with the situation, his face filled with an emotion he felt suitable for the moment, nothing more than raw anger it was. The unmoving gaze was accompanied by deliberate slow breathing, like he was fighting something back and loosing at that.

"You are my guest, Monty," the bearded man, now as turbulent as a wild sea somehow managed to make a statement, though his voice changed from being an additional tool of business to that of a captain who tries to manage his ship struck by a storm somewhere in the middle of an ocean, raw and shallow.

"Surely he is trying his best to hide something behind this burst of anger which may very well be guilt," thought the observant investigator in his sharp and canny mind, but before he could react, the Master continued, "And I am your host Sahib. Allah forbid even prior to any desirable occurrence, the situation here gets worse before any conversation between the two of us commences. It will be better for both of us if we mutually decide not to talk about immoral people like Scarlett White."

And then he picked one of the pouches of pan masala from the table and courtesy his experience and opened it in one try with all the strength of his fore limbs. He took out the powder straight on his left palm and sprinkled some tobacco powder from a small tin can kept on the side of his closed laptop, which Monty had not noticed till that time. Filling his mouth with the mixture, he was silent for some time, with his eyes still staring wide on Monty's face through the circular glasses and lips moving up and down, right and left as he chewed the tobacco masala mixture using his yellow but well arranged and equally sized teeth, fitted firmly in his bony jaw which was not clearly visible due to the thick beard.

A couple of breaths were necessary for Monty to quickly find his composure and continue the conversation after it had paused in a weird manner. He decided to go straight on the main point, and said, "Yesterday night, Scarlett White was murdered in her bedroom, and I am here to investigate about that crime. Pardon me if I sound rude, but request you to cooperate with me. And let us not humiliate the dead by calling her immoral." The look of authority, the virile confidence in the body language and the charming deep voice were the three things that never seized to let anyone move out of a conversation with Monty.

Not only was Master Shams-ud-din unable to speak due to the succulent mixture filled in his thick lipped mouth, but also because words had completely left him as he was in a state of utter shock. The bright eyes that were burning with anger a few moments back, now turned wide as Monty stared in them through the round frame of the spectacles, trying to figure out the difference between guilt and shock, or perhaps between an actor and a non-actor. Those lips had seized their movement and the chewing of the pan masala paused, to be followed by a spitting of all the remains straight into the blue and red dustbin.

Monty could just imagine the sparks in the brain of the Master, desperately trying to connect all the dots and consequently causing a short circuit in his own mind. The Master looked like a goggle eyed toy from one of those claw trap machine full of soft and cute toys at the fun fair for little children to play for. "Judging from his reaction, there are just two possibilities – first that this man really did not know about the crime at all and second that he was an expert actor" thought Monty and decided to continue the critical interrogation to find out the truth.

"Sorry to say Sir but the sad part is that she is no more and the bad part is that she was murdered," Monty said in his attempt to continue the cross examination as it slowly changed into a discourse.

With his widened eyes set point blank on the wall behind the head of the guest, Master Shams-ud-din replied, "We have lost that brightly glowing star yesterday, which was perhaps just a luxury but not a necessity in today's dark sky. May the Almighty Allah give her an easy and pleasant journey and shower blessings on her grave, Ameen." This statement was followed by a shutting of his tiny eyes, quite possibly in remembrance of Scarlett White, and an awkward silence once again filled the room. The only things making some kind of noise were the two rotating blades of the table fan on the left corner of the teakwood table.

The silence did not stay for long, maybe less than a minute was all it could survive. Master Shams-ud-din opened his eyes with a sudden jerk and the jerk was such that it had the momentum to even upright his neck. The anger had faded away completely and what was left was an emotionless bearded man sitting there without any expressions on his square face. He just sat there motionless and speechless, like a decorated lifeless mannequin placed next to the entrance of a popular cloth store.

Even an injured bird fights against all odds to fly high up in the blue sky, and even a chained elephant at a circus has the strength to break free if it so feels. Similarly, the investigator out on a mission had no other option but to continue his interrogation in order to get all the answers to his tricky but significant questions, necessary to solve the mystery. So, he continued, "Relax Sir. How do you know Scarlett?"

The stone face mode that Master Shams-ud-din had now entered, reminded Monty of his own friend and apprentice, Chetan Prasad. The Master chose to talk over being a silent mannequin and therefore he replied, though still looking into the wall behind Monty, "I don't think I must call a dead person immoral, but Monty Sahib, since you are investigating this crime and I wish the convict is punished as severely by the law as possible, I am ready to cooperate with you over this."

"Thank you Sir. The law will indeed take its course but you need to cooperate with me so that I can provide substantial evidences to the courts."

"The truth dear Monty is that Scarlett was one of the, if not the most arrogant woman in this city. I agree that she was a beauty contest winner, but does that honor allow one to have an exaggerated sense of one's own importance or abilities? I don't think so at all, and I am sure that you will also agree with me."

Monty just shook his head keeping his left hand on his chin, playing with his crisp jaw line and continued listening to what the suspect had to say.

"She was full of what the youngsters nowadays call attitude and that too in the worst sense. She treated others as if they were lower class individuals. The pride did not let her realize that fate keeps on changing in lifetime. The mirror remains the same, only the image created by reflection in it changes every time."

And then he picked up a mirror, of the size of a Bollywood magazine, from next to the dustbin and showed it to Monty. "Look Monty, this is your image, handsome, young, muscular and well built." And then he turned it towards himself, saying "See now it shows my image, bearded man with perfect adoption of the Sunnah, forty six, not muscular and though once well built like you, now on the decline." He then quickly kept the mirror back from where he had picked it up but kept observing the reaction of the guest from head to throat, not getting any clues though from the experienced and skilled interrogator.

Monty raised his left hand from the chin to the back side of his hair as it had been blown away out of order by the strong breeze of the ancient table fan and as he was correcting it, Master Shams-ud-din continued his speech, "Monty Sahib, today I will tell you the philosophy of a gentleman's life within a minute – If you give me the permission."

"Permission granted."

"For most working gentlemen, it gets tough to pass time after the Sun has set. The boredom while waiting for night starting even from the evening may sometimes kill the spirits of a man but the years are eloping as quickly as the breeze would from this fan when there is a power cut, without any of them even realizing it."

It did not take much time for Monty to understand clearly that the dialogue was going either out of the context or too deep, and Master Shams-ud-din, the shrewd business man was playing all the dirty tricks, that may have proved to be successful in business to divert the main issues. Interrupting the philosophical speech of the Master, Monty said, "Your words are pure gold Sir and the logic you give is one in a million and the most accurate for any given situation, but I am here to talk about Scarlett and her murder. Let us go back to the topic. How do you know her?"

Master was indeed a sharp witted and scheming business owner apart from being a creative craftsman. He understood that the ploys he used to manipulate his regular clients to trick them into paying highly even for little work, would not work with a pragmatic investigator like Monty. So he quickly decided to move to his plan B of communication. Raising a good portion of the left side of his visibly strong body and tilting towards the right, his left hand reached for the inner pocket of his pajama and pulled out a small pouch of pan masala of the brand Zuban. And he threw it on the table, between him and his guest.

As soon as Monty saw the sealed pouch of Zuban, he realized that he had seen a similar red colored pouch on Scarlett's dressing table. This was not a local brand and not even sold in Kanpur. But, obviously, Monty did not want to reveal even the most diminutive details of his private investigation to his wise suspect. On the other hand, Master Shams-ud-din with all his sharp powers of judgment of his tiny eyes continued observing the facial reaction of his decent visitor, maybe to understand the actual depth of the investigation.

"Zuban pan masala. Is this available in Kanpur, Sir?" exclaimed Monty in a shaky voice with a couple of halts in between, and the black eyes fixed at the red and green pouch with as much concentration as a hungry lion has in its eyes while watching from distance an innocent lonely deer having the green grass to fill its empty stomach.

"Haven't you seen this before Monty Sahib?" replied the Master with an expression of a cold white stone.

Realizing that severe grilling was on from both sides, Monty, with a shake of his head, said, "Things that aim to be mysterious always end up not being so mysterious because there is always a mistake committed by them, of trying to crave for serious attention. This looks like it is new to Kanpur but I have a peculiar feeling that I have seen it somewhere."

"Scarlett was fond of Zuban, Monty Sahib." A smile appeared on the coated lips of the Master, though somewhat hidden from the outside world due to his impenetrable beard. This was a cynical smile indeed and not a real grin, but a fake one for sure.

"So how do you know Scarlett?" questioned Monty with his arms rising up till his broad shoulders in an authoritative expression of cross examination.

"It is a long story. Kindly don't interrupt me as I share with you the truth."

"I am here for that."

"Monty Sahib, Scarlett was a regular customer here. As I told you before, the most influential and the rich ladies of Kanpur visit The Powerful Horse Boutique. We specialize in making ladies attire..."

And he was interrupted by Monty, who was on the verge of losing all his patience as the Master was slyly trying to avoid the main topic again and again. Perplexed, he said in his deep voice, but at a volume much higher than normal, "I am here to know about your story with Scarlett, not about other ladies of the town."

On observing that the guest was falling short of patience, Master Shams-ud-din's sheepish grin widened and he continued, "The caravan of dreams stops only for a moment or two and then we wake up, not knowing which path to take. I am coming to the main topic of our discussion Monty Sahib, but request you to maintain patience till the end of my dramatic yet true story."

"I am sorry Sir but I cannot operate at the pace of Nature. I have loads of other genuine tasks to complete, so I request you to be precise with your words."

"Then here we go. Scarlett White was a regular visitor here at the Powerful Horse Boutique. She was indeed the glamour girl of this town, partially because of her rare and extraordinary beauty and partially because of the most fancy and over priced outfits she wore. She loved to dress in the most amazingly crafted chic attire along with matching high heeled stilletos.

She was not only alluringly elegant with her looks, but also had a sublimely imaginative wisdom. She used to design those graceful and dazzling charismatic dresses herself and get them stitched from the most fancy and overpriced tailor in the town of Kanpur, sitting here in front of you. Not only her own but she even designed outfits for other models participating at various pageants and get them stitched too, by me and my skilled team.

Her fashion designing was as pure, poetic, spirited and marvelous as a Ghazal. The inner soul of even an ordinary human with little or no understanding of any type of designing would get totally shaken up after a glance at her designs from the corner of his admiring eyes."

And then there was a pause, followed by a couple of deep breaths and a stare at the Zuban pan masala pouch by the tiny eyes from within their sockets and through the shield of the Mahatama spectacles. Total silence filled the cramped workroom as the sound of the rotating blades had become too familiar background score and its presence was no longer felt in Monty's ears. With his left hand still on his chin, he continued to carefully listen to each and every word spoken by the craftsman.

"She was very much fond of Zuban. Monty Sahib, this tasty and addictive pan masala is a specialty of Rajasthan. My former good friend Gaurav Singh from Ajmer is the sole dealer of this majestic brand and he is the one who used to send it for me till the end of last year. I used to gift one or two pouches of this pan masala to Scarlett every time she visited my boutique. This went on for almost a year. I had to finally break my friendship with my dear friend Gaurav due to some unforeseen circumstances which I will let you know if you are interested."

"Sorry to hear about your broken friendship but is that related to Scarlett in any manner? If yes, then go ahead, otherwise we can leave it to be discussed in our next meeting."

"No, Monty Sahib not connected to Scarlett directly but yes, Gaurav Singh was no doubt in touch with Scarlett till last night as he used to supply to her

Zuban. And the tale of the end of my friendship with him is related to you and me in my opinion."

"Then be precise Sir, and without any out of the context dialogues, tell me why did you put an end to your friendship with Gaurav?"

"We were close buddies. When I went to Rajasthan with my wife, he and his family hosted us for a dinner and we had all the traditional dishes of that place like Dal Bati, Churma, Alwari milk cake and Balushahi. So, when he visited Kanpur looking for a wholesaler for Zuban, I invited him for some home cooked lip smacking Mughlai dishes at my modest residence. All was well until he posted a couple of selfies with me and the food we ate on social media. That spread online like any lethal fire spreads in a dense forest. Politically motivated people, and you know we have them in such huge numbers that don't even come close to those from anywhere in the world, raised religious issues on his post. It was at that moment that he decided to end friendship with me as he was absolutely brainwashed by his own group of friends against being friends with a bearded man with a green turban like me."

"That is unbelievably sad."

"And I was the also the one who introduced Gaurav to Scarlett so that she can keep getting those pouches from him directly as per her need. And the two of them maybe in touch with each other till yesterday, as you say she was murdered the last night."

"Are you trying to blame him for the murder?"

"No. He is too good, probably as innocent as a cow. He can never even think about such an act."

"You said you are not in touch with Gaurav. Then, how do you have a new pouch of Zuban in your pocket?"

And the Master hesitated in answering. He thought for a moment with his eyes closed, behind those round glasses and then replied with a blank expression, "Now I get it privately couriered by my other friends from the royal state of Rajasthan." These were the only words he said with his eyes looking down and not on the face of the observant visitor.

"That sounds good. I request you to continue with your and Scarlett's dramatic story," said Monty, noting the stumble from the Master but not reacting on it.

"Your wish is my command, Monty Sahib. Normally, she had a candy coated tongue but it was utterly the opposite when her head was full of umbrage. Her body language was full of pride and a little bit of arrogance due to her egocentric and self opinionated personality.

Scarlett's nature and behavior kept on changing from bad to worse over the months, especially after her divorce with Mr. Hargurjeet Singh, who I believe is one of the most humble human beings on earth. Her malignant nature turned even more malicious after my friendship with Gaurav broke and I could not offer her Zuban for some months when she visited my place, though she was getting it secretly from him.

The stitching offered by me was still perfect and I can guarantee that no other tailor in this entire town could stitch those outfits for her and her models with as much delicacy and hard work as we did for her. Even when there was nothing wrong in the finished dress, she used to get angry at me and my team and try her best to point out mistakes. We were always honest and sincere with our work for her, but she was full of irritability. She wanted perfection, and though, thanks to the Almighty Allah, we are too blessed to be perfect at our craft, and our results were also perfect, still her nature was beyond our comprehension.

Maybe the separation from her husband was the real cause of her ill temper and impatience, but that is just a probable cause. Whatever the reason be, the manner in which she started conducting herself towards me and my sincere team, was not acceptable at all. Things escalated too far as she did not hesitate using abusive language towards all of us, especially Sarfaraz and me.

All limits of tolerance were crossed on the day that marked one full year of her divorce, the twenty sixth day of December last year, when she came here in the morning to collect the special attire for her evening party. We had worked so hard on that complex outfit that even a doctor performing a life threatening operation will not work with so much concentration and precision, but as usual, she spotted a mistake. I don't think I should call that a mistake. It was not one.

The argument she raised was about the placement of the button higher up on the neck. I am an experienced tailor, Monty Sahib, and I know what I am doing. Using all the practical knowledge I possess and the observations I have made over the years, I had deliberately placed the button a little higher than where she wanted it to be placed. Being a girl, even she should have understood the actual reason behind it, but instead, she started abusing and blaming me for spoiling her so called divorce party dress.

I agreed to change the place of that button as per her wish. We always cater to the needs of our clients. True professionals we are. There was no point of abusing and shouting. It was just a two minute work for my dedicated team, but her anger had crossed all limits and she slapped me tightly in front of all my employees and a couple of customers."

And then there was a long pause. Monty could see that the tiny eyes hidden behind the round spectacles were had already filled up to their brim. They could burst forth anytime but the man had seen so many years and was strong enough to prevent the burst. The chin well covered by the salt and pepper beard trembled like that of a small child. The throat choked and the eyes were closed as if the darkness would soothe him.

"Are you serious?" exclaimed Monty with his eyes widening like those of a guiltless buffalo who finds itself sitting leisurely on the railway track with a fast moving train all of a sudden coming towards itself. His left hand left his chin and was now placed on the uneven teakwood table.

"You heard it right, she slapped me right on my face" continued Master Shams-ud-din, not in his typical business tone but in a one that clearly demonstrated his urge to cry, perhaps overwhelmingly but somehow he suppressed it and managed to speak.

"Twenty sixth of December was the day and 1PM was the time when I decided to put an end to all kinds of communication with Scarlett White. After slapping me, she walked out from my boutique and that was the last time ever I saw her."

"This was indeed overly dramatic," pointed Monty, observing the expressions which twisted more than a river full of water in its wide course towards the ocean, and the consistent body language of the excessively emotional suspect.

"Only Allah knows what she thought of herself. Extreme amounts of arrogance coupled with a bad sense of pride indeed results in one's own disaster. I am a man with intense self respect and she tried to violate it in front of my employees and customers. Expecting a second chance from me would be termed as foolishness.

Not only did I stop taking work orders from her after this incident, I even stopped receiving her calls and responding to her pointless text messages. She tried her best to contact me after that for a couple of months, maybe to apologize, but I did not give her any chance."

The deep breath of the Master that seemed to be hesitant in his lungs a while back, now returned to normal. The sigh that managed to escape the lips passing through the thick filter of the salt and pepper beard, was slow as if his brain needed that time to process what he had just said or remembered. The tiny eyes glued at the forehead of the visitor to spot his reaction to all the words that had been said.

Almost nothing seemed to etch upon the detective's handsome but inscrutable face. Monty, being an investigator, would never let any fascination ruin his game, so expecting a response from him was lack of judgment on the part of Master Shams-ud-din. Continuing the investigation, Monty tried to confirm, "So, when was the last time you saw her or speak to her?"

"Eight and a half months Monty Sahib, as I told you. Neither did I meet or see her, nor did I speak to her over the phone. I did not even reply to her text messages."

"They say people who seek revenge dig not one, but two graves. Did you not feel like taking a revenge of that slap on your face?"

"I did think about it. That stinging slap did echo, not as much on my skin as it did on my mind for some weeks. But, I was so helpless. Never can I go against the teachings of the Prophet and dare to think about raising my hands on a woman. These limbs of mine are made for tailoring, not for violence. I wanted to move on and that is exactly what I had done. Out of nowhere you came today with the news of her murder and made me remember the things that I never wanted to."

"Maybe in order to take revenge of the stinging slap, you..."

Before Monty could even complete the sentence, Master Shams-ud-din smacked the table with flat of his right hand just like an enraged bully hits an innocent lad at the college. This was not a gesture of kindness but a signal of something weird to follow. He hit so hard that it stung his own hand but he did not want to show his pain. The friendliness and enthusiasm in his tiny eyes turned into a rage, not just fearful but brutal. All his blood had reached his head, turning it red and boiling, with resultant fumes trying their best to escape from the slight gap between his gritting teeth. Even his tone turned louder and violent.

"Shut up. Yes, I do hate Scarlett more than a mother hates the ruthless murderer of her kid but this does not mean that I was involved in the plot of her murder.

May Allah bless you with some commonsense. Sarfaraz, Abdul, Zafar come here. Where are the three of you? Come inside, right now."

The wooden door behind Monty opened with a creaking sound of pressure and the three humble tailors entered without any knock. Led by Sarfaraz, Abdul and Zafar too had a sense of urgency this time on their stern faces. Monty turned his neck towards the left for a moment with the black eyeballs glued to the corner of the white portion of his eye, only to observe that all three of them took their positions surrounding him from three sides. Surely, a savage brawl was on the cards any moment presumed Monty as he turned his head in its normal position. With a deep reassuring breath, he gathered all his strength into his muscles and prepared his body for defense, clenching tightly the fist of his right palm.

"Thanks to the Almighty Allah, I was born several years more than a decade before you Mr. Monty. I have more experience than a foolish investigator than you. Especially because of my profession, I meet a lot of females regularly but never have I ever met a more arrogant, insolent, shameless, bad mannered, uncultured and abusive lady than that Scarlett." He turned towards Zafar and Abdul and continued, "Despite being professional tailors, we found too difficult to cope with her presence around us here at this boutique then think about the sorrowful condition of her husband." Turning his eyes straight towards the forehead of Monty, he said, "Go and ask her husband about her murder. Don't sit here any longer to waste our precious time. We have a lot of work to finish." And then he clenched the fist of his left palm and staring at it said, "I have left punching people a long time ago as I hate the pain that blazes up my arm when my fist breaks someone's jaw. So, get out of my office and never in my life show me your face if you want it to remain as handsome as it is now."

As he felt a mild touch of a human hand on his left shoulder from the back, Monty quickly stood up on his muscular legs. The armchair, anyway, was not as comfortable as it appeared to be. Making a fierce eye contact with Master Shams-ud-din, he said, "I am doing my work. Sorry to hurt your sentiments but I will be back if I find any evidence or require any more clarification from you, even if that is against your will."

As the touch of the human hand on his shoulder turned from mild to aggressive, Monty using the strength of his shoulder, pushed it away and turned towards Sarfaraz who was about to push Monty out of the workroom. "I am going buddy. Don't escalate things so much beyond proportions that they get difficult for you to breathe." Sarfaraz was not nervous anymore. He seemed to have no effect of Monty's statement. Abdul and Zafar pushed Monty out of the workroom. The push was not intense but clearly a sign that no further conversation was possible with Master Shams-ud-din, who kept staring at the investigator with his bloodshot eyes, full of anger.

Monty quickly came out of the open door of the workroom without looking back, as he wanted to avoid any kind of unnecessary fistfight. He rushed towards the shoe rack, picked up his matte black branded shoes and left the boutique without actually wearing them. Instead, he carried them in his bare hands to avoid any form of violence inside the boutique. The three tailors accompanied him till the main door of their boutique, not allowing him to even look towards the Master and observe his reaction. They did not speak using their lipless mouths but their aggressive actions revealed their inner thoughts, as expressive as the eyes of a trained Kathak dancer.

The pavement was dirty and even littered with some ghee covered papers, boxes and napkins from the sweet shop as people visiting there paid scant attention to the clean and empty dustbin placed at the corner, opposite the doctor's clinic. Monty did not want his expensive socks to get smelly, greased and soiled. So, he entered Dr. Ram Agarwal's clinic looking for some free space to properly wear his polished shoes, but there was none. The patients were stuffed in there like the green grass on a fertile land during the rainy season, the only difference being the unbearable smell of sweat. Not even an inch of free space was available as the doctor continued his consultation strangely with around six or seven patients simultaneously, with all of them standing around his head and speaking their hearts out, louder than the others.

Monty came out gasping, trying to find fresh air, left with no other option but to wear his expensive and waterproof shoes on the filthy pavement itself. He did not seem much excited this time about the sweet aroma that Mishra ji used to cunningly to invite the people into his shop. His mind was in a conflict leading to thoughts in random directions but leading to nowhere exactly like a heavy wrecking ball being pulled by several horses, each in a separate direction.

After wearing the shoes, Monty rushed towards his Challenger, got into it and sat on the comfortable leather seat. Some are scared of the dark, some of the height while some of the insects, but Monty was not scared of any of those. The thing that scared him the most was the confusion in his own mind, full of inconclusive thoughts leading to intense and continuous electrical sparks flowing through his spine to add to the dilemma.

Although he sat in the comfort of his own locked car, yet he was shaking. His brain was constantly searching for a reassuring sign, like the mobile phones search for network signals when the airplane just lands, still at the runway. Sadly, all attempts made by his brain failed. There was no one he could talk to as the teddy behind would always refuse to speak and his apprentice Chetan Prasad was on a leave. But, there was something Chetan gave to Monty before his departure. The trembling left hand of the nervous investigator reached the dashboard and opened it through the flick of the handle from his thumb. It took less than a minute to pull out the special cigarette, the ointment of relief in such hazardous situations. This was also an indication of the fact that that day's hard work had come to an end.

The lighter was in the back pocket of Monty's trouser. He took it out using his right hand, lighted the cigarette and kept it back. Monty inhaled it slowly, his brain and body taking absolutely no time to process the relief. He felt that his lungs and heart were covered with a warm blanket. The smell of burnt paper and its flavored contents, worse than the smell of burnt coal, filled the in the car but to the smoker, it felt like he was inhaling a flower scented deodorant. Taking small draws of the long cigarette, he turned on the ignition of his Challenger on and with the shift of the gear on the reverse mode, moved back, changed gears and then taking left turn, drove away slowly straight towards the setting sun, through the network of the patchwork with the filter of the burning cigarette stuck in between his pristine lips.

Chapter VII

Fight for right

Normally, this was not the case but at that time, Kanpur was weirdly silent as if it had ended the night before. The sun however was still fiercely determined as it bathed the streets in a rosy glow, creating an illusion of a scene from a retro romantic movie. The rich natural hues turned brighter more quickly than expected due to thorough absence of fluffy clouds. Even when some were drowned in their self-generated grief and hardships, there were others who got inspired by the beauty of the ineffably blue sky.

The spokes of both the wheels blurred, each strand together and unique, all at once, as Chetan Prasad pedaled in the direction of the pleasant breeze, literally flying at a speed that could rival a cheetah. His bicycle was not anything special but perhaps the cheapest one available at any bike store. The tyres seemed to be new however the bicycle was certainly more than half a decade old. The black paint had started to fade at various spots on the metal, especially towards the rear and the luggage carrier had come off.

Despite being a stern man with practically no expressions, the anticipation of meeting his dear friend and boss after a gap of an action-packed day had wired Chetan's body like he was plugged into the mains. He felt that his brain was in a fast forward and there was no off switch. As he reached the apartment where Monty resided, even before he could park his bicycle, he saw Rita Mishra sitting at the side of the main gate, on the pavement.

She was dressed in the sweat stained white t-shirt over the blue shorts, exactly the same outfit she wore the previous day. The bruise of her right leg, above the knee still seemed to cause her agony as she sat on the pavement, barefoot, with the dirty rubber slippers kept next to her. On seeing Chetan, she stood up straight on her feet, surprisingly with lightning fast movement of her limbs, despite the injury.

"Good Morning Chetan. I was waiting for you since a long time. I knew you will come today," she said in a tone that could not hide her excitement. Her lean hands trembled and her eyes turned wide as every cell of her body began to vibrate with a nervous kind of energy.

"Good morning Rita, I like it when women wait for me and you know that, don't you?" said Chetan, parking his bicycle on the pavement just outside the open gate of the apartment, looking towards the Challenger parked inside through the corner of his right eye. He went on to slowly dust the mud that had turned the area around both the knees of his blue jeans to brown, perhaps when he kneeled down outside a temple on the way.

"Yes my Lord. That is why I was waiting for you," she said in a satirical tone as she grabbed his left arm, the one that had peculiar red scar near the elbow visible clearly as his white collared shirt was half sleeved.

Chetan turned for the first time and looked straight into her face that had no makeup, her willowy frame, her oily nose and flat cheeks, finding beauty deep in her unblinking eyes. Making sure that there was nobody watching them, he leaned towards her, close enough till their foreheads touched against each others'. As her timorous feet stepped over his white sneakers, the smell of her ponytail flooded his senses which he found too tough to resist. He slammed his lips to hers, nearly knocking all wind off her lungs. It was slow, soft and more comforting than any words can ever be. His hand rested below her ear, his thumb caressing her flat cheek as the two breaths mingled into one.

The fun was however cut short when he himself pushed her away observing the arrival of the security guard at the gate of the apartment. She stepped back and said, "Waiting for you is always worth it Chetan Prasad," feeling much better especially after getting a nod and extracting a transient smile on the poker face. As the guard went pass them towards a casual gathering of a couple of hawkers and a housemaid on the opposite side of the road, she continued, "I am not feeling well since past two days. You were not here and I could not get the pill for this bloody recurrent migraine as I did not know the name of it. Life became an unimaginably cruel torture for me, the one which I just survived, not lived."

Chetan's motionless eyes showed the kind of gentle concern an old man has for his grand children but his lips remained as brown as rust, albeit slightly wet. He laid his left hand lightly over her right shoulder, and instead of flinching, she seemed to be soothed by it. In a soft voice, he tried to calm her down, "Don't worry Rita, I am back and I have with me the medicine you require." His right hand went straight into the pocket of his jeans and out came a couple of tablets wrapped thoroughly in a clean sheet of white paper. "Today I will offer you two tablets. Have one right now and the other one in the evening for complete relief."

Rita took both the tablets from Chetan with an expression of delightfulness similar to that of a hardworking cricketer when he is awarded his maiden test cap. "Thank you", was what she said with her little eyes fixed at the two medicinal tablets, "and today I have a special request for you." Chetan heard with a lot of attention as she continued to speak.

"Nothing is ever free in this world. Everything I give you is a debt for you and vice versa. Don't think I am in love with you or anything of that sort. You provide me these medicines in exchange of the fantasy talks and inappropriate dates but today I went ahead to the extent of a kiss. I hope you can understand that I need something extra from you today." Her tone changed from gentle to rough as her words gathered weight with Chetan left as confused as a weak opposition's leader in a democratic Parliament to reply, "What do you mean?"

"Don't act so innocent Chetan Prasad as if you have never seen me unclothed before and dehumanized me then with your evil intents." She said in a low yet audible voice, perhaps referring to any past love affair between the two. He simply turned his gaze to her, swift and emanating with resigned sympathy and said, "because, I have not. Are you out of your mind Rita, do you even know what you are blabbering?"

Raising the finger towards her lips, she said, "Shut up. You know that, I know that but the world does not know that. What if I scream right now and lodge an FIR against you stating what I just said? Sadly you and your boss will be in no position to prove me wrong." And then she pointed towards an aged man standing all alone, dressed in white kurta pajama, with a mobile phone in his hand and fiercely staring straight at Chetan's forehead. "That man is my uncle and he has already clicked a picture of you kissing me here. When a person can kiss openly in a public place, it is very easy to imagine what he can do in private."

"What do you want?" asked Chetan as few droplets of sweat accumulated near his thin hairline.

"I am quitting the job from your boss Monty's house with immediate effect. Go and tell that lone owl to never ever try to contact me in his lifetime. If he wants to, remind him that my uncle has a copy of the CCTV footage of Monty's floor of yesterday morning, when he opened the door of his flat to allow me to enter inside. Luckily, for extra security, the camera has been installed on the wall opposite to the door of his flat. Only thing visible in the footage is that he was absolutely undressed, wrapped in just a thin towel when I entered the flat where obviously there was no third person. I think you know what the police will do if I complain against both of you."

"I will inform him about your resignation. Is there anything else you expect from me?" said Chetan with his eyes closed, perhaps falling short of ideas to tackle the situation. He was taken aback but he did not want to show that he was taken aback with what was being said to him.

Rita's thin lips turned up towards her poking nose, making a thin moon like shape as she continued in a tone much gentler than before, "What I expect from you Chetan is that you keep providing me with these medicines as and when I need them. These are the only ones that cure me every time the brainless migraine attacks me. My uncle will call you whenever the need be and you can hand these divine tablets to him."

"Done," said Chetan as he appeared somewhat relived that Rita's wish was not going to fall as heavy on his pocket as he initially imagined.

And then there was a silent conversation as the two of them started to stare into each others' eyes. Chetan finally looked away, tears of separation from Rita after a short but romantic relationship with her, threatening to blur his vision. She wore her dirty rubber slippers but before walking away, she kissed gently on the brown cheeks of Chetan. It left a little wet mark, a shallow pool of saliva on his left cheek. His mind felt a pleasant buzz but then she walked away with her uncle, away forever.

The sigh that escaped Chetan's wet lips was slow, as if his brain needed some time to process what exactly had happened. His eyes remained fixed at the pavement, on the exact path through which Rita Mishra and her uncle had fled. Then he took an about turn, a turn towards the gate of the apartment and away from the pavement as he walked inside, gaining momentum with every step towards the staircase and then upwards towards the first floor, refusing to turn back even once.

A strange fear travelled in Chetan's veins as he prepared himself to ring the doorbell of Monty's flat but he somehow controlled it from making it to his facial muscles or skin. As he was lost in the imagination of the exact area that the CCTV on the opposite wall might be covering, the door opened. Dressed in his regular uniform of black infernal tuxedo over elegant black shoes, Monty appeared absolutely ready to continue his mission.

Chetan's complexion remained pale and matt despite meeting his chief and his eyes as steady as if he was a middle aged woman shopping for rice. He let out an understated sigh and entered the flat quickly with expressions that suggested that nothing much had happened.

"Such an eventful night followed by the lively day yesterday and I got to know about it today and that too when I called you casually. This is not fair chief. Had I not called you in the morning, you would have gone on to interrogate the third suspect all alone, and who knows this case would have wrapped up and I would have come to know about it only when the Government awarded a medal to you," said Chetan angrily to his chief, who in turn had a pleasant and kind expression on his face, perhaps amused by his apprentice's irritation.

As the two of them sat on the two plastic chairs, next to the circular table in the middle of the hall of the flat, Monty said in his normal deep voice, "I have narrated to you the entire episode on call and I hope you have noted down all the major points of my yesterday's conversations into your document."

"Yes I have," as Chetan nodded, he took out three special cigarettes from the pocket of his white shirt and kept them on the table, next to the ashtray that contained the burnt remains of another injurious roll of paper. With his eyes turning towards the crossed visiting card of Master Shams-ud-din which lay next to the ashtray, he continued, "these three were the only ones I could manage to bring this time. It was difficult to get more as the police are turning much stricter with every passing day against all kinds of smuggling, especially of these expensive tobacco free rolls which only the elite have access to."

The smile from Monty's face disappeared as he was lost in thoughts, definitely not the ones of the author whose books are pushed back into the shelves after a quick reading of their first page, but those, which if visible would be inverse explosion, crazy chaotic twists and turns all leading up to perhaps only one word – Achievement. People who have tasted success are always those who focus on their goals and those who are yet to climb that ladder, need to focus much more. Monty certainly belonged to the latter group. The less number of cigarettes did not matter to him as he was focused solely on his mission of solving the murder mystery. Coming straight to the point, he enquired, "What time did you schedule my appointment with Hargurjeet Singh?"

"Right after speaking to you, I called his manager and he informed me that Hargurjeet has very little free time before he leaves for Kerala for a vacation day after tomorrow. When I took your name, he scheduled the appointment on an urgent basis at noon today at Hargurjeet's farmhouse. Due to his commitments, we will have only a few minutes of meeting time with him," said Chetan, changing his tone from that of an irritated friend to that of a responsible apprentice.

Monty, as a general rule, hid his emotions. Perhaps, he had figured out through his experiences that they were extremely confidential and therefore his face was blank at most times, as if lost in deep rational thoughts. But that day was different. He was going to meet the third and final suspect of the murder and that helped excitement creep up into his mind resulting in a sweet, joyful laughter that seemed to echo through the walls of the hall. All of a sudden it stopped and Monty got back to his serious being, asking, "What is the exact time now Chetan?"

"It is ten so I guess we have around an hour before we leave. By the way, where your diamond studded gold wristwatch is Monty Sir?" asked Chetan as he observed the bare wrists of his chief, a sight that was not common at all.

Checking the lengths of the three cigarettes on the table, a wry smile appeared on Monty's face as he explained, "Glad that you noticed it missing from my wrist Chetan. Turn on the GPS enabled location tracker of my chip in your mobile. We have an hour to find my dear watch."

"Oh! Not again. Last time you forgot it at Simran's bedroom! Do you remember how long it took to get it after her husband refused to unlock the door?" replied Chetan with his hands going up in the air and an expression on his face resembling that of a student burdened with extra homework during cricket world cup finals.

"That was because Simran preferred bare wrists but don't worry, this time it has been stolen. Before I see a shock on your face let me tell you that the thief, Rita Mishra is actually a beautiful soul but forced by her pernicious uncle to do things which end up looking ugly."

"I see. I met her on my way up and no wonder she told me to inform you that she will not work for you anymore," said Chetan with a poker face that was as familiar to him as are the ingredients of a birthday cake to its baker. Without wasting any minute, he began to load the mobile phone application on his smart phone to trace the exact location of Monty's watch.

"Just two lanes away towards the south," he proclaimed when the desired location was easily traced by the customized application used by the investigators.

"I know you have developed a feeling once again for Rita. Be calm as I assure you she will be back to work from tomorrow, if not tonight. I think she cooks delicious food anyway. Let us leave now as it might take longer than expected to reach Hargurjeet Singh's farmhouse." As Monty said this, the look of determination in his black eyes coupled with the slight buzz around his tremulous lips gave an impression of the adventure he was expecting on the way.

The two got up from their respective plastic chairs almost simultaneously and the first thing Chetan did was to pick up the three cigarettes from the table and put them back in the pocket of his shirt. "Expect all of these to turn to ashes by the end of the day today," he said, showing signs of confidence to his chief. Meanwhile, Monty picked the keys of his esteemed Challenger from the bed in this room and both of them left the flat, making sure that it was locked properly.

Monty drove the Challenger following the mobile application on a road that was not as crowded as it would normally be, not because the population was under check but because of the heat generated by the scorching sun. He had taken the round shades back from the teddy seated at the backseat, who might be having a tough time without them just like Chetan. The distance was not too much and the mobile application spotted that the special watch was inside a small and temporary residential structure, just two lanes away.

Monty parked the mighty Challenger right in front of the door of the hut like structure between two high raised buildings. Probably it was made shift arrangement by a laborer working on a nearby construction site. The entire hut was of the size of a small storeroom, the one where grandparents do not allow their little grandchildren to enter while playing, fearing they might see something there which they never wanted them to. It was made of a tent like material, perhaps a mixture of filthy blue plastic and thick brown cloth. There were obviously no windows but one door like opening, perhaps smaller in size than a normal cupboard's door.

"Let us not waste much time," said Chetan looking towards his chief as the two of them got down of the Challenger.

"I will surely get my watch in sometime but what I pray to the Gods is that she actually turns out to be a beautiful girl from the inside so that you too are not disappointed," replied Monty with a sarcastic smile on his face enough to make Chetan blush for a moment, as he entered the structure through its opening, followed by his buddy and apprentice.

As they entered inside, the scene shocked both of them and their solemn faces fell faster than corpses in cement boots. Their brown skin turned grey as their mouths hung with lips slightly parted and eyes stretched as wide as they possibly could. Rita's profoundly immoral uncle was laying only in his white pajama on a narrow made shift bed, made of only dried stalks of grain, the ones that are used as fodder. As he tried to sleep, Rita was occupied in giving him a back massage with her bare hands.

The heat in there could melt a metallic rod as there was no fan. Let alone fan, there were no lights too. How could there be? There was no electricity connection in that temporary residence. The battery operated mobile charger and an emergency light bulb were placed near the door itself. There was no toilet too. Only a couple of steel plates, two glasses and a cooking vessel were kept on the floor next to the so called bed, along with a stove and a rather small gas cylinder. There was a small red colored suitcase containing clothes probably of uncle and aunty as Rita's collection of two tops and one party dress lay on the floor in the corner, next to half a dozen worn out slippers.

Rita stopped the massage, her mind ordering her body to mask all the fear but her eyes could not. She knew that a show of weakness would serve as an inlet for the enemy to surge through. All those years she had spent with her uncle helped her maintain a poker face in odd situations. She started the conversation in a diffident tone but a false show of confidence in her body language, "I told you I will not work anymore. Why are you here? Go away."

Even before the investigator and his apprentice could react, her uncle reached for his mobile and dialed a number which was probably in his fast dial list, shouting, "five get five," on the line and then disconnected the call. It was obviously a codeword that left Monty and Chetan aware of the possible danger. Retreat would be a disaster thought Monty as he quickly replied to Rita in his normal tone and deep voice, "I came here looking for my gold watch. Kindly give it back to me." As he said this, he took off the black shades as they were just not needed inside that dwelling, and kept them safely on the bed, next to the relaxing uncle. Chetan on the other hand, stood still near the door, anticipating the entry of some of the unknown helpers as the uncle had possibly called for them over the phone.

"I don't have it," shouted Rita at the top of her voice as her uncle got up on his feet staring right at the top of Monty's forehead using his tiny brown eyes placed deep into their sockets and with the company of a raised brow. He was a man who had aged several years ago but not from his heart. It seemed that the wrinkles on his dark face were there to glorify his skill and experience in petty thefts and irrelevant arguments. Though he was old, his biceps and triceps would put many young men to shame, proving that he was strong enough to defend himself if need be.

"We know that it is somewhere in this hut," said Chetan, marking his presence as he looked straight into the eyes of his former girl, trying his best to make her say the truth, but she turned her gaze away.

"Shut up and get out," ordered the uncle in a raspy voice that was as unpleasant to the ears as is the beating of random items by a small kid inside his playroom.

"I will get no pleasure in taking you down old man. It is totally unnecessary. Give me my watch as fast as you can because I have urgent meeting to attend," said Monty in a tone that was possibly stricter than that of a warden of a boys hostel, revealing an unseen aggressive side of his otherwise serious, solemn and sensible character.

"When it comes to fighting, I never play by the rules," said the old man in his hoarse voice, followed by a strange laughter with his crooked mouth half closed, as there entered five tall men probably in their mid thirties. All of them were dressed in a grey colored uniform, signifying that they were all laborers from the construction site in the lane. The men were well built, not from work out at the gym but naturally due to the nature of their work. They looked physically so strong that it seemed that their one punch would be equivalent to ten punches from an average man working at any office.

Monty and Chetan watched each one of them enter turning their heads by not more than ten degrees. Their hearts hammered but they kept their posture casual with no hint of hesitation. The laborer, who entered at the last, closed the door like opening by dropping the curtain behind him. The humble residence now turned into a vulnerable wrestling ring ready to host a life threatening no holds barred match, two versus six, perhaps seven with Rita included. The empty space left there was as less as the space between two cards in a pack.

"Welcome my guests with some sweet music," said the old man with a look of burning fire on his face and exactly in the tone of an evil commander of infiltrating terrorists. Following his orders, the laborers went in for an all round attack on the duo.

"Show me you are better and I will bow to you and learn. Perhaps you want a fistfight, fine with me, as a general rule, come empty handed and we will see who leaves this place with pride and own belongings," said Monty as he angrily stared at the old man and began the fight with a back dropkick at the chin of one of the attackers, instantaneously taking him down with pain and perhaps a broken jaw with the unbearable impact of a heavy leather shoe across the little face.

"One down, five to go, bring it on," shouted Chetan as he slapped the falling man with the full swing of his right arm, making sure that that man had no chance whatsoever to even stand up within a couple of hours.

One of the four standing men bent down with a sudden jerk trying to push Monty by his waist in an attempt to make him fall down on all fours. Years of training at the gym came handy as Monty moved with lightning speed towards his left and tucked the bald attacker's head, as large as a basket ball, underneath his right armpit and wrapped his own arm around it like ribbon on a birthday present. Pressing his left forearm against the attacker's twisted face, Monty grabbed his right wrist, threw that hairy and muscular arm over his own left shoulder and lifted the attacker in the air through his solid thighs. The man must be around eighty kilos heavy but the ease with which Monty lifted him up clearly proved the kind of weights he was used to train with at the gym. As the attacker was lifted in the air in an upside down position with his feet almost touching the ceiling, Monty was swift to freely fall backwards, slamming the attacker's back to the hard floor below, maybe breaking a bone or two of the thirty three that are a part of the human spine.

The cry of agony from the attacker was worse than the cry of the goat whose kid is slaughtered in front of her helpless eyes by the laughing butchers for selling the fatty chumps at good profits. Monty had no time to even look at the suffering man as he got up on his feet incredibly quickly.

Meanwhile, Chetan Prasad jumped over towards the steel utensils and picked up the two glasses while one of the attackers picked up the steel plate that lay on the floor. Chetan threw the glasses, one by one at the laborer, using them as missiles shot directly at the enemy's base camp but the man with the plate defended the first glass perfectly with his plate and attacked the second one as if he was a batsman trying to hit a six out of the park. The glass flew in the air and hit Rita on the sweet spot below her right ear. Luckily her hands were up there as she was trying to duck under the misfired missiles, preventing any kind of injury to her.

The short and stout attacker standing next to Rita took out the leather belt from his trouser and began to swirl it with all his might in all directions faster than the speed of rotation of the blades of a high flying chopper. The only difference was that he swirled it aimlessly, though with the sole intention of whipping Chetan or Monty right across their face. Monty was quick to bend over and push that mindless fellow, striking his rib cage with his hard right shoulder, generating a thud louder than the sound of a gunshot. The clash was so intense that the laborer lost the rotating belt and it went flying into the air only to hit his own unaware friend on the back of his neck, taking him down with its momentum to fall with his bearded face hitting the half a dozen worn out slippers kept at the floor.

The laborer who was short in height and wearing a dusty safety leather boot, perhaps the one that firemen wear on duty, kicked Monty on his blazer from the back. The power he could manage on the kick was not enormous due to the absence of any running or swinging momentum but Monty was sure that his coat got dirty, and he could not tolerate a spoiled boot mark on his prized possession. "You need a high five, on your face, with a wooden chair," shouted Monty as his eyes turned red in rage and an expression of anger that could scare even a ghost, but unfortunately not that particular laborer. "There is no chair here you fool, instead I will use my boot for a high five on your face to change it from handsome to ugly with just one blow," he replied. All he wanted to do was fight. He repeated his ferocious kick, this time dirtying the black trouser, near the right knee, making Monty angrier than before, not by his kicks, but by his arrogance.

"Come again, aim for my face." Monty invited the laborer to try another kick. As the attacker charged towards Monty in an attempt to kick his nose, Monty raised his right leg at an angle larger than ninety degrees to the floor, and used the momentum of the attacker to deliver the sole of his shoe as hard as a rock, to the forehead of the assailant. The difference in heights of the two helped Monty strike exactly where he wanted to, leaving a mark of his shoe's sole right from the receding hairline to the wedge shaped nose of the attacker, passing through the space in between his eyes. The short heighted laborer turned out to be stronger than what Monty had expected. He did not fall down but lost all momentum after the collision, giving Monty time to jump up with a twist and kick him with the soles of both his shoes connecting one below the other right across the chest to take the opponent down. The hapless laborer fell backwards slamming his head against the hard floor and Monty landed over him, maintaining his balance, thanks to the strength of his arms. It was certain that the poor guy had slipped into concussion but the marks of the boot on his clothes had angered Monty so much that he did not end there. He went on to slap both the ears of the defeated man simultaneously with as much power as he could at that time, disorienting his brain cells to the extent of him losing cautiousness.

The time that Monty took on teaching the perfect lesson to the short guy, gave opportunity to the bearded laborer to pounce over him. Monty was sitting on top of the unconscious laborer when this man jumped over him from the back and sat over the investigator, pushing his face down on the chest of the guy below. Using the power of the muscles of his forearms, the attacker pulled Monty's arms and placed them across his thighs, locking both of them in the crook of his knees. After the attacker had his opponent's arms precisely where he wanted them, he reached forward cupping his hands in a manner so that his fingers were interlocked. Then he grabbed the Monty's chin in his cupped hands and leaned back, pulling on Monty's chin and applying tremendous pressure to his back. It was not only the pain that made Monty cry in agony, but also the fact that this move completely immobilized him.

At the same time, the laborer carrying the steel plate threw it exactly at Chetan's head, taking him down with a sudden blow. He then picked one of the two tops belonging to Rita from the floor, swirled it clockwise to form a spiral weapon and charged towards his enemy, shouting, "You are dead." Even before Chetan could stand up, the laborer attacked him from the back, wrapping the cloth around his neck, trying to choke him up by pulling the two ends in the opposite directions.

Rita's old uncle took this opportunity to humiliate his guests even more. He opened the red suitcase and after a few seconds of search, took out the diamond studded watch that belonged to Monty. With the watch in his hands, he walked towards its trapped owner. He bent slightly over Monty's locked head, making sure that the guest had to look up to him and said with a crisp smile, "I told you I don't play by the rules. Before you pass out, make sure that you see this watch on my wrist." He then began wearing that on his right wrist with his smile growing wider than before.

Monty was not in the position to speak. He knew if he opened his mouth, the cup of the hands of the attacker would slip to his throat, blocking the passage of air in and out of his lungs. Chetan on the other hand was on the verge of passing away due to the continuous application of pressure on his throat. He looked towards Rita making an eye contact with her and shouted, "Suitcase!"

All that Rita was at that moment was urgency. All other emotions were pushed away from her being. She picked up the already open suitcase using both her hands, dropping a few dresses from it on the way up to her shoulders and threw it right at the face of the laborer who was trying to choke Chetan. The attack was sudden and unexpected and it hurt badly as the suitcase was heavy. The man fell down on his back, the top slipping away from his opened fists, giving Chetan the opportunity to stand up on his legs. He wasted no time in pushing the man sitting on the top of his chief with both his hands, resulting in the unlocking of Monty.

As Monty and Chetan both rose steadily to their feet, ready for the assault, the remaining two laborers instead of fighting, joined hands and went out of the dwelling through the door with dropped shoulders, saying, "When his own niece is not on his side, why should we waste our energy?"

Rita's uncle turned to face her. There was no trace of white in his eyes or a shade of brown on his face.

Everything was red while the wrinkles turned purple with the cold. As her breath changed from regular to panting gasp, Rita knew that the burning stare would last only as long as it took him to think of the most brutal form of punishment he would use to discipline her. She had no courage left in her to keep her eyes open.

He moved towards her and raised his right hand in the position to slap her tiny face. The slap was as loud as a clap and stung the face unimaginably hard. It was an open handed smack and had left a red welt behind on the left cheek. Just below the eye was a small cut where the iron ring had caught the soft skin. Rita staggered backwards with her eyes watering and opened them to see her uncle clutching the left side of his face in pain after getting that tight slap by Chetan.

"I am sorry, I never wanted to hit a senior citizen. That is just not my culture. But I had no other option as this man was proceeding towards slapping you. As a devotee of female Goddesses, I cannot let a man slap a woman in front of my eyes," said Chetan to Rita, trying his best not to stare at the mark his slap left on the old man's face by looking down on the hard floor where the laborer with a broken jaw lay quietly.

Staring at the bruise above Chetan's eyebrow, that had begun as a purple stain but had now sunk into the socket itself giving it an appearance of a black eye, Rita said, "Hope that mark made by the plate will go away soon because I am in love with you and I don't want to go for a dinner with a black eyed man. You never leave my mind, you are always with me, mentally if not physically. You are the cause of my stability in this world full of chaos and I desperately need you. Uncle is mine too and I hope he has realized the grave error he did till this time and I thank you for making him realize his mistake."

"You are the only one in my heart and soul. You are the only one I buy those migraine pills for and trust me, I will keep buying them till I breathe my last. And do you know why I don't let you know the name of that medicine? It is so only because I want to be close to you in your distress," as Chetan said this, he walked up to Rita slowly and pulled her closer to him, wrapping his arms around her. This embrace was warm and his strong arms seemed very protective to her. She hugged him back with her fragile hands around his waist, not wanting the moment to end.

"One tight slap was all that was required to open my eyes that had remained closed since decades. Perhaps that slap should have come much earlier, anyway, I thank you Chetan," said Rita's uncle, who had realized the wrong he had done all across his life. His mouth set into a semi pout as he turned to Monty to say, "I am sorry Sir. You are my guest and guests deserve God like treatment at the host's place. I committed a grave mistake. Please pardon me." As he said this, he reached for one of his kurtas, perhaps the most expensive one from his little collection and started cleaning the shoe marks on the trouser and coat of

Monty, only to be stopped by the investigator with a raised left hand and a pat on the shoulder by the right one.

"I am happy that you have realized your mistake. Give me my watch and allow Rita to live her life. If she wishes to work, let her come to my house tomorrow as I love the food she cooks. Maybe one day she will be a top chef, who knows?"

The old man immediately handed over the diamond studded gold watch to Monty, who wore it on his wrist. Along with the watch, the uncle also handed over the shades that Monty had kept on his bed and Monty put them back on as he stepped out of the door saying, "You have an entire lifetime for romance my dear Chetan, but now we are getting late as we need to catch the third suspect before he runs away to Kerala."

Chetan followed the instructions of his chief by pulling off is arms from Rita, though he was a bit reluctant to do so. Before leaving, Rita and he bent and touched the feet of the uncle for his blessings and then Chetan left the dwelling following his chief as they sat in the esteemed Challenger. "You need to fly sir as the time left to the appointment is just twenty minutes."

"Fasten your seatbelt," said Monty as they drove away from there, leaving the scene creating a cloud of dust behind the Challenger's silencer.

Chapter VIII

Being affluent is a curse or a blessing?

The brakes of the Challenger were applied with a violent jerk and all its four tyres came to a halt, kissing the patch on the side of the road opposite to the destination. The shriek of the tyres on the application of brakes was as deafening as the roar of a hungry lion. Why would it not be? They had been facing the friction in the heat for over twenty minutes of nonstop drive in the top gear, a drive that did not care about the howling traffic from both sides on every single street that led to the farmhouse.

The gate was exactly in the middle of a fifteen feet wall, as white as a dove, and was fashioned from black iron. It looked similar to the ones that appear in story books, artistic and pretty. It was rectangular in shape with bars from top to bottom. Chetan was quick to get down from the car and rush towards it, pressing his nose into the gap and moving his black eyes side to side with utmost care. He saw a couple of muscular guards in black, who seemed more like the bouncers of a night club, staring back at him from the inside with the facial expressions of a wolf ready to pounce over its prey.

"Why put a gate with bars here fellows if you don't want people to look inside?" said Chetan calling the guards towards him. And then he went on to tell give them the details of the pre-booked appointment with Hargurjeet Singh. They seemed to know about the meeting and without wasting any time, they opened the gate, allowing Chetan to enter in, followed by his confident and stylish chief who left his car unlocked after parking it next to the gate. As they walked in, their smiles grew of their own accord with a nervous excitement of meeting the third suspect.

The artificial noise was piercingly silent in the entire farm, which measured around four thousand square yards, if not more. Green was the only color visible on all sides. The grass on the narrow walkway was nicely trimmed and adequately watered. On the left were plants with green leaves and delicate petals. Scattered among them were the beautiful birds and cute little squirrels that played in the sun with the innocence that cannot be matched by humans. The songs of the birds, scampering of the little squirrels and the subtle movements of the flora combined to form a voice of the nature, the song of the garden, especially for those who listen with more than just their ears. Surprisingly, there was just one gardener who stood on a five feet stool, engrossed in trimming the over grown portions of a tree at the corner.

Towards the right of the walkway, there was a parking area with a couple of luxury SUVs parked, both matte black in color, along with a silver colored motorbike that seemed to be imported straight from Japan. The observant eyes of Monty noticed the sticker on the rear side of the bike that contained the symbol of a lawyer and a small sized text that stated advocate. There were also six or seven bicycles parked behind, as if hiding from the front view. The three feet tall white wooden fence that acted as the boundary of the walkway on both its sides was obviously a new one. Pale white cedar planks that were yet to see a drop of rain, stood unvarnished in the blistering August sun.

The way in which the guard who was accompanying Monty and Chetan walked, made it seem that he was in a hurry. His steps were not long but they were rapid like a speed walker, obviously without the odd twisting motion. There was no option for the guests apart from increasing their pace of walking too as the bearded guard was armed with a pistol that rested silently in its dull brown leather cover at the side of his black trouser. Tenser than a tiger in his hunt, Chetan walked with his hand on his forehead not just shielding his face from the sun, but also covering the black eye. Monty on the other hand, preferred to glide down like a slinking panther, as if it was not grass but marble below his expensive black shoes with eyes that squinted to let in only enough light to navigate. He was clearly thinking about the questions he had to put up to the suspect, knowing very well that each step was taking him closer to the former husband of Scarlett White.

The trio finally reached the farmhouse that was a single storey aesthetically pleasing midsized bungalow in itself, especially because of the breathtaking scenery surrounding it. Though it wore the color of unfinished wood, probably because it was not as new as the fences on the way and had clearly weathered several years by harsh climatic elements, it was a treat for any house party organizer. It faced the world proudly and defiantly with a rusted tin roof and a sagging porch. Its entry was through an ancient wood and glass door that opened straight into the hall.

The interior was magnificent and the creativity of the designer left Chetan awestruck. The twenty light bulb chandelier that hung from the middle of the ceiling was perhaps the most expensive one that even a rich ladies' man like Monty had not seen lately. It illuminated the brown walled wooden hall with the yellow that gave it an effect of pure shining gold. On the left wall, there were several certificates, newspaper cut outs and other documents, all framed in maroon and blue background glorifying the achievements of Hargurjeet Singh's father, a notable former Member of the Legislative Assembly.

The right wall was comparatively vacant but that was self evident because it hosted three wood and glass antique doors, all of which were closed at that moment. The wall exactly opposite to the entry door had a large fireplace, perhaps very useful in the winters, stationed exactly towards the left of the plastic switchboard that contained exactly four switches and a socket. Above that, there were a couple of small fans with their blades in cage, similar to table fans, fitted on the wood that were not really required at that time as the breeze from the window between them was enough to keep the hall pleasant.

In the middle of the hall, there was a four seat black dining table, not the one that average people use at their homes, but the one which was made of Pink Ivory and had a figurative painting embedded inside the thick glass at the top. That piece of art portraying a Chinese couple in love sitting on a rock, would sell in several lakhs if presented in an auction, let alone the table. All the four black designer chairs that surrounded the table, two on either side had a cushion at the seat and back for comfort but no armrests.

Three of those chairs were already occupied and on one of those that faced the entry door, sat the tall, fair and handsome Gabru Sardar, Hargurjeet Singh. The grey colored Patiala Shahi turban on his disc shaped head had a tinge of blue to it and it completely covered his ears, acting like a lid of a warm casserole. The blue of the Pagri was in contrast with the blue of the cotton jacket that he wore that had an unused bright red hood with an orange tinge. As the steel colored thick zip of the jacket was open from the front, his inner round neck t-shirt that comprised of three colors, bright red on the top, white in the middle and blue at the bottom, was clearly visible.

Sitting next to Hargurjeet, was a twenty something young woman with a charismatic and fascinating personality. Maybe the makeup she wore was of the finest quality, but it was surely overdone. She had curled her dark locks that seemed to dance between black and brown, hanging more in waves than curls over her tiny yet attractive pretty face. The apparel which the lady with chocolate brown skin chose for the occasion was a combination of a sleeveless and open shoulder top made of cloth that had the color of jute with a couple of red flowers embroidered on it and a pitch black cotton miniskirt that was pitch black in color, revealing her flawlessly waxed legs much more than what the guests had expected for their formal meeting. On the other side of the table, opposite to the glamorous woman, sat a middle aged bald man in a plain white full sleeved shirt tucked into a white trouser over his white artificial leather shoes.

"Mr. Monty is here," said the guard to the man in white and immediately rushed out of the hall closing the door, without even looking towards the standing guests or the sitting host.

"Finally the hero we were all waiting for is here. Welcome Monty C Dhingra!" said Hargurjeet as vigorously as a housewife explaining the cleaning work to a new maid. His voice was cheerful and matched one of the famous Punjabi singers. He stood up revealing his torn blue jeans, the fashion of the day and proceeded towards his guests with open arms and his big luminous eyes probably staring at his own image on the round black shades of Monty. Though his thick gold chain made no noise, the purity of its shining metal would put even some famous rappers to shame. Although Monty was initially reluctant, he had no option but to respond with wide arms to the hug offered by the suspect to him, a hug that only the best of friends give to each other and that too when they meet after years. Hargurjeet went on to give a tight handshake to Chetan too before pulling the chair next to the middle aged man and offering it to Monty with an open left palm. He then returned back to his place with the energy of a three year old, leaving Chetan standing behind his chief but still pleased especially after smelling the masculine scent of the suspect's perfume.

Before sitting, Hargurjeet pulled the woman's chair closer to his own chair with a facial expression of urgency and his crooked fingers touching his heavy beard near his cone shaped chin. Luckily the thin man did not have to apply much power as the woman was petite. After the adjustment of the chair, as he bent to sit, he said, "AC please stay closer to me, the man who steals girls is here." And supported by the middle aged man in white, he himself burst into a weird kind of laughter letting the gap between his thin lips perfectly expose the nicely set white teeth. The frown from the sudden pull of the chair changed to the beginning of a smile on the lady's lips that were glittering pink with the perfect shade of lipstick.

Not too impressed by the joke, Monty, sitting with arms folded and resting on the table, began the real conversation with his body bending slightly forward, "Hargurjeet, I am here to sort some facts, not for jokes." The up and down movement of the woman's eyes, which were as deep as the Bay of Bengal, signified that she was impressed with the investigator's personality and voice.

"Man is on earth to live, not exist, MCD, I hope you can introduce the black eyed gentleman standing behind you before we initiate any talk," though he was still in a joking mood, he said something which even the contemporary philosophers would be proud of. The long but thin eyebrows rose up with a slight tilt of the lady's awkwardly skinny bare neck towards Hargurjeet.

"He is Chetan Prasad, my apprentice, but I hate one sided introductions." Her smile widened with her pink lips rising up to her elegantly straight and delicate nose as she seemed to enjoy the conversation.

"This man, sitting next to you, is the lawyer who is handling one of my court cases. His name is Mr. Swaroop Tandon." Monty turned towards the middle aged man who moved his hand forward for the obligatory handshake, surprisingly with loose grip. He had a dark skin tone and a thin but dark moustache below his long and swollen nose. When he was shaking hands with Chetan, Monty observed the double saffron thread tightly tied on his right wrist. It was exactly same like that of the man near Scarlett's house at the night of the murder.

"And Monty Bro you might not see the big bindi on her arched forehead or a plate of fish on this table but this pretty lady here is Anjana Chatterjee, my sweetheart. I am going to get married to her on the first of October. She is probably the most beautiful female in Kanpur." As Monty turned towards Hargurjeet, he saw him blush with his cheeks blooming red that did not go very well with his tight skin.

As Monty and Chetan turned towards Anjana, she attempted to hide her face behind her chalk shaped fingers, her cheeks turning to a color that would rival the rose pink hue of her nail polish, shining brilliantly through the gaps. She turned her head towards the guests but averted her gaze, looking downwards with a nod of the head to greet the duo.

"Congratulations to both of you!" exclaimed Chetan but his usual poker faced manner did not compliment his words.

"Thanks!" Anjana said. Her tone was as sweet as that of the cuckoo while her accent was suggestive of her Bengali descent.

"I hope the introductions are over. Ms. Anjana, the color of your lipstick goes very well with your attire today," said Monty with his head tilting slightly towards the right, making the lady blush a bit more. Then he removed the shades from his eyes and handed them over to Chetan, who arranged them behind his shirt, similar to a famous actor of Bollywood. He then turned towards the suspect, saying, "We must come to the main agenda of this meeting now."

"Hargurjeet has a great choice. I think he is the one who has gifted this lipstick to Anjana," said the lawyer diverting the conversation away from where it should go. He sounded similar to the man Monty heard at the site of the crime. There was no anger, no joy, no resentment and no sadness in the manner he spoke. It was almost robotic. He was possibly the same man but not drunk at that time.

"Yeah, right Swaroop Uncle. But this is just a small thing. Four months ago, when she passed her post graduation examination, I gifted to her the black luxury car which she is presently using. And oh boy, doesn't she like it!" replied Hargurjeet with a sense of pride but sounding arrogant, as expected from a billionaire's only son.

"But I drive it only when Haggu sits next to me," interrupted Anjana, adding fire to the fuel that would lead to burning the mind of any sane common man if present in that hall, but not the experienced duo of Monty and Chetan, both of whom had no interest in the materialistic belongings of the couple.

"Absolutely true," agreed Hargurjeet as his warm and soft hand moved around her middle for a perfect cuddle, as if that was the only antidote left in this world.

As the drama continued, the lawyer, Mr. Swaroop turned towards Monty to ask, "Monty ji, some cynics might argue with me on this but I would like to make a bold statement. According to my personal opinion, it is unfortunate that some women nowadays seek advantage of the prevailing laws, using some of their loopholes in an improper manner to suit their own agenda. They approach the police or courts with false complaints and cases, especially against the rich men to extort as much money as they can. In fact, I come across such cases in the court on a regular basis. How do you find the best women from the fresh lot?"

"A good question Sir," said Chetan raising his left arm up with an open palm and bringing it down on the left shoulder of his chief, "only the men who are inexperienced tend to be incompetent when it comes to finding the right woman for themselves. Monty does not invite them, but such unskilled men themselves come to him offering their females and giving money in return."

The atmosphere turned serious as nobody in the hall seemed to like the answer given by Chetan. Though Monty kept silent, gender objectification was never something he would support. Had he chosen to respond to the man in white, it would have sparked a time consuming debate which would pass almost the entire time allotted by the rich man for that meeting.

"Ok Hargurjeet, allow me to leave now. Tomorrow is Thursday, the day of Sai Baba, a lucky day for me. I will submit the notice against that fraudulent woman tomorrow," said the lawyer as he stood up, ready to leave the meeting, getting only a nod from Hargurjeet.

"Don't call any women fraudulent Mr. Tandon. They are the ones after God who venture happily into the lap of death to give birth to a new life," said Monty with his eyes focused directly at the middle of lawyer's broad forehead, "Please remain seated as I have a couple of questions for you."

"Nice dialog Monty but my reference was to the housemaid who falsely alleges attempt to rape charges against Hargurjeet. All she wants to shut her mouth is a mere two lakh rupees in cash. Ask me those questions as fast as you can because I have too little time left to reach the court," said the lawyer, turning still exactly where he was standing.

"Where were you after midnight, when fifth changed to the sixth?" asked Monty, trying to clear his doubt about the man.

"Ah! So you do remember me? We met that night near Scarlett White's house. I must say that your memory is too good."

"What were you doing near her house?"

"If you mind your own business Mr. Monty, life will be less demanding. I had visited there with an important work which you don't deserve to know," said the lawyer as he began to walk out of the hall, only to be pulled back with a gentle force by Chetan.

"Which level of madness is this?" shouted the lawyer, raising his voice louder than the buzz of an alarm clock and throwing away Chetan's arm from his elbow with intense anger turning his face as red as a drop of blood from a fresh wound.

"Tell me why you went to her house that night?" asked Chetan, pressing his elbow against the shoulder of the lawyer.

"Relax guys," screamed Hargurjeet, who was silently watching the dramatic scenes till a second back. "Uncle went there to meet Scarlett and convey to her the message of my second marriage."

And all the five pairs of eyeballs turned towards each other in the hall, as what followed was complete absence of words for a few moments with the sound of deep breaths acting as background score to the silence. Confusion, anger, drama, glamour, question and its answer, everything was trapped within those walls of the farmhouse's hall.

"Don't be so silent gents, are you guys preparing a political speech in your minds," said Anjana, trying to calm the atmosphere as she loosened her black leather stilettos for extra comfort, signifying that they were probably new ones.

"I am here because Scarlett was brutally murdered on that very night, moments after I met Mr. Tandon outside her house and I am investigating that crime," said Monty coming straight to the point, the style he preferred the most. He looked towards Hargurjeet as Chetan fixed his eyes at the lawyer's face.

As the lawyer's eyes met Hargurjeet's, their facial expressions told that both of them had a five second communication of certain thoughts by means of unknown senses. The lines on the forehead of Hargurjeet chiseled all the annoyance, delight, bitterness and shock off his face, turning it almost impersonal. Meanwhile, Anjana and Mr. Tandon too seemed completely empty from the inside, absolutely emotionless.

"So now Mr. Tandon, can you please tell the actual reason why you visited Scarlett's house that night?" asked Chetan sounding angrier than ever before and his eyes still staring the lawyer as if he was not a human but a shot of tequila.

"Two days have passed and neither the police, nor the press has informed us about it," said Hargurjeet who now appeared a ghost like shadow of his actual self.

After a long thought, the experienced lawyer replied, "I met her on that night, conveyed the message and watched her burn. She was physically cent percent fine till the time I left her house, and happened to meet Monty just near the gate after exiting it. And then I went to my own residence. If you remember Hargurjeet, I called you telling how much she hated the news of your wedding on the call that very moment. This man, who calls himself an investigator, entered her house perhaps after I had left that locality itself and now claims that she was murdered. Even after two full days have passed, the police and the press have no clue whatsoever of the crime but this womanizer cum detective is here to blame me for the murder. I would like to declare that he himself is the one behind this killing and he may have even hidden the dead body somewhere and is now simply wasting our time, trying to blame us for his own deadly act. Hargurjeet, if you permit me, I would like to call the police right now and get these two arrested without a second thought." The lawyer sounded confident and did not hesitate even one bit to call Monty a ruthless murderer, let alone a womanizer, an adjective that absolutely turned off Monty.

"I never came here looking for a fight. I am a calm and composed man by nature, but no one can sit back, relax and watch himself get blamed for a crime he was not involved in, unless he is a defective nincompoop. And certainly, I am not. I see a coward in you Mr. Tandon and have analyzed your cheap moves too. You have a little devil sitting on your tongue, but my creature is greater. Come you trainee, come, and see what a true master can do," replied Monty, not exactly boiling in anger but appearing ready for a verbal spat or even a physical brawl as he stood up, his nose almost touching the lawyer's nose as they locked their eyes against each other's.

"Calm down guys, don't summon my inner monster. It does not play nice. Maybe she was actually murdered but by someone else, or, who knows, she might have committed a suicide," said Hargurjeet as he banged the table hard with both his hands, making a loud noise to divert the attention of Monty and the lawyer, away from each other.

"We are here to find out the truth," said Chetan, trying to enter the conversation, still without a hint of any expression on his brown face, which surprisingly appeared to have grown a thicker beard compared to that in the morning.

"A Minister never leaves his chair to address the poor voters committing suicides outside his office. I have a lot a work pending at the court before appearing for one of my clients. No more time I can devote to your baseless talks. If you wish to take the conversation with me further, you may visit my chamber. Goodbye," said Mr. Swaroop Tandon, coming back to normality with every breath he took. He walked out of the hall through the door, without even looking at the desperate investigators. Although Chetan wanted to hold the lawyer back, he did not move an inch as Monty gestured him not to.

"AC, you may go and change to your swimwear, I will quickly send away these guys and join you in five minutes or so," said Hargurjeet to his fiancée. The gorgeous woman stood up and without saying anything or looking towards the investigators, left the hall, through one of the three doors on her left, her walk representative of her modeling aspirations.

"Keep calm Haggu, don't let any Monty, Shonty or Chetan ruin your day," said Hargurjeet to himself with his eyes closed and taking exactly three slow breaths. Then he opened his eyes and said to Monty, "there is some peace now, let us straight come to the agenda of your visit. I will answer all your questions, shoot them one after the other, as many as you can in the next four or five minutes."

"I have heard a lot of stories about you Hargurjeet Singh," said Chetan as he sat on the chair next to his chief, left uncomfortably warm and vacant after the exit of the dubious lawyer.

"Who in this town has not? All those rumors you may have heard about me from all your sources, are true. I am the God you should worship the most," said Hargurjeet as his voice changed from that of a Punjabi singer to that of a villain of a movie. The stare he gave to Chetan was enough to intimidate the apprentice to the degree of making him lower his gaze down to the painting on the table.

Raising both his hands slightly in the air, Monty asked, "Mr. Tandon was talking about a housemaid alleging rape charges against you. What is wrong?"

Hargurjeet raised his left leg, followed by his right leg and placed them on the table in a crossed position, with a loud noise, right in front of Monty's face, almost breaking the glass in the process. As he pointed towards his velvet red shoes with thick white soles, and said, "Look at my shoes. They cost around three lakh twenty thousand rupees. When I told that idiotic woman to clean them properly using a wet cloth, she did it with a dry cloth. That triggered me. Though I practice Yoga every morning and that has really transformed me from a wild animal to a courteous, kind and pleasant man, I still hate it when an ordinary servant does not follow my instructions properly. So I scolded her, not more than one or two Punjabi abuses falling out of my mouth in intense anger. I went on to tell her about the price of these shoes and that is when her little brain froze. Since that very moment, she wants to extort money. She has fallen to the extent of putting false allegations on me. I will not spare her even if that would require me to turn to the wild animal that I once was."

"What would the former wild animal do to her?" questioned Monty as he too raised his legs, placing his black shoes on the table, behind the back of the Chinese couple, with the pointed soles facing Hargurjeet.

"Not only did that wild animal believe in free speech, it also believed in mute, torture and violence. I would have shut her filthy mouth, stuffing it with these shoes as deep as she could take and then had her hung upside down on a tree facing her own house. And after that, order her idiotic parents to beg for mercy for not teaching her manners." As Hargurjeet said this, a sadistic wry smile came on his face, similar to that of a question paper setter when he sets possibly the most difficult question paper for the final examination. Though he smiled, the smile did not last long as he continued, "But that was past. Now I am a gracious man and I thank my girl Anjana for this transformation, and of course, Yoga too."

Chetan and Monty looked at each other with expressions that proved that telepathy still exists. With his right arm in the air, Chetan replied, "Don't you feel ashamed when you go too much overboard with your words and actions?"

"Feel ashamed? That should be the regular job of your parents you black eyed apprentice," said Hargurjeet, seeking pride in his statements.

Though Chetan was as angry as raging bull, he had been trained enough in the past by Monty to not lose his calm in such situations, and with his chief next to him, he found the composure to maintain the rate of his inhalation and exhalation. Monty, meanwhile, removed his legs from the table and placed them on the floor, as did Hargurjeet. He said in a tone that friends use to talk to each other, "Hargurjeet's father has been a Member of the Legislative Assembly in the good old days and still has transcendent political relations. Am I correct, Hargurjeet?"

His eyes brightened, and shone like a school boy who got a good rank in his class, as Hargurjeet replied, "Agree with you Monty. It is due to my dad that I know that by mistake if I venture into something erroneous, I would come out of the crisis sooner rather than later. Still, I would not like to trouble my dad for lame things like a case against an ordinary housemaid."

With a nod of his head, Monty, winning over Hargurjeet's trust with his words, came straight to the point, "So, Hargurjeet, what is your reaction on Scarlett White's murder?"

Both, Monty and Chetan could feel the panic that began with the tension growing with every breath on the face of the suspect. Hargurjeet's breathing became more rapid as he felt a cluster of spark plugs right in his abdomen. With his heart racing faster than normal, after a weird pause of ten seconds, his eyed scanned the guests as he replied, "Who killed her? How was she killed?"

"That is exactly what we want to find out and need your cooperation for it," said Chetan, not letting the excitement or the anger make way up on his rather dull face.

Coming back to a fifty percent of the normal condition, Hargurjeet replied, "There are many ways to waste time Monty and you have perhaps chosen the worst one. Do you need some financial support in your business of debauchery? If you do, I will help you my friend. If not, I will advise you to concentrate on it as these criminal investigations will not take you anywhere."

"I feel I waste my time only when I repeat myself. Investigations are my primary business, and I am doing it with full responsibility. Tell me all that you know about this murder," Monty replied, oozing confidence not just from his words, but also from his body language. The fact that these types of cynical jibes would end pretty soon did not let his spirit dampen by more than a bit.

"Scarlett is, or rather, was my wife. Around one and a half years back I divorced her and that was the time I decided that never will I ever in my life keep any kind of direct contact with her." Hargurjeet sounded confident too.

"So what was your lawyer doing at her place?" asked Chetan, rubbing his eye with his palm as it had started to pain more now primarily because he did not get time yet to apply any kind of ointment to it.

"I too don't like wasting time on repeating things that have already been said."

"Why did the lawyer kill her?"

"I don't think he did. Was he carrying any weapon with him when you met him?"

"That does not prove he did not kill her," chipped in Chetan.

"Shut up you black eyed small time apprentice."

"How many times have you spoken to Scarlett since your divorce?" questioned Monty, not losing patience despite the pain in the neck that Hargurjeet was.

"Never have I ever. Even if she comes back to life, I will never speak to her under any circumstance. Knowing her reality, even you guys would not if she's back."

"What reality?"

"I don't have time for these meaningless talks. Anjana must have already changed. I need to go for a swim now. You guys may leave." As he said this, Hargurjeet stood up in an attempt to leave the conversation midway.

Monty had judged the nature of the suspect very well. Instead of using force or any type of intimidation, he chose to use words that would stop the suspect from running away without completing the interrogation. He stood up, almost simultaneously with Chetan, and said, "You cannot just catch a girl like you catch a fish. If you were lucky enough to have Scarlett, it is only because she let you. Remember that Hargurjeet."

The urgency evaporated from Hargurjeet's body. His rapid walk out of the hall halted before he reached the door, as if a bullet train had applied emergency brakes to allow the grazing field cows to cross the track. He turned and Monty could see that his focus was right at the skull of Monty. Immediately he knew that he had crossed the invisible line and offended the sensibilities of the suspect. Hargurjeet's anger came as fire, as it burnt hot and fast.

"She was like the carpet I walk on. When the carpet gets old and worn out, I throw it away and buy a new one," he said as his eyes turned red in anger, matching with his velvet shoes.

"Oh, so you got offended by the statement which I just made! You must go away and not listen to the ones which I am yet to say." Monty knew that it was only an eruption of a volcano of words that could extract the required information from the spoiled brat. The plan worked perfectly well as Hargurjeet came back to his chair and sat there with his forehead resting on both his palms, elbows on the table as he drew in slow breaths.

"Listen Monty," he said after a pause. "Bouncing of remarks from one side to the other like a table tennis ball, will lead to nowhere. You must understand that she married me only for the sake of money. There was a time in the past when I thought that my obsession of her was love and that is when I proposed her for marriage. She agreed. To be loved only for money was a torment. In the struggle to appear happy in the society and in the compulsion to be exactly what needs to be admired, there was isolation. For almost a year of my marriage, I was locked behind a mask, hiding from even my near and dear ones. But when she crossed the limits other than capital offences, I could not take any more. She demanded a home as living on the streets would lead to her end, so I gifted her one of my personal leisure houses and some money along with a car for her daily needs. That was the end of our relationship."

"That is really unfortunate," said Monty as he sat on his chair, with a facial expression that revealed his sympathy with the suspect and proved that his acting skills were not so bad.

"What lines did she cross?" asked the curious apprentice.

"She had a secret affair with an ordinary poor man Sooraj Singh, the man who probably still works as her driver."

"These girls, I tell you Hargurjeet, are torn between the nostalgia for the close ones and an urge for the strangers. What sort of a man is that driver?" said Monty, pretending to have never heard the name of the driver before, as Chetan stood behind him, as serious as a man who just suffered a heart attack.

"Nothing more in rank than a disgusting tiny legless larva of a cockroach that lives in decaying matter, Sooraj is perhaps a backstabbing dog who breathes everything apart from loyalty to his masters."

"How do you know him so closely?" asked Chetan.

"He is the son of my father's servant and stayed at the servant quarters at my residence during his young days. He once brutally killed a street piglet for food, and threw the remaining bones in our backyard. That was the time when my father, a vegan purely because of his demand of justice to animals, kicked him out of our house. Years later, he emerged into my life as Scarlett's lover. I thought of getting rid of him but Yoga has made me such a changed man that I cannot stand any violence around me."

"But I heard one of your former girlfriends died two days before you got married to Scarlett. Were you not practicing Yoga then?" questioned Chetan referring to the news article about the suspect that he had read in a leading newspaper a couple of years ago.

"If you want to see a miracle, you got to be friends with me and if you want to be a part of one of those, then be enemies with me," replied Hargurjeet with a smile blooming up on his face as he seemed to turn normal.

"What do you mean?"

"I am staunch worshipper of Lord Shiva. Mondays are the days when I don't consume alcohol and also don't eat non vegetarian food. I know most people do it on Tuesdays, but Monday is my day. Thanks to the Lord above that on Mondays, they eliminate my enemies from my life. I think you are talking about Faizana, the unlucky girl who was killed in a truck accident, two days before my wedding with Scarlett. I had already broken up with her, still she wanted to disrupt my wedding. She had threatened to create nuisance at my party. Gods did not like it and she died in that accident. She was so unfortunate that she did not even get the time to regret her actions. Even Mrs.

Suman Saha, the famous gynecologist you may have heard about, died on a Monday after she was murdered brutally by her own driver. She had refused to abort a four month pregnancy of one of my maids, only a week before her death. The story of Mondays does not end there. Though I publically declared it on a Wednesday, the actual day I was officially divorced to Scarlett was a Monday too. And now you guys are saying that Scarlett was murdered this Monday."

As he completed his speech about the miracles of Monday, Hargurjeet stood up and rushed towards the door where her fiancée had entered, saying, "I got to go for a swim now guys. Both of you can leave." Even before the guests could reply, Hargurjeet had ended the conversation in possibly the most abrupt manner. He reached the door in no time as he took steps much larger than normal, leaving Monty and Chetan all alone in the hall.

Meanwhile, Monty sat on the chair with his back pressing against its rest, as his feet twitched to the music only he could hear. His face turned as passive as it would in deep sleep. Chetan moved closer, touching his chief's shoulder, placing his right palm on the black tuxedo lightly. Monty turned his eyes towards his apprentice and smiled, that smile which he usually wore at the end of a working day. His voice tumbled out softly, "One."

Chetan immediately reached for one of the three special cigarettes from his shirt's pocket. Luckily all of them were as safe and clean, unlike what he had expected, especially after the fight at the temporary lodging. He offered it to his chief, who took it without any hesitance, a sign that declared that it was the end for the day's toil. He took out the lighter from the back pocket of his jeans and lighted the cigarette for Monty.

As Monty inhaled slowly, his nerves relaxed in response to the smoke and he felt his lungs being wrapped by a warm blanket. Those small draws helped him a lot in getting rid of some of the stress that had accumulated into his precise but admirably balanced mind. Although those special ones were free of tobacco, their smell and the taste were just as bitter. Perhaps that was what gave Monty the comfort. As he leaned back a little more on the chair with the smoke blowing out of his lips, he sprinkled the ash down right on the cemented floor, next to his black leather shoe. He stared at the cigarette between his fingers but the thought in his mind was obviously something different. Addiction was in his mind, not only of the cigarette, but also of solving the mystery as soon as possible.

The silence was interrupted by the bearded guard, who banged the door open and entered inside, jumping with as much urgency as he would if he stepped on a wasp. He was the same guy who had guided the duo to the hall and was still carrying the same pistol in its dull brown leather cover which appeared not as an attachment to his black trouser, but as a part of his body. "Exit is this way," he said in a rude tone, pointing towards the door from where they had come in. Chetan stood up immediately and began to walk towards the door with the guard, while Monty followed them, putting his shades back on as he walked out of the door.

Chetan and the guard walked like the people from the armed services. The steps they took had a marching quality to them. Monty was in no hurry though. He was smoking, walking and observing simultaneously. The blue skies were no longer clear, even the sun was not as bright as it was when it came, perhaps dimmed by the haze created by the pollution flying over with its source particularly from the factories, leather tanneries and vehicles of the city. The chirping birds had flown away, possibly towards the villages, to avoid the brown and black appearance of the sky. Even the squirrels had gone into their burrows.

The hardworking gardener seemed to have taken a break as he sat on his haunches behind the two matte black SUVs with the smoke from the bidi in the middle of the forefinger and index finger of his right hand, covering his face instead of the Japanese motorbike that had disappeared. "Old man, will you like to smoke this one?" said Monty to the elderly man as he pointed towards his cigarette. The gardener stood up on seeing a handsome young man in a black tuxedo talking to him.

"Never have I ever smoked a cigarette sir, it is the one thing that only the rich deserve. Though I have the desire to feel one across my lips, I don't have the money to waste on such luxuries," said the fifty something man, who had aged much beyond his actual years.

Monty walked towards him, taking note of the registration numbers of both the SUVs in his mind as he offered the gardener the remaining half of his special cigarette, saying, "Breathe in the warm air uncle, it will fill the emptiness of your lungs. Throw that regular bidi away. Watch a puff of smoke around your face whose scent is a hundred times better than that bidi."

"But I have just two more left for the day," interrupted the frowning Chetan. He was clearly not appreciative of the seemingly kind gesture by Monty.

"No worries Chetan, let the old man have some fun too," replied Monty with a smile on his fire engine red lips, as broad as his own shoulders but not false like the one on the guard's face.

Though the old man was initially shy and reluctant to accept the tip, he did throw away his bidi, putting it off with the torn sole of his slipper, radiating his eagerness. He did take the half cigarette with a weak but grateful smile and immediately put it across his thin and somewhat pale lips. In return, he offered a crisp and proper salute to Monty but chose to remain mute.

Monty and Chetan crossed the cage like gate of the farm and reached the Challenger without uttering a word to each other or to anyone else on the way. As they sat in the car, Chetan quickly took out the second last cigarette and lighted it for his chief. With the smoke coming from his pristine lips filling the car like the haze outside, Monty said, "Tell your girl to dress up brilliantly, and hope that your black eye heals soon as we are going out together for a dinner tonight!" Chetan nodded as even he wanted some fun after the hectic day. They drove away from the farm with the wheels tightly hugging on to the grey road.

Chapter IX

Time moves so slow yet so fast

Chetan Prasad checked his profile picture for the fourth time in as many minutes. It had already got a well deserved thirteen likes from his dear friends and cousins. After all, he had just chosen social media to announce his love-hate relationship with Rita Mishra. The picture which they clicked a moment ago was coldly luminous and though the filter used was a bit misty, it was very pleasing for the viewers. What stood out in it was Rita's transformation from a helpless maid to a radiantly attractive lady. It was possibly the Chetan effect.

Instead of the usual wrinkled and filthy clothes, she was dressed in a splendid and effeminate one piece black dress, covering her body from the seemingly unprotected shoulders to the three inch brown wedges. Her spotless pink cheeks and big fastidious eyes clearly proved that she had spent a good amount of time at a beauty parlor before coming for that modestly lavish dinner. Though Chetan was dressed in his usual blue jeans and a tucked in shabby grey shirt without many expressions on his face, in that particular image, all thirty two yellow, irregular teeth were clearly visible between his dark brown lips, as he had bent on his left knee, holding the hands of his love.

The picture was obviously taken by their boss, who sat all alone at a corner, looking around the busy tables and the dance floor. The lounge was almost full. An old couple with one glass of wine each studiously bent over their meals. A group of young women, in their thirties were busy in their gossips and giggles, as were a couple of elderly couples, who dined on the table adjacent to where Monty was drinking.

Both, Chetan and Rita were going crazy. The music near the dance floor was loud and it made their skin tangle and their lungs feel like mush. They had joined the other amorous couples there, jumping in a huddled group like toffees being shaken in a box. 'Let the bottles open, let the alcohol flow, take a peg of whiskey my dear men, forget the pains and glow!' was the song that made Monty tap his feet, joining the bass and his heartbeat into one.

By the time the song was over, Monty was done with a couple of pegs of whiskey. He raised his eyebrows to signal Chetan to come back to the table. Literally nobody on the dance floor was bothered about the sincere diners who sat on the wooden chairs away from the loud music, but those wily eyes of Chetan were not late in noticing the signal. Though he liked the new song, he had no other option but to come out of the floor, almost dragging his girl with him against her will. Quickly he sat opposite to Monty, with Rita taking the chair adjacent to him.

The noise level was high, as was the smoke level, but at least the three of them could listen to each other clearly at the table, than somewhere near the dance floor. Adjusting the button of his tuxedo which had got a just a little bit loose during the fight at Rita's uncle's hut, Monty said, "I have ordered a full Butter Chicken with three Lachcha Parathas."

"So why did you call us here? The waiter will take time to bring the food," said Rita adjusting the strap of her new dress and applying another coat of lipstick to the already red lips.

"I called Chetan, and he can't let you dance alone," replied Monty with a cutely bashful smile similar to that of the Lord Kamadeva.

"Yeah I can't," said Chetan with his shoulders and arms almost burning with shyness as he looked towards the black hair of his girl, which had completely hidden her ears.

"To succeed in our mission, we must have single minded devotion towards it," replied Monty as he observed Rita staring at the couple who just shared a passionate kiss at the dance floor.

"We have finished interrogating all the three suspects but the mystery still remains unsolved. Who is actually the guilty man?" said Chetan as he turned serious, going back to his original poker faced persona.

"What is the most powerful weapon in the Universe?" asked Monty.

"Nuclear bomb," screamed Rita. She was so loud that the elderly couple turned their bossy eyeballs towards the trio. Her constant fidgeting was obviously irritating

Monty and he stared back her. That look from those beady eyes was enough to discipline her as she sat quietly, looking down at the napkin that lay next to her folded hands on the dining table.

"It is the Trishool, the trident used by Lord Shiva," replied Chetan, closing his eyes momentarily in respectful remembrance of the Lord.

"Exactly, and though Sooraj Singh appears a religious fellow, he had three reasons to kill Scarlett, and I have three clues that point towards him," said Monty as he signaled the waiter to repeat his drink.

"One was obviously his rather bitter and uncomfortable relationship with Scarlett which he wanted to hide from his wife, what could be the other two Monty?" asked Chetan as even Rita turned attentive.

"During my meeting with him, he emphasized several times that he is a poor guy. His wife is medically not fit and he has two children. Scarlett was exactly the opposite. Jealousy, as you know Chetan, is irksome to others but a torture to the jealous. And of course the greed is known to be the cause of all dooms," said Monty as the waiter made a new peg for the good looking guest.

"Even I have doubt on him. Perhaps he lied about his relationship with Scarlett to you. Why did she call him so many times on a trot just before getting murdered?"

said Rita proving to Monty that the new lovers can never keep anything secret.

"Yes, why would anyone call her killer so many times just minutes before getting killed?" Chetan seemed to agree with his partner.

"The first probability can be that Sooraj called himself using her mobile to confuse the investigators, or perhaps just to prove that he was not present at the crime scene. Secondly, I don't think Scarlett was suffering from epilepsy. How come that full new strip of seizure control medicines lay next to her bed? The irony is that Sooraj's wife did not take her tablet the next day as he had dropped it on his way back just a day before, possibly at that very time when Scarlett called him." Monty and Chetan looked at each other in the eye, not able to believe what they just heard as this was indeed the first time ever that Rita made such an apt statement.

"And that makes sense as Sooraj was well aware of her house's interior having worked there for a good number of days. And not just that, he knew the exact details of her investments too, as you said he spoke about them without any thought," opinioned Chetan as the waiter arranged the plates for their dinner.

"So you guys believe Sooraj is guilty?" asked Monty.

"I think so," said Chetan, followed by a shake of the head from Rita.

"What about the brown cross on the visiting card of Master Shams-ud-din and the fact that I spotted a pouch of Zuban pan masala at the crime scene?"

"But why would a religious man like him do this?" said Rita as she once again adjusted the strap of her dress.

"He was tightly slapped in front of his employees and customers by her. And as far as I have understood from his words, he regularly had heated verbal exchanges with Scarlett. His employees look decent but they get as wild as particularly hungry and enormous Royal Bengal tiger on the command of the shrewd Master; It is quite possible that they had a role to play in this plot," replied Monty as the waiter brought the chicken dish and Chetan instructed him to serve. He obeyed and after serving them, he left. The food smelled nice and looked delicious, especially the leg piece which he served to Monty.

Taking in the first bite, which was seriously hot, Chetan continued, "But the Master had no idea about the interior of Scarlett's house. So I don't think he is the one behind this murder."

"By that logic Hargurjeet had the best idea about the interior as it was his own property before the divorce," said Rita licking her finger that had the gravy dripping from it after she had taken her fourth bite.

"The lawyer Mr. Tandon exited the scene before the gunshot. So, possibly he is not the one behind the murder," countered Chetan.

"But then, the lawyer may have visited just for diverting her mind and Hargurjeet himself did this or someone from his gang of armed men may have done it. Anyway, it was a Monday and he has a fantastic history related to it. I still remember the smile that came up on his face when he told Chetan and me about the tragic deaths of the people who go against him. Believe it or not, all of them died on a Monday," said Monty, raising his brows and the glass as he finished his third peg, signaling a repeat to the waiter.

Then, he continued, "So what must have happened was that the lawyer entered Scarlett's house and informed her about the second marriage of her ex husband. Both of them smoked together, possibly Scarlett smoked the cigarettes and the lawyer enjoyed the hookah. After he left, she got upset and took out her wedding album, maybe to shred it and with it put an end to all her memories of Hargurjeet. She called Sooraj for her personal hedonistic comfort but he did not answer any of her calls, possibly because he did not want to cheat his wife anymore. The killer entered her house in the meantime, shot her dead hitting exactly at her ear canal so as to not create a bloody mess and escaped before I could catch hold of him."

"But I have a doubt," said Rita, "why would any girl meet the lawyer or any stranger for that matter, so late at night and that too in just her under clothes?" Monty and Chetan once again looked at each other and then at Rita, impressed and outdone by the remarkable point that she just made. She continued, "And why will a crossed visiting card of a person she slapped long ago, lie in on the floor of her house on her murder night? I now think that someone from Master Shams—ud-din's gang is guilty of this murder. The killer reminded Scarlett about the slap incident and in sheer impassioned rage she crossed the visiting card and threw it away."

"Then what about the tablets?" interrupted Chetan.

"She might have purchased it to give it as a tip to Sooraj as she must be aware of his wife's epilepsy. Unfortunately Sooraj did not turn up that night," Rita was ready with her answer as Monty took a large bite of the leg piece, watching the unexpected one do all the talking.

Backing her, he said, "Master Shams-ud-din told me that Scarlett was an ardent fan of Zuban pan masala too. If that was true, how come only one pouch of that brand lay on her dressing table? This proves that the killer had mistakenly dropped that pouch there. All I can say is that never have I ever seen anyone other than the Master consuming Zuban."

"Correct, and regarding your question Rita about Scarlett meeting the lawyer in her under clothes, I think she might have changed after the lawyer went away," said Chetan in an authoritative tone but some of his words still sounding unclear.

The food finished and Monty asked the waiter for the bill. It dinner was probably on him. "This case has given me a headache. How do you guys operate without any trouble?" said Rita as she seemed to give up despite being the one who sounded most logical. The waiter brought the finger bowls and they washed their sticky hands.

"If your migraine is back, then here is its cure," Chetan said, taking out a tablet from the pocket of his wrinkled shirt, where he kept his chief's cigarettes. It was wrapped in a paper tissue and he quickly opened the wrap and took it out. He offered that magic tablet to his girlfriend who smiled and immediately ate it with the water in her glass, as if she was waiting for it since ages. The little episode brought a wide smile on both their faces.

As the music got louder, the dry ice smoke that had restricted itself to the dance floor, now reached till the dining tables and those white vapors reminded Monty of his protocol. He said to Chetan but looking towards Rita's gigantic smile, "Light one cigarette for me." This obviously meant that the day's discussion was over. When a mischievous smile engulfed the pristine lips trapped between those tremendous jaw lines, it was clear that Monty had already declared the guilty in his mind. Chetan did as ordered, lighting that tobacco free special cigarette for his chief with the candle that was placed in the middle of their table.

The time was exactly eight minutes to midnight by Monty's diamond studded gold watch. He paid the bill through his platinum debit card but told Chetan and

Rita to remain seated where they were. As Rita was busy checking her own looks, perhaps feeling superior and insecure simultaneously, Monty walked towards the dance floor with the burning cigarette in his left hand. It was not a walk, it was a stride like that of a knight with his armor glistening, sword clanking and helmet in the hand. The dancing couples noticed the handsome man and thought he would join them, but were disappointed as he went straight to the DJ, asking him to stop the music for some time. Though the music stopped, the silence was obviously not there as the crowd jeered making as loud sound as a battalion would during their war cry. Monty took the microphone from the DJ and climbed up on the stage placing his left shoe on the DJ's table and the right one on the chair. With the microphone in his right hand and the cigarette in his left, he began his announcement.

"I know each one of you want the music back and therefore, I will keep my speech as short as I can, but trust me guys, I have something really important to share," he said. The crowd turned silent. They did want the music but also wanted to hear what Monty had so say. Meanwhile, Chetan and Rita also walked towards the stage, with Chetan using his mobile to make a video of Monty's speech.

"Hearty congratulations to my dear friend Chetan and to his girlfriend Rita," as Monty continued, Rita blushed, hiding her face with the rough of her palms for a moment to avoid the look from the crowd, while

Chetan's raised his right hand to acknowledge the people.

"This night dear friends should not be remembered just as the new couple's proposal night, but also as the night that will change my life forever. My grandfather used to say that complete faith and dauntless courage lead to commendable achievement. I had faith in my abilities to challenge adverse situations. I had the courage to fight against inherent, inescapable danger. I thank Chetan for being on my side during my internal struggle against those probably insulting taunts and heavily satiric jibes. I will also like to thank all those people who continuously jeered me, taunted me. You guys made me push my limits. Today, I will win this unvoiced battle against all of you cynical, perhaps childish humans who doubt on the natural but extraordinary capabilities of Monty C Dhingra, the private investigator. Even the faultless police and the ever reliable crime bureau usually take months and sometimes years to identify the murderer. They have access to forensic science, but I have none. They have the media by their side, but I have none. They have large teams, but I have just Chetan and now Rita. The gorgeous diva of Kanpur who was crowned the undisputed winner of two fascinating beauty pageants, Scarlett White was cold bloodedly murdered at her quiet and utterly unknown residence after midnight on the sixth day of August. The police and the crime bureau may still be investigating the crime. I, a spectacularly worthless womanizer, as some may think, have successfully finished my investigation in less than two days. And now, in this formal announcement, as the clock strikes twelve, I declare that the owner of The Powerful Horse boutique, the extremely clever Master Shams-ud-din is her killer."

Monty expected an instinctive and overpowering response from the crowd, but there was none. In fact, their reaction was immensely cold and savage. They were as silent as the people around a child's grave. Instead of answering questions like why and how, Monty wanted to ask them what exactly had gone wrong. Even the DJ stood still at the corner of the stage, not even ready to look at Monty in the eye. Surely, this was not the commendable achievement that complete faith and dauntless courage would result in. He wanted them to be impressed by his capabilities but instead they stood as still as dead, not even talking to one another. What was more surprising was that the enthusiastic waiters had stopped their work too, freezing silently at their respective places.

In the mournfully silent atmosphere where it seemed that even raising the brows was taboo, Monty turned his beady eyes towards Chetan, who had stopped making the video and was looking towards the floor with his head down, his nose almost perpendicular to the dance floor as if he was a nursery kid trying hard to hide his face after being punished by a strict teacher for not doing his homework. Rita, on the other hand, was perhaps the only one smiling in the crowd but that smile too was not the one that anybody would expect immediately after the critical announcement. It was the one that had her lower lip tightly bitten by the upper one, spreading the red color of the lipstick till almost her sunken chin, surely not the way anybody would desire.

Then he heard the sound of approaching footsteps of perhaps two people. Whoever they were, they seemed to be either heavily armed or members of a gang who consider themselves untouchables. The echo made by those footsteps was monstrous as if specifically made to declare their arrival to the silent gathering. Curious to see who were they, Monty climbed on the top of the DJ's table, throwing away the microphone on the stage but still holding his special cigarette firmly in the space between his thumb and rigid fingers of the left hand, sprinkling the ash on the dance floor as if that was the new dry ice.

It is never good news when a couple of police officers in their uniform enter any premises at midnight. Monty could see two men clad in khaki wearing shining brown shoes walk towards the dance floor. One of them; the inspector was an epitome of authority with his gun hanging idly near his hip and a couple of silver stars on either side of his collar, while the other was a rigidly attentive constable carrying a staunch little lath.

Though he did not want to show the level of his nervousness, Monty could feel the adrenaline being produced by not just his adrenal glands but also the neurons. His ears turned from brown to red as did some of his muscles below the opaque tuxedo purely because of the increase in the blood flow to those parts. Never in any situation, had he ever complained of any symptom of high blood pressure but the significant rise in his breathing rate made Monty realize that something within him was not normal. Despite looking around in search of the answers, his eyes led to nowhere as the focus was in some way not there. The awkward silence of the crowd and the heroic entry of the police officers into the lounge were not the factors that made him edgy, instead it was the profusely prodigious confusion that highly strung his brain.

The inspector walked towards the stage, passing through the voiceless mannequins with a body language that related clearly to his undisputed authority. The constable followed him closely, looking at the faces which in turn looked at the floor, as if they were all accused of any horrendous crime. As he approached nearer, Monty could feel his vigorous and unnecessarily broad moustache crossing the threshold before any other part of his dark and huge body. After several marching steps, he came to a halt as stiffly as a soldier, turned around and began to look at the crowd with his hard coal black eyes.

"There he is, catch him," the implacably exacting inspector ordered the constable, pointing his swollen crooked finger towards Chetan Prasad. His natural deep masculine voice sounded as if he used the microphone attached to a couple of low bass speakers.

The alert constable moved towards the apprentice in a flash, catching hold of Chetan's left elbow. Though he was grey haired and lean, the muscle power that the constable possessed was unmatched. Frightened by the sudden attack on him, Chetan stared blankly at the constable's clean shaven but wrinkled face with wide, horrific eyes. With his shoulders literally trembling with fear, Chetan tried to run away, pushing the policeman but his attempt obviously went in vain. The constable was quick to grab Chetan's right arm, pulling his own arm around his back. That hold stretched the pectorals and the shoulder joint of the apprentice, immobilizing the arm completely. Chetan gave up the idea of running away and surrendered. The crowd was behind the constable anyway and would have surely caught Chetan even if he managed to pass the trained policeman. The inspector meanwhile took out a metallic handcuff from his pocket and passed it to one of the guests standing next to Chetan, who quickly handcuffed the apprentice's right hand to the constable's left hand, leaving Rita in shock. She needed some time to comprehend what had just happened but perhaps the urge to urinate had taken over other things and she ran towards the washroom like a nursery kid running to his parents after the school got over.

Even Monty's weary but undaunted brain did not understand that why did the officers arrest Chetan. He inhaled quickly but his system did not respond to the smoke the way it should. Neither did his lungs feel as if warmed by a blanket. Masking his anxiety with a look of seriousness on his face, he requested the inspector, "Sir, the guy you have just arrested is my apprentice, Chetan Prasad. I am Monty, the private investigator and he works for me. I think there is some kind of misunderstanding on your part. I request you to release him." Though he said in as much confidence as he exhibited at the crime scene, his lips trembled and even some of his words were not as clear as he would have liked them to be.

Nevertheless, even though his looks suggested otherwise, the inspector was courteous. He seemed to understand the effect of alcohol on human body. Maintaining his calm, he replied making sure that he was audible not only to Monty but to all the people including the waiters who stood in the last row, "This man Chetan Prasad was on our wanted list from a long time. As you all know, innocent citizens of our opulent city, especially the youth, are constantly falling into the traps laid by the active drug mafia with its base in other countries. Modest citizens are being tricked into consuming drugs. Some of them don't even know that they have fallen into the category of addicts, as they are not told that what they are consuming is actually drugs. Twenty two people from our city have already lost their life due to this very active racket, and hundreds of addicts are not able to realize the difference between the reality and their imagination when under the influence of the powder. The government has started free rehab programs for those who have been tricked by people like this Chetan Prasad and his gang. Earning money is never a bad idea but playing with someone's life to get some cash, is crime. Be assured all of you that the police will take all possible steps to eliminate this nuisance from the society. Together, we will fight and achieve victory in this war against drugs. Jai Hind."

"Jai Hind," the crowd screamed, each one of them shouting at the top of his voice. Drugs indeed are life threatening and no sane individual would fall for that powder unless tricked. Every parent wants a healthy child and every child wants healthy parents. Some individuals from the crowd wanted to slap, punch, kick or perhaps break Chetan's bones, but both the officers told them not to as this war they believed should be non-violent.

Meanwhile, Rita came back from the washroom. Perhaps she had washed her face and with it most of the makeup including the lipstick which she was so fond of. There was no music but she began to dance. When she flowed around the crowded dance floor, it appeared as if that was the only way her body knew how to speak. Her personality, her sensuality burst through into a vibrant picture of her soul. The crowd could not believe their eyes, but the policemen could. The inspector announced, "This is what I meant when I said that people under the influence of drugs cannot differentiate between the reality and their imagination.

I think she has been drugged and the culprit is already in our custody." Chetan had already closed his eyes with his head down but as usual, without any facial expressions. He knew that this was the end of all his dreams to be a crorepati.

"Oh Sir, look at that man on the stage," said the constable, pointing towards Monty with his raised brows.

Even before all the members of the gathering could turn their wide open eyes towards the stage, the dynamic inspector snatched the remaining half cigarette from Monty's hand in a grossly rude manner. The sudden advance and the pull left Monty extraordinarily infuriated. The anger that boiled deep in his system was an obvious one as it was possibly the last cigarette of the day. It churned within his muscular body, hungry for destruction. Seeing his cigarette in the inspector's hands, he said, "The pressure of this raging sea of annoyance would force me to say things I do not want to. Return my cigarette."

And he jumped towards the inspector in an attempt to get his roll back. The inspector was quick and experienced. He threw the cigarette right on the dance floor and as quickly as an attacking Kalaripayattu fighter, he stepped on it with the heel of his brown shoe extending from the wet filter to the burning end. Not just that, he tapped it thrice with the hard sole making sure that the cigarette turned unusable not only for Monty but for anybody. The event was so out of character for both Monty and the inspector, so far from what the crowd could have imagined that most of them stood still, staring with their mouths open.

"I take no pleasure in taking that down young man," said the inspector as he could see the wide spectrum of emotions in the black eyes of Monty, "but it was necessary. It is better to hurt your desires now than to heal the damage they would do to you later." Monty moved forward to literally grab the inspector by his collar but some anomalous signals from his brain controlled his helpless empty handed rage. The inspector continued, "I have not swung a punch yet and I already see you quiver. This is not because you are afraid but because you are under the influence of drugs. That was not a cigarette my friend, it was a roll of drugs supplied to you by your apprentice. Look at that lady still dancing behind the crowd," he said as he pointed towards Rita, "she is also suffering. I hope you get well soon my friend." Monty stood in his place, still not ready to believe the truth. Never before in his adulthood had he been in a situation where he did not know how to react, so he decided not to utter a word and looked at the crowd and the inspector blankly.

As the inspector and the constable began their walk out of the dance floor, literally dragging Chetan with them, Monty tried his best to make an eye contact with his apprentice. The eyes that were once filled with so much purpose and love were now replaced with the ones filled with bitterness and hate. The only thing that showed any resemblance to the old friend was the outward structure which inhabited the miserable soul. The old friendship was over forever, but the old friend Chetan did not raise his eyes even once. Perhaps he did not have the courage to face Monty, or Rita ever again. He just walked out of the lounge silently with the inspector and the constable. Monty almost never cried but that was because his crying was in a different way. His tears turned into concrete actions, his obsession for solving problems. The impregnable strength of his mind somehow managed to control his urge to smoke. "So guys, remember Master Shams-ud-din is the killer of Scarlett White. It might be in the news tomorrow, but I am the first person to announce that today," he shouted at the top of his voice looking at the crowd but once again got confused seeing the placid reaction of the crowd. They stood still as if they had gathered there to mourn for the passing away of a life well lived.

Once again, he heard the sound of approaching footsteps but this time of three people. With the help of his sensitive ears he could make out that two of them were wearing either pure or artificial leather shoes while the third one was in pencil heels. The only announcement of their arrival was a slight drop in the air temperature and the descent of absolute silence. He peeped from the gap between the cold people in the crowd and the place where Rita was still dancing. The police inspector was back and perhaps he left the guilty Chetan in the SUV, confined within the watchful eyes of the constable. But he was not alone.

Accompanying him was a gorgeous lady, maybe in her late twenties and a middle aged man with a thin but dark moustache below his long and swollen nose. All of them walked casually towards the dance floor. Monty noticed the glamour from bottom to top, finding it hard to believe. Those black pencil heels might be at least five inches tall, if not more and they added up to her natural height to raise the top of her silky smooth and lengthy black hair to a minimum of six feet. She was dressed in a revealing one piece dress that had a beautiful design of fresh green leaves on a plain white background, exposing her carefully waxed straight legs from the slightly muscular thighs to the tender feet at the bottom and the flawless shoulders at the top. The three line text on her right thigh was the cherry on the top, but unfortunately, not many in the crowd could read Greek.

The mental strength of Monty's brain seemed to be lost as his brain formulated no thoughts other than to register that he was shell shocked. With a little effort of his muscular jaws, he closed his mouth and then looked at the tip of his shoes before glancing back to the new entrant. He rubbed his eyes from both his sweaty palms to make sure there was no problem with his vision. Though he had had four pegs of whiskey and smoked exactly half roll of drugs, all the intoxication seemed to have flown away or perhaps not. The lady that came with the inspector to the front row of the crowd, exactly opposite to Monty, was none other than Scarlett White. The way the middle aged man walked next to her proved that he was in a romantic relationship with her. He was Mr. Swaroop Tandon, the lawyer Monty met outside Scarlett's house and during his visit to Hargurjeet's farmhouse.

She pointed towards Monty with an extension of her open left palm. The inspector moved forward, grabbing Monty by his right arm, said slowly in his left year, "You are under arrest. If you cooperate, we can walk out without a fistfight." Monty found the inspector so annoying, especially his hard touch despite the refined look of seriousness that he had. Mr. Tandon and Scarlett meanwhile disappeared from Monty's vision, perhaps mixing well with the other members of the gathering.

Though Monty was shocked, he could not do anything. He was helpless. Trying to sound normal despite the attempt by his shivering lips to curb his voice, he politely asked the inspector, "How? Master killed Scarlett. I investigated. And why are you arresting me?" Even somebody who knew Monty reasonably well would have said it was someone else speaking. Not just the tone, but the quality of his voice had suffered a drastic downfall.

As the inspector requested the crowd to give them way and he began to walk towards the exit along with the cooperating Monty, he explained in a low volume, "You have many charges against you Mr. Investigator, right from IPC 307- attempt to murder to IPC 506- criminal intimidation and from IPC 451- Trespassing with intention to commit a crime to IPC 511- attempt of theft. Fearing a possible fall from the bed due to her epileptic seizures, Scarlett White regularly sleeps on the floor and that is where you tried to outrage her modesty and snatch her mobile. She says you could only manage to steal a visiting card from her house, which anyway she was about to throw in the dustbin. Other offences like possession of illegal arms have also been registered against you as Scarlett White, in her FIR against you, has also submitted pictures of you with a pistol in her bedroom. You entered her house late at night when she was alone, taking advantage of the fact that she had forgot to lock the door after her close friend, Mr. Tandon, left her house as she was busy, trying to call a taxi for him late at night. She goes on to say and that you fled moments before the police arrived."

With the eyes that held pain untold, Monty replied, "but Master Shams-ud-din had killed her. I heard the gunshot. It sounded to the one when my father shot my mother. There was a pouch of Zuban pan masala too at the crime scene."

"Shut up and stay away from your apprentice. I have understood that it wasn't you but the drugs that you mistakenly took that caused this utter nonsense. And don't talk too loudly about that pan masala. It isn't. It is a different type of drug that is smuggled through Rajasthan."

Monty lowered his head but said, "I have the license for my pistol and I did not fire a single shot."

"I hope that you don't get the harshest of punishments for all the crimes you did not do in your senses. After all, preparing your crime report and presenting the facts to the court is my job and I don't charge as much as some of the others," a weird smile appeared on the inspector's face as he said this, proving that he was not as innocent as he initially appeared.

"Thanks Sir, but make sure that Chetan Prasad...," as Monty was about to request the officer, the inspector interrupted saying, "Don't worry, I have good contacts with the jailers. Though I am taking Chetan and you to the same jail, I will make sure that you both are kept in different cells." And they began their walk towards the big door of the lounge.

The lawyer, Mr. Swaroop Tandon, standing in the middle row of the crowd with a glass of whiskey in his right hand, made a desperate eye contact with Monty and said, "You must stick to petty crimes Mr. Womanizer, as that is all you can do. And if you love your life, don't do drugs."

Monty wanted to literally slap the lawyer. He was so angry that even his breathing stopped but he was helpless. He walked away with the inspector, out of the lounge, closing the big door with a gentle push from outside.

"Sorry for the disturbance guys, the party is not yet over," screamed the DJ as the music began, louder than before. The crowd had been waiting for a long time exactly for this moment. Though the dance floor was like an abused chess board with spilled drinks and a couple of broken glasses, they did not mind. Even the elderly couples joined in the fun. The dancing queen Rita was visibly tired and sat at a wooden chair to relax, her narrowed eyes perhaps blankly looking for the men she had come with.

Towards a vacant corner of the smoking zone, there stood the gorgeous accuser, all alone, adjusting the lacy strap of her magnificent dress in the middle of her flawless left shoulder. Her close friend, Mr. Swaroop Tandon walked slowly towards her, making his way from the middle of the dancing enthusiasts. Putting his left hand in the only pocket of his usual white shirt, the experienced lawyer took out a thin and long cigarette similar to, if not same as, the one that Chetan supplied to Monty. She requested the passing waiter for light and he did exactly that. She inhaled slowly and like a canon, her body pushed out the smoke in rapid, deliberate bursts. Hazy rings, mostly circular in shape, floated upwards, distorting and twisting along their wayward path. The bitter smell around her proved that the fight against drugs was going to be a long one as there was not just one, but multiple disingenuous vendors operating in the city, as well as other parts of the country.